# GRAB

# BAG

# 9

A Gay Erotica Anthology

# BarbarianSpy
## FOR LITERARY HEAT

This book is copyright © habu 2015
habu asserts his right to be known as the author of this work.
Published by BarbarianSpy in 2015
Cover design © S Bush 2015
Cover image: Manipulated, © Wrangel | Dreamstime.com
ISBN E-book: 978-1-925190-63-2
ISBN Paperback: 978-1-925190-64-9
All rights reserved

BarbarainSpy
Toronto, Australia

# Grab Bag 9

by

## habu

# Table of Contents

# Introduction

Ninth in the series of an eclectic collection of gay male short stories by habu, the fifteen stories of Grab Bag 9 offer up a wide-ranging cornucopia of lush gay fiction from the romantic to the rough. The stories all were written in the second half of 2015 and are run in the order in which they were dropped by habu's Muse, most often in the morning in that half-awake period as he was contemplating facing a new day.

The stories in this collection range from the historical to the contemporary and from the introspective (e.g., "What Friends Do" and "The Oldest Ball 'Kid'") to the tongue in cheek ("I'm So Sexy"). In setting they range from the greater world (e.g., "Widows of the Prince" and "Not in Kenya") to specific locales in the United States, where the setting is almost a major character of the piece (e.g., "Halfway" and "Summer's End at Spirit Lake"). They include pieces written for erotica contests ("Naked, Not Nude," "Ever Rest at Evernew," and "Summer's End at Spirit Lake") and short stories written on request for readers ("Thirty-year Anniversary" and "Hanging Off the Appalachian Trail"). And, as always, there is the stray police detective or spy story ("Inevitable Case").

The first story in the collection, "Naked, Not Nude," written for a Nude Day contest deals with the difference between naked and nude, which, however, becomes a moot point in this story. In "Ticket to Ride," a young man willing to give it all up for tickets to a basketball game gets almost more than he can handle. "Widows of the Prince" deals with the problems of a man being the life partner of the ruler of a postage-stamp-sized principality, which are exacerbated when the prince has a show wife and dies early. In "What Friends Do," a male modern dancer takes on a sex escort job for a dancer friend who needs the rent money but is not up for the challenge of the escort job. "I'm So Sexy" is a slightly tongue-in-cheek story of the efforts of a college to recruit as a professor the sexiest man alive.

The "Inevitable Case" is another in the series of NYPD detective stories in which the detective is steeped in the vice he is charged with policing. In this one the detective finds himself handed a case where he has been intimate with the victim and is related to the suspect.

A couple of the stories were written by request of readers. Thus, "Thirty-year Anniversary" was written for someone who wanted to see a story in which a casual coupling of raw lust could hold its interest for the men involved for thirty years. A second, and much (much!) different requested story, "Hanging Off the Appalachian Trail," packs in a big punch of rough orgy BDSM sex with lots of toys and an outdoor hiking trail session.

Carrying the BDSM theme to a new continent, in "Not in Kenya," a British policeman is sent to Nairobi to cut down the cases of Kenyan policemen assaulting young gay men but gets deeper into the case than he had planned.

In "After Poker," a young man coming to Florida to lose his male-male virginity finds more than he sought in the wake of a poker party. The other players at the table get a little special action after the game as well. Remaining in the States, this time at the annual Washington Citi Open tennis tournament, in "The Oldest Ball 'Kid,'" the fictional number three American men's player finds that the fictional number three German tennis player's help in seducing young men to share comes at a price.

In an historical piece going back to France in World War Two, "Chameleon Love," the young male prostitute of a small French village has to balance loyalties and decide who to respond to when his village is occupied by German troops. "Halfway" continues with a prostitute who also is a transvestite. He's abandoned in Halfway, which is half way between Philadelphia and Harrisburg, and which features a gay adult bookshop with a convenient pole in the club behind it and allows the transvestite to contemplate the future.

The collection ends with two more, but very different historical pieces, "Ever Rest at Evernew," is a vampire antebellum time period piece set in the plantation region of Natchez, and "Summer's End at Spirit Lake" is a romance dealing with race issues in mid-fifties Georgia.

# Naked, Not Nude

About the time the top-down convertible stopped just down the road, waiting for him to catch up, Brady realized who it was. He should have been faster on the uptake, he thought. Who, other than the guy living five houses down from his parent's house in Titusville, Florida, owned a restored, cherry-red 1967 Impala SS convertible? Of course, what could he do other than walk up to the car? Dive into the bushes? The guy had stopped to give him a lift.

Brady's dad had made him stop mowing Mr. Wheaton's lawn three years earlier when Brady was in high school. His dad wouldn't say why, but it was right after Mrs. Wheaton moved out and took the kids. The whole neighborhood was buzzing about whatever had gone bad between the Wheatons and wouldn't talk to their kids about it. The Wheatons had seemed like a Ken and Barbie couple up until then.

He hesitated for a moment, but only for a moment. He needed to get back to the college campus from bumming a ride to his parent's house to raid the secret stash of money he had there, while they were vacationing over in Tampa. He was hitching it, and Mr. Wheaton had been good enough to stop the car. Brady needed the ride. He thought too of pulling his T-shirt back on. There was a thought in the back of his mind that he probably should do that. But he didn't. He also didn't want to think about how he'd been told he'd get a car to stop faster for him if he was shirtless—because if he thought about that, he'd also have to give some thought to what he'd had to do a couple of times to get the rides he got. But he had to admit that it always worked—and it wasn't like he didn't give out at college from time to time.

As he reached the passenger side of the car, he heard his name being called. "Brady? Brady Buxton? That's you, isn't it? Where can I take you?"

"You headed to the center?" Brady asked as he looked up and down the road before pulling open the heavy door of the old land cruiser. "If so, I'm on your way. The college by the causeway out to Merritt Island. If not, no problem. I'll get another hitch."

Walt Wheaton worked at the Kennedy Space Center, as did most of those Brady knew in Titusville, including both his own mother and father. Brady didn't know what Wheaton did there, but he assumed it must be physical, because Wheaton was in top physical shape. He did a lot of running up and down the streets in the neighborhood in just his athletic shorts and runners, and it didn't look like he had an ounce of fat on him. Not bad for an older guy. He must be in his late thirties at least, Brady thought.

When Brady opened the passenger door, though, he stepped back, his eyes going big. "Whoa," Brady both thought and said. Mr. Wheaton might look stripped down during his neighborhood runs, but he was even more stripped down than that now. He was naked.

"What?" Wheaton said, and then he laughed. "Oh, yeah, I didn't think. It's become so natural. Climb on in, Brady. I won't bite. I'm on my way out to Playalinda Beach, on the northeast edge of Merritt Island. Here, I'll cover up, if it will make you more comfortable." As he said this, he unrolled a beach towel that had been stuffed in front of the center console and spread it across his lap.

That hadn't been in time to hide from Brady, though, that the man was built big and that the sandy-red hair on his head was just as sandy red elsewhere.

"Still got the Impala," Brad said, nervous for something to say as they got on the road.

"Yep, still got the old '67 Impala Supersport. Wouldn't let go of it for the world. Happy my wife didn't want it. I'm livin' alone in the house now, you know."

"A 396-4BBL-V8 engine," Brady said.

"Yep. You remembered. I'm impressed."

"I've always loved this car."

"I always would have given you a ride. All you had to do was ask. I'd still like to give you a ride. So, off we go; go ahead and climb in."

Brady swallowed hard and decided it was time to change the subject. "Playalinda Beach? Isn't that—where you are headed?"

"Yes, that's a nudist beach. That's why I'm . . . well, you know. Do you know what Tuesday is? And, get in the car. Neither one of us can get to where we're going if I don't get this buggy going down the road."

"No, what's next Tuesday?" Brady said, as he slid into the seat, but kept as close to the passenger door as he could after he'd closed it. It was a big boat of a car, so there was distance between them—which Brady thought was good. Bucket seats, which also was good. He was having a bit of a problem with tension and response. He was a player—in sort of an exploratory way so far. He'd just never thought of doing it with Mr. Wheaton. Now, with his father's admonitions going through his brain and certain things maybe clicking into place, thoughts were entering his brain. He was fighting them off, though.

Included back there in his brain were thoughts about Mr. Wheaton he'd had when he was mowing the guy's lawn. Not thoughts he should have been thinking then—and maybe shouldn't be thinking now. The guy was a lot older than he was and he lived in Brady's parents' neighborhood.

"Tuesday is National Nude Day," Wheaton said, as he pulled the car out onto the street and pointed it at the Atlantic Ocean. "Both my wife and I are nudists. Well, my former wife, I guess I have to say. We met at a nudist camp. Not something we followed in the neighborhood, of course, but we'd go to beach camps now and again. It's all natural and comes comfortably for me now. I'm sorry if I wasn't thinking about how it looked when I picked you up. But I was driving directly to Playalinda Beach for the weekend. They're having a big celebration to mark the day. And it's not something I'm supposed to go to dressed."

"Uh, it's OK," Brady said. "But, uh, is it really feeling so natural to go around naked?"

"Naked's not a word we use for it, Brady. Naked is being stripped of all your clothes and exposed to emotions and senses—if you know what I mean. Nude is a lifestyle. You're still stripped, but it's of inhibitions and all the baggage we have to carry around all day in regular society. When you're nude and with other nudists you just are stripped of all the baggage. Thoughts of sensual don't enter into it."

"But, uh, doesn't it get embarrassing? Isn't it sometimes, you know, arousing—and easy to see?"

Wheaton laughed. "Not for experienced nudists, like me. You get used to it. Older and out-of-shape nudists, of course, don't cause much trouble for those not yet fully immersed in the practice. It's not about sex—not when you really get into it. It's more about freedom. Hardbodied and young and attractive people sometimes make controlling yourself difficult, but nudists understand. They take someone showing arousal in their stride—just like being given a verbal compliment—like me telling you that you are sure looking good these days—which you are. You must work out a lot."

"Yes, some," Brady answered. He couldn't help letting his eyes gaze at Wheaton's towel-covered lap to see if he was showing any of the signs that Brady himself was experiencing. But the towel was so thick and bunched up that he couldn't tell.

When the trajectory of his gaze rose to Wheaton's face, he saw that the man was looking at him instead of the road and had a little smile on his face. And the gaze hadn't started at Brady's eyes. It had moved up from his young, cut torso.

Embarrassed—and feeling something else he was fighting—Brady said, "If you turn right up there, my dorm is down the street a bit." He wasn't sure, but he thought what he said came out more like a squeak than his normal voice.

As the car stopped and he opened the door, Wheaton said, "Remember, it's nude, not naked. We're not talking anything prurient here. It's just a natural, back-to-nature lifestyle. You might give it a try. I'd love to take you to one of our gatherings, if you're ever interested."

"Uh, yes, thanks," Brady answered. "And, uh, thanks for the ride. Thanks a lot, Mr. Wheaton."

"Call me Walt, Brady. You're grown now. What, nineteen? Twenty?"

"One, going on the other. Thanks again for the ride. See you around."

"I sure hope so; you know where I live," Wheaton said, flashing Brady a big smile before he got his land yacht back in gear and on the road.

Brady couldn't stumble into his dorm fast enough.

* * * *

Brady had to hold his T-shirt in front of his crotch as he entered the dorm and hit the stairs to his floor.

Maybe if he studied nudism deeper, he could be as casual about it as Mr. Wheaton was and as easily separate it from sexy and arousing as Mr. Wheaton did. But he couldn't do this, and he found not just finding Mr. Wheaton naked—or nude, as Mr. Wheaton put it—in his car out in public disturbing and, yes, arousing, but it also didn't help that Mr. Wheaton was a hunk and a half or that Brady had been known to fantasize about older men—and, at one time, about Mr. Wheaton himself.

When Brady got to the floor his room was on, he didn't go straight to his room. He stopped at the resident adviser's door and knocked.

"Yeah, whata ya want?" came the sleepy reply. "I'm tryin' to study here."

"It's me, Brady," Brady said in a tone pitched to be heard beyond the closed door but, Brady hoped, not up and down the hall. All the guys on the hall knew what it meant when a guy sought out the resident adviser on this floor, and it wasn't to get guidance on studying or on toothbrush etiquette.

"Come." And then when Brady was standing inside the door he'd closed behind him and was looking down at the bed where the resident counselor, Kenny, was stretched out in all his football linesmen glory in just briefs and socks, having been awakened from a nap, Kenny asked again, "What do you want?" But this time he didn't ask it the gruff way he had before knowing who was knocking on his door.

"I want what you've been wanting me to want. I got a raging hard on and I need it bad."

"It'll be more than a blow job."

"I understand."

"Come 'er."

Kenny sat up on the side of the bed, as Brady stumbled over to him. Then, rather than pulling Brady down to sit beside him on the bed, he pressed the younger man all the way down on his knees between his spread thighs, pulled his cock out of his brief slit with one hand, cupped the back of Brady's head with the other, and brought Brady's mouth down to open over the head of his cock. "If this is what you came for, this is what you get."

As Brady showed that he'd done this before, Kenny murmured, "Awww, nice," through his released breath. "Be good to Kenny and Kenny will be good to you. Been waitin' a long time for *you* to come to Kenny."

They were sixty-nining on the bed when Kenny pulled back and asked. "Why today?"

"Just creeped out about something, I guess," Brady answered.

"Some guy's advances creepin' you out? Some creepy guy after you?"

What do you mean? Brady thought. Whose advances would have creeped me out more over this semester than yours? But what he said was, "I creeped myself out more than anything—seeing something I wanted that's been in front of me for some time. Surprised and scared the shit out of me. But, we just gonna fool around here, or are you gonna nail me?"

"You know I'm gonna nail you. You knew at the start of the term I was gonna nail you. You've just been playin' hard to get."

Their sixty-nine turned into a struggle of how that was going to happen. Brady's experiences had been pretty vanilla and furtive up to that point. Kenny liked variety, though, and positions that showed off his size and his strength. Brady was trying to keep his head from bouncing off the floor at the side of the bed or for the strain of his weight to fall on the back of his neck by palming his hands on the floor in an effort to keep his head off the concrete, as Kenny, sitting on the side of the bed, grabbed Brady's hips, with Brady's ankles hooked on Kenny's shoulders, and jack hammered Brady's channel with a thick, throbbing cock.

Brady was nearing exhaustion when Kenny hauled him up on the bed and on top of him as he lay stretched on his back. "Like a reversed crab," he muttered, as he brought Brady on top of him, nudged Brady to place his feet on either side of Kenny's hips, with his legs bent, and grab for the railing of the headboard over their heads with his fists. Grabbing Brady's hips in his hands again, Kenny skewered Brady's asshole with his cock and pulled Brady's channel on and off it.

A short time later found Brady stretched out on his belly on the bed, grasping the rails of the headboard overhead and slightly raised on his keens, as, reversed and on top of Brady, Kenny grasped the legs at the bottom of the bed and put his pelvis into motion, mining Brady's channel in a reverse thrust. Pumping and pumping . . .

. . . Until Brady collapsed in exhaustion, and Kenny just rolled him off to the side on his belly, reversed his body on top of Brady, saddled himself over Brady's buttocks, and rode him to a taunting completion, while Brady moaned and begged for the total fuck he was getting to forget the one he feared he really wanted. One thing he'd forgotten and shouldn't have was that Kenny was on the college gymnastics team.

"There, forgot what was creeping you out?" Kenny growled in Brady's ear as he covered him close from above after shooting off and left his signature hickey on the side of Brady's neck.

"Yes, God you wore me out," Brady murmured. And indeed, Kenny had worn him out, and Brady now recalled what guys had said about Kenny—not to go with him without expecting a full workout—and to remember that he was on the gymnastics team. Brady had been fucked before, but never for as long and in as many positions as that. Kenny's attentions should have satisfied him for many days to come. But Brady wasn't entirely truthful. All the time Kenny was fucking him, Brady was thinking of the mature man's hunky naked body he'd just left, driving away in his cherry-red, 396-4BBL-V8 engine 1967 Impala SS convertible.

∗ ∗ ∗ ∗

By the time Walt Wheaton had made it across the causeway onto Merritt Island and then northeast to Playalinda Beach and had run the gauntlet that got him onto the nudist beach, Brady had already been pretty much nailed by Kenny and Walt was panting heavily to do the same to somebody.

He had lusted after that Buxton boy for all the years the kid had mowed his lawn. He had sensed some interest coming from the other side that he thought could be cultivated and only had been waiting for the kid to be legal. But in the meantime, he got caught in the act with another guy, which had led to the unraveling of his marriage and being shunned in the neighborhood. The Buxton kid had gone off to college, and Walt hadn't seen him around after that. Seeing him today—grown a couple of years hunkier—had put Walt in a mood that he couldn't ignore.

Marching up to a tent with a familiar rainbow emblazoned on its side, Walt jerked open the tent flap and, in the dim lighting of the canvas, providing protection from the sun, saw the not-so-young, but not-too-old and well-preserved stretched out body of fellow nudist and investment banker Charles Laney. Charlie was lying full frontal toward the front of the tent. Conveniently, he had been wanking off, and thus was hard and ready to go.

"Spread your legs and give me your ass," Walt growled. "I got a load to drop fast."

"I thought you'd never ask," the slightly effeminate Charles purred, grabbing and stuffing his pillow under his butt, spreading and bending his legs, putting his feet flat on either side of the blow-up mattress, and giving Walt an "It's about time" saucy look.

Walt slid down onto his knees between Charles' spread legs and reached up with a hand to grip Charles' throat and hold his head and shoulder blades flat on the surface of the mattress. Charles gasped and groaned, struggling a bit to arch his back to provide a straighter trajectory for the penetration, but Walt struck fast, true, and deep and immediately went into a rhythmic pumping action that had them both groaning and straining against each other to get full mutual benefit of the spiking.

Pulling out and shooting off on Charles' thigh, riskily not having taken the time and patience with a condom, Walt collapsed on top of the banker, younger than Walt only by a couple of years, but thin and willowy to Walt's muscular hunkiness, and slightly limp wristed.

Charles had already ejaculated. He wrapped his legs around Walt's thighs, holding the more muscular man to him, hoping that Walt would fuck him again—he'd wanted Walt to fuck him for the longest time; it's why he'd joined this nudist group. And, although recognizing the danger of the lack of protection, he had reveled in the skin-on-skin friction of the fuck and regretted, despite everything, that Walt hadn't come inside him. He ran his fingers lightly over Walt's shoulder blades, torso, and buttocks as Walt's panting decreased. Running his hands back up to Walt's head, he pushed his fingers through Walt's luxuriant sandy-red hair, whispered in his ear, "Fuck me again. Please fuck me again. Just as ferociously as that." Then he tried to bring Walt's face around for a kiss on the lips, but Walt wasn't having any of that. Not a sucky-face kiss with this wimp.

This had been the release of tension and frustration, not a romantic tryst.

"Fuck me again, Walt," Charles whined.

"In a minute," Walt answered. "If you've got a—"

"You can bareback me. I'm clean. I want you to bareback me," Charles murmured.

"If you don't have any rubbers in here, it won't happen again."

With a sigh, Charles reached over and unzipped the duffle bag he'd brought with him. He had been living in hope for this attention from the magnificent Walt Wheaton. So, of course he had a couple of condoms with him.

After the second, doggy position, fucking, Walt lay on his back on the mattress with Charles stretched out beside him on the sand.

"I've been wanting that," Charles said. "But I don't know—"

"It doesn't have anything to do with you," Walt answered. "You know we aren't supposed to get into any sex here—it flies in the face of the principles of nudism."

"We don't have to do it here. I'll give you my phone number. My house or yours—or a motel—I don't care."

"Not likely to happen again," Walt said. "Just had a blast from the past. Something I wanted to get into a couple of years ago. Lost control. Had to spike someone. Gotta work that out of my system, though."

Walt rose and quickly left the tent, looking around the beach to make sure that no one had seen him. People were just starting to gather for the Nude Day celebrations. He wasn't supposed to be into this kind of shit here. People got tossed out of the nudist scene for losing it like this.

Good thing, though. Now he wouldn't be walking around with a hard on thinking of Brady Buxton—if he could keep himself from thinking about Brady Buxton.

When Walt was gone, Charles moved back to the mattress and started slowly jacking off again. He was disappointed that Walt didn't promise more of a hookup. But it was Walt's body that had gotten Charles to pretend

20

he was a nudist. And it had happened once. So, it would happen again. He lay there, purring, smiling, and stroking.

\* \* \* \*

Walt answered the knock on his door at dusk two days later.

"Brady," he said, surprised.

"Do you really believe all that shit about nudism being different from being naked and some sort of pure back-to-nature philosophy with no sense of arousal or sex—and if you see another nudist and get hard it has nothing to do with sex?"

"No, Brady," Walt answered with a smile. "I became a nudist to shop naked bodies for who I'd like to screw. How about you?"

"I've seen a naked body I'd like to screw me," Brady answered, almost breathless.

"Driving a 1967 cherry-red, 396-4BBL-V8 Impala SS convertible?"

"Yeah," Brady said quietly.

"You want to come into my house, Brady?"

"Yeah."

"You want to come up to my bedroom, Brady?"

"Yeah, I want to come up to your bedroom."

# Ticket to Ride

*Will ride for one ticket to Saturday's Stingrays game and dinner. Box 482. Include pic/stats.*

The notice at the Tampa underground newspaper was short and simple and was accompanied by a thumbnail photo and URL to his Web page at a gay dating site. Ryan hadn't tried this approach before, but he'd been told it worked for other guys—as long as you didn't get too picky. He really, really wanted to go to the semipro basketball game. The Stingrays were hot, hot, hot this year, especially that power forward Shane Thompson. Ryan just hoped he was advertising in time. The paper hit the stands Monday; he probably should have given it more than a week.

By Thursday he decided the scheme was working as far as offers went—he knew there wasn't anything a guy interested in such stuff wouldn't be interested in when they checked out his photo and Web site—but out of a dozen contacts there were a dozen toads. Most of them so old Ryan was surprised they could walk to the seats in the basketball arena.

Thursday night he was panicked. Friday morning he was resigned that he wasn't going to the Stingrays' game the next afternoon. But when he checked the box at the underground newspaper's office, he found one envelope. Inside the envelope what he found was not the requested photo and stats, but an actual ticket to the game and copy of a menu for the exclusive Charter House restaurant right on Tampa Bay.

He was leery about not getting stats, and now he was faced with the decision to take the plunge or sell the ticket. It didn't seem ethical to sell the ticket, though, assuming it was a real ticket, which he'd only find out if he tried using it. What the hell, he thought. By today even some of the toads who'd answered his ad earlier in the week were looking better and better. This wasn't a promise of a ticket; it was the ticket. He went home to decide what to wear. It would have to be both sporty and a bit dressy if they were going to the Charter House. Good thing that, as a male model, he had great taste and fit and had just about any event covered in his closet.

Surprise, surprise. The ticket got him into the arena on Saturday afternoon. He'd decided on tailored trousers, an expensive polo shirt that fit his cut physique like a glove, and tasseled leather loafers with footsie socks that looked like he wasn't wearing any. Oh, and black mesh bikini briefs, with a pouch that pushed his junk out front. An even greater surprise when he entered the arena was that the seat was a great one, down just off the floor and at the side of the court.

The guys on either side of the seat, which Ryan lived in fear that he'd find was a duplicate ticketed seat and he'd be the one very publicly tossed out of it, were already there and in place. Both were burly and middle aged. Both were expensively dressed. Both were toads. And neither showed enough interest in him for him to even begin to ask which one of them was his date. Each had a young bimbo on the other side of him to mesh with during the time outs.

Ten regulation minutes into the game, he found himself spending more time trying to figure out how to solve this mystery then following the play on the court, although the Stingrays were on fire—or rather their star power forward, Shane Thompson, was on fire. The short forward, Jared Jackson, was being great on helping Thompson get into position, but Thompson was finding the basket from nearly every spot on the floor. He was making the basket three times for every miss.

At the ten-minute mark Ryan's mystery was solved. Jackson was giving Thompson body protection as Thompson went for a shot, which he made, but a player on the other side, desperately trying to reach Thompson before he could make a shot, fouled Jackson. The collision was one that the solid Jackson withstood, but it sent the other player to the floor with a howl, writhing on the floor, and grabbing at a wounded limb.

As the medics came onto the floor and others gathered around the downed player, Jackson turned to the stands—he was nearly within reach of where Ryan sat—winked directly at Ryan, and called out "Dinner at the Charter House. Stay put afterward. Someone will come for you."

The men on either side of Ryan turned and hit him with questioning looks, and all Ryan could think of, while he was blushing, was to swivel his torso and head around and look up the rows behind him as if the message was being sent further up in the stands.

He trembled and fidgeted the rest of the game, unable to get completely comfortable for the hard on that just wouldn't go away and that he was sure the men on either side of him were aware of even though the game was such a slugfest and their dates were so demanding and needy that there wasn't much opportunity for their minds to wander.

A ticket for a ride.

Ryan could fill in the stats for Jackson himself, with the help of the glossy program the guy sitting next to him was leafing through. Six eight and 240 pounds. Solidly built. Ryan was five nine and 150 pounds soaking wet. Ryan could only hyperventilate at the possible other stat that was significant. The man's hands were the size of baseball mitts, and his feet were at least size thirteen. And as far as a photo, Ryan didn't need any. There were photos enough of the handsome, chocolate brown player, with dreadlocks down to his shoulders, tattoos all over the body that was exposed in uniform shots. And he was right out there on the court for Ryan to watch his movements resembling those both of a dancer and prize fighter.

There was no doubt about it; Jared Jackson was a black bull. And probably as virile as a bull. Was it only one ride Ryan had promised? It was a good thing that the play on the court had justified a roaring cheer in the crowd, because Ryan could hear himself moan.

\* \* \* \*

"Hold still and open for me," Jared murmured in a deep, soothing voice.

"Go slow," Ryan whimpered. God, it had to be almost eight inches. And thick and throbbing. Ryan had nearly had to unhinge his jaw getting it into his mouth, although Jared had been good and undemanding about that—like he'd been about everything so far. It was Ryan who wanted the bragging rights of throating it all—if he could. Which he couldn't quite.

They were standing in the middle of Jared's plush bedroom, with the floor-to-ceiling windows looking out over Tampa Bay from many stories up, a bedroom that was dominated by a king-sized bed, which Ryan was looking at with both arousal and trepidation. Jared had also asked him to stay the night, and Ryan had agreed. Jared had also made clear that he would fuck Ryan multiple times, but he had couched it as both a request and as an experience Ryan didn't want to miss. The man was a smooth-tongued devil. Ryan had agreed to it all.

But with the mushroom cap of an eight incher already buried inside him up to the rim for the first time, pulsing and coaxing Ryan open . . .

"Oh, fuck, be good to me," Ryan cried out. He was standing—or had been standing up to a few seconds ago, naked, with Jared, also magnificently naked standing behind him, his arms wrapped around Ryan's belly and chest. Ryan had lifted and turned his head and Jared had lowered and turned his to go into a deep kiss as Ryan felt the pressure of Jared's strong arm pulling Ryan's feet off the floor, the small of his back dragging along Jared's upcurved, rock hard, throbbing, jet-black cock until the bulb of the cock slid between Ryan's butt cheeks and pressed at Ryan's entrance.

Jared had already been on his knees behind Ryan, an arm wrapped around the smaller man, holding him upright, and his other hand encasing and stroking Ryan's cock, with time outs to pull on and squeeze Ryan's ball sac, while Jared's long, pink tongue ate out and teased open Ryan's hole.

There was no way, though, that Ryan's channel was going to be open enough to comfortably take the cock— at least not the first time.

Jared had whispered, "Don't worry, we'll get it to fit like a glove the third or fourth time," which was said soothingly enough and probably was meant to reassure, but it only made Ryan hyperventilate.

"Open to me, baby. Open to me," Jared hissed as they groaned in harmony on the slow deep penetration, Jared slowly pulling Ryan's channel down on the jet-black staff.

He held there for a moment, buried to the root, as Ryan moaned, "Oh, shit, oh Jezus. It's so big. Oh fuck." Ryan's face was buried in the hollow of Jared's shoulder and he was gripping Jared's biceps with the nails of both hands.

"Let loose and slowly bend forward. Reach for the floor with your hands," Jared commanded. "Don't worry, I've got you. We're about to go downtown with this." As Ryan slowly jackknifed forward, reaching for the carpet and letting his head dangle as Jared bent his knees and went into a half crouch, taking the weight of the smaller man on his beefy thighs. His hands went to clutching Ryan's waist on each side. He started to pull Ryan, doubled over and suspended in front of him, on and off the cock, slowly, but with increasing depths of slide.

Throughout, although he was fucking Ryan with a mammoth cock, he took it slow and handled Ryan gently and tenderly.

Jared had been a perfect gentleman all evening. At the end of the game, Ryan had remained in his seat until an usher came to him and escorted him to a private dressing room, with a shower, where Jared appeared and let Ryan watch him shower and dress. When clothed, the basketball player looked more stylish and ready for an expensive restaurant than Ryan did.

He drove to the restaurant in a Jaguar roadster, advised Ryan on the menu as if he ate there regularly, which, as far as Ryan knew, he did, and expertly selected the wine, pronouncing French like he was a native. Ryan wouldn't know if he was doing it well, but the waiter seemed impressed, which impressed Ryan.

Jared was a smooth conversationalist, certainly more glib than Ryan was and able to cover a wide range of subject matter. This wasn't at all what Ryan had expected to find in a black basketball player—or in any guy he hooked up with to get a ticket to the game, for that matter. He was completely disarmed—at least until they got to Jared's apartment and where swaying against each other, half undressed, in the center of Jared's bedroom, and Ryan had gotten the measure of Jared's cock with his hand.

Even then Jared took it slow, taking charge of completing their undress, taking time to kiss and fondle, whispering encouragement and assurance. And then fucking Ryan slow and easy, standing, with Ryan doubled over and being held buttocks to groin.

Jared filled out the bulb of his condom before Ryan came a second time. Ryan had been so keyed up that he'd come with Jared kissing him and stroking him through the material of his trousers in the garage parking space even before coming upstairs to Jared's apartment.

After the standing fuck, Jared gently carried Ryan over to the bed and laid his back down on the edge. Leaning over to kiss Ryan on the lips, he then moved his mouth down Ryan's body to his groin and swallowed his cock, causing Ryan to shudder and groan—and eventually to come again. After that Jared stood, moved between Ryan's thighs, pressed his forehead to Ryan's, and kept Ryan's eyes captured by his as he entered Ryan's channel again and slow fucked him to another ejaculation.

It went on like that off and on all night, with Ryan expecting the hunky basketball player to get more physical, more demanding.

But he never did. He was gentle and tender with Ryan, doing everything he could to open Ryan to the size of him. And by the morning Jared had managed to ream Ryan to his specifications. "You'll thank me for this," we whispered to Ryan before they rose from the bed, which Ryan didn't think about at the time and only understood later. Jared fixed Ryan a big breakfast, and drove him back to his own apartment.

It was a date that totally exceeded Ryan's expectations. When he got up to his apartment he realized that nothing had been said about them meeting again. He regretted that. In addition to the sex—and the tender attention that went with it—Jared was in a position to comp game tickets to Ryan. The ticket for a ride concept had no downside when it was with Jared.

For the next couple of days, Ryan wondered if he'd try to contact Jared through the team office—which might just tick Jared off—or put another ad in the underground newspaper.

Tuesday's mail obviated his need to think further about that.

* * * *

Scrawled on the envelope Ryan pulled out of his post-office box at the underground newspaper was the phrase "Ticket to Ride." Enclosed was a ticket to the Stingray's basketball game the next Saturday afternoon. But there also was a piece of notepaper that merely said, "Six nine, 250, and nine by two."

Ryan smiled. He thought Jared Jackson was bragging just a bit. Ryan was a pretty good at measurements and even the game program on the Stingrays that Ryan had looked at as the guy sitting next to him at the previous Saturday's game had logged Jared in at six eight and 240 pounds. The programs usually exaggerated on the big side. Monday's sports casts had said there was a trade in the offing that might send Jared to St. Louis, and that had bothered Ryan—he wanted to see Jared again—but that must have fallen through or was for sometime down the trail.

On Saturday afternoon, Ryan arrived at the basketball arena looking forward to a repeat evening with Jared. This time he'd dressed a bit more upscale for going to a ritzy restaurant after the game but sexier underneath—a gold lamé G-string pouch. He bought a game program, which he hadn't done the previous Saturday, because he thought he'd get Jared to sign it for him. Leafing through the program, though, he was unable to find the listing for Jared.

He mentioned the omission to the usher at the top of the section his ticket was for.

"Jared Jackson? He's history, man. He was traded and hauled ass out of here last Monday for St. Louis. Trading him was a mistake, if you asked me. He was a real stud."

You don't know the half of it, a surprised and confused Ryan thought. But he just thanked the guy and got directions to his seat, which was as good and as near to the playing floor as the one from the previous Saturday had been. He do his best to enjoy this game; the ticket conduit through Jared had been a good, albeit short lived, one.

Once again, it wasn't that long into the game when there was a lull in the play and Ryan was looking through the program again, willing Jared's photo and stats still to be in there, even though he wasn't among the players on the floor. The guy nudged him and pointed to the court when Ryan looked up.

The Stingray's star player, the power forward Shane Thompson, was standing and staring up at him from the edge to the court. He raised one of those arms of his that was famous for his wingspread, pointed directly at Ryan, and growled, "You."

At that moment Ryan understood what he meant—and also now understand the stats that were written on the notepaper that had come with the ticket for today's game. He just hoped to god that those around him didn't understand what Shane meant—what he wanted—what he obviously assumed that Ryan would give him.

\* \* \* \*

"Cute," Shane said, with laughter in his voice, as he unsnapped the side straps of Ryan's G-string, pulled it away, and tossed it on the floor of the same room in the locker room area where Jared had let Ryan watch him shower and dress the previous Saturday.

"Guess that means you're a pro and I don't have to go easy."

Ryan gulped. That hadn't been the meaning he'd intended—and he hoped Shane was joking about that.

It was obvious to Ryan that there was to be no dinner in a fancy restaurant and no erudite conversation with Shane as there had been with Jared. Also no romantic, gentle, and tender lovemaking in a plush apartment overlooking Tampa Bay.

As soon as Ryan had been escorted to the room and the usher had departed and shut the door behind him, Shane, coming naked out of the shower, pushed Ryan down on his knees and made the young man give his nine by two—which Ryan now readily believed he had—a blow job. Then it was Ryan's upscale clothes being stripped from him and tossed aside, and Ryan being hauled up and tossed, back down, on a massage table.

Off came the gold lamé G-string, and in, painfully, went the power forward's thick fingers in Ryan's channel. Then some tonguing, but in short order Shane giving Ryan all nine thick inches in the ass in a vigorous pistoning. It was now that Ryan understood—and appreciated—Jared's whispered comment that he'd be glad that Jared had reamed his passage to the needs of a big cock.

It wasn't all night. It was just that once, in the private locker room. But to Ryan it felt like a steamroller had driven over him, backed up, and driven over him again. It was nothing like Jared. The two of them had fucked repeatedly throughout the night, but Ryan had not been as exhausted, bruised, and totally fucked by Jared as he was with just the one taking by Shane.

Shane showered again afterward. Ryan was still lying, spread out on the top of the message table, panting and moaning, as Shane dressed. Before the basketball player left the room, having thrown a twenty-dollar bill on Ryan's shuddering chest and growling, "Jared said dinner was supposed to come with the lay. Get yourself something nice from McDonalds," Shane also dropped another envelope on Ryan's chest.

When Shane was gone and Ryan was able to sit up and look at the envelope, he saw that it had "Ticket to Ride" written on it in an elegant script. Inside was a season ticket to the skybox section.

Ryan was to learn the next Wednesday night when he appeared at the next Stingrays' home game to check out what this latest ticket was all about that his seat was in the club owner's skybox. When he entered the box, the faces of four middle-aged, not-fully-in-shape men in expensive clothes looked up at him with assessing eyes.

Ryan wondered which of them he would have to service to pursue his interest in watching Stingray home games. With his luck, it would have to be all of them.

# Widows of the Prince

They say you can't pick who you love. I picked Auggie not out of love but because he was a sweet, hungry, and willing bottom when we were both students at Stanford. It didn't mean much to me at the time that his full name was Prince August Maximilian Ormandy and that before we graduated from Stanford he'd risen to be monarch of a postage stamp-sized princedom on the Mediterranean that maintained its independence by hosting a world-famous gambling casino, being a tax haven for professional athletes, and providing a flag-of-convenience home for questionable-activities shipping vessels. When I let Auggie take me home to his Mediterranean paradise with him, I continued to call him Auggie in private, but I soon learned to call him My Prince in public.

That didn't mean that he was in any way "my prince" when I had him writhing under me with my hard dick working his channel.

It did mean, however, that I had to carefully remain in the background, ever mindful of a Byzantine political game of chess that would have impressed Machiavelli and the Borgias. I had done far better at Stanford than Auggie had and came out of college with far better prospects—if you didn't take into account that he was the potentate of a square mile of pure gold and had nothing to prove by doing well in college. The reality was that most everyone in my new home thought of me as Prince August's valet. Only his closest associates knew of me also as the close friend and confidante that he liked to have near him, and although even a few of them suspected that in private, behind locked doors, I fucked the shit out of him and he delighted in that, they didn't voice it in more than whispers among themselves. His wasn't a lese majesty type of princedom, but he paid so well that no one wanted him to fire them.

The valet cover—not really a cover, as I had to perform the function—helped explain why my bedroom was connected to his. This continued even after he had married, as tradition demanded he do, to the woman his father had picked out for him in a negotiated deal for money before the man had breathed his last.

Madeleine was a Hapsburg from the industrial northern German city of Hamburg. If I were to be asked to show an image of an ice maiden, I would flash a photo of Nordic blonde Madeleine—all very nice tits and ass; long, long legs; and cold, cold blue-eyed stare. She came with attitude, a discerning suspicion of my place in the scheme of things, and two thugs to guard and be totally devoted to her. That both were fucking her, sometimes as a threesome, taking her together, was something I made it my business to verify.

I didn't tell Auggie of this, though. He either already knew it and didn't care or he didn't know it and didn't care.

I held my own with Auggie—being his only functional spouse—through the night after the wedding. Madeleine conceded the position voluntarily on the wedding night, helped by the convoluted wedding ceremony customs of the princedom, which I observed from the fourth-row position from where the line of "staff" started. The full-day ritual left both bride and

34

groom exhausted, and Madeleine begged off the nuptial bed until both were more "up" for it. The prince agreed, and as they maintained separate bedroom suites, Madeleine retired to her room, and I shut and locked the doors of the master bedroom suite to the world, while the prince lay, exhausted at the foot of the massive, gilded, four-poster bed, still wearing all of his wedding finery.

As I undressed the Mediterranean-dark, handsome young man of androgynous beauty and slight and trim stature, I was functioning as the valet of the prince. When I took his cock in my mouth and gave him suck, he was My Prince. But when I crouched over him, lifted his right leg to my shoulder, slid my thick cock inside a channel that had been well-reamed by my specifications, and started to pump to the sounds of his groans and moans, I was the master and he was my bride. Symbolically and atypically, I wasn't sheathed with a condom. This was Auggie's wedding night. I was not ready yet to cede my position as his lord and master in the bedroom. I seeded him, my bride, twice in the night before withdrawing to my own small chamber connected to his.

Madeleine's chamber also was connected to his, but I had made sure that door was locked. But I made no attempt to stifle Auggie's groans and small cries as I fucked him hard and deep. I wanted Madeleine to hear and know.

She was to make no overt indication that she knew the lay of the land. She also knew her purpose, as did Auggie. The prince's primary responsibility was perpetuation of the line. As a Hapsburg Madeleine understood this well too. On the third night after their wedding, she opened her chamber door and her legs to the prince, who did his duty, knowing that it was his duty. Within weeks Madeleine was pregnant and less than a year after the marriage, she had provided the prince with a male heir, Maximilian Gregor.

The struggle for ascendance over the prince between Madeleine and me continued for a year and got nasty—at least on Madeleine's part. I had to watch what I ate and I had to be careful not to be alone with Madeleine's two thugs. Unfortunately, I didn't watch what I drank enough. The pressure got to me, but rather than withdraw—there really wasn't any reason I could give that I clung to Auggie—and on too many nights I drank so much that I couldn't control myself.

That's when Madeleine changed her tactics drastically. We were alone. I was three quarters to the wind in my cups and she was all tits and ass enticement. When she produced a second child for the prince, a girl, Marta, the child had distinctively red hair—nothing like either Auggie's Mediterranean looks or Madeleine's Nordic ones. But very much like my own Irish heritage. Madeleine didn't let me forget the circumstances and held over my head the threat of telling August. It was petty, yes, but I could well understand that her frustration would lead to seeking some form of revenge.

So, I told Auggie myself that in a drunken stupor I had fucked Madeleine, stressing the circumstance of what naturally happens when a man has two spouses. What I left out was that it had been more than just the once and that chances were good that his daughter was actually mine. Auggie chose me, which was the beginning of the descent of Madeleine, but also, I fear the beginning of the end for Auggie—and for me.

Auggie spent less and less time in Madeleine's bed chamber and more and more time with the door from his chamber to hers locked. I now had him in bed every night. He had produced an heir and spare for the princedom. He considered his responsibilities in that realm fulfilled. I can't say how exhilarated I was that he turned from her back to me. At the time I didn't analyze that, though, and give it full value. It only was after he was dead that I realized the challenge he had faced and the choice he had made—and why I had stuck around through thick and thin. During that time we enjoyed a companionship that was much the same as would be found in a strong marriage. He could always escape the demands of his monarchy with me for a taste of normalcy, or he could count on me being an unbiased sounding board. I would have been honest and forthcoming even about Madeleine, who had had no say in either the marriage or having found that Auggie had an avenue of release and companionship before she even came into the picture. To Auggie's credit, though, he never used me to stoke a dislike or resentment of her.

The breaking point was when Madeleine found Auggie and me "going at it" herself, something she had avoided actually seeing and thus that she heretofore could deny.

We were in the cabana by the pool at the palace. I had Auggie on all fours on a lounge bed and was hunched over him and mining his ass deep when I saw the door of the cabana open. Madeleine stood there in the doorway for the longest moment, not saying anything, just staring at us with those washed-out blue ice-maiden eyes. I saw her eyes narrow and an expression of disgust float across her face. Then she was gone.

The next day we were in Switzerland, skiing. As a mere valet, I was some distance behind Auggie and Madeleine when they raced down the slope. I had no idea where her goons were, but when I got to the scene of the "accident," where Prince August had veered off the course and into the trees, smashing his body against one, Madeleine and both of her thugs were there, bent over his body.

Madeleine was a widow—and the regent of the princedom on behalf of her two-year-old son. I was a widow too. But one without status or place—or recognition by anyone now alive.

\* \* \* \*

I wasn't even invited to the funeral. A widow of the deceased—his chosen widow, I had to believe—and there was no place for me in the church. I watched the caisson pass from the third row back on the street, two blocks from the church.

Now, I've come back to the palace to pack. I fully understand that, in the battle of the widows, I have lost. At least I can go back into my world and make a new start.

But why do I feel so sad, wasted . . . and empty?

Perhaps because for me it wasn't really a game for ascendance, but was a battle for my chosen life—and life mate.

I hear them at the door. They haven't bothered to knock. They've just pushed the door open and are standing there—Madeleine's thugs.

I drop the shirt I'd just folded on the bed next to the suitcase. I'm not going to need my suitcase. I can see it in their eyes.

"Time to go," says one.

I sigh, all of the fight out of me. They say that you don't choose the one you love. That is true with me. I thought I had chosen Auggie because he was a sweet, hungry, and willing lay. Why didn't I know until now that it was for love—and that with him gone now, I didn't really give a shit what happened to me? A widow's surrender.

# What Friends Do

I'd gone to the kitchen in Jay's apartment to get myself a sparkling water from the fridge—we couldn't drink what we'd really like to drink during the performance season—when his doorbell rang, and he let his landlord in. I just stayed out of sight in the kitchen, because I knew this was going to be unpleasant and I didn't want the landlord, who I'd heard was a real ass, to get the idea that I'd moved in with Jay after Dalton died. Which I hadn't, and I didn't think there was any chance Jay would let me.

And therein was the rub. This was a good two-bedroom apartment in McLean Gardens almost within sight across Wisconsin Avenue of where both Jay and I were principal dancers with the Washington Ballet. It was a ten-minute walk to the theater for Jay. I had to take the bus from a much lower-rent part of Washington, D.C., and had a studio apartment that wasn't anywhere near this nice. Jay had lived with Dalton, who was quite a bit older than Jay was and who had a high-level job in some government agency down near the Mall. They'd been a couple for a few years, although Dalton's employers and friends probably didn't know it.

I did, though. Jay and I had come through the dance schools together and now were both principal dancers with the premier modern ballet company in the capital. We were tight—not go-to-bed tight, of course, because we were both bottoms. And we were such good friends that we didn't begrudge the principal roles the other one got. There was enough for both of us. In fact, we each were leads in the two casts of the current *Petite Mort* ballet by Jiri Kylián that was in production. That's why I came to the kitchen for sparkling water rather than a beer. A male dancer pretty much shows it all on stage. We had to be in perfect trim.

If there was any difference between Jay and me it was that he was long term and consecutive with his bedmates and I was casual one-night, no entangling relationship stands. He preferred them older and regular Joes; I rotated between rich and flamboyant, white sports muscle, and black bulls. I was up for variation, interesting positions, and a bit of rough and Jay was strictly vanilla and romance.

"I'm good for the rent," Jay was saying in the other room. "If you'll just float me for a couple of months. Dalton's estate has to settle, and then I can pay it all. I could do a third of it a month until then. I don't want to move. The location is great, and I don't want to have to move all of this stuff. Just a couple of months, please, before I can get back onto schedule."

"We can maybe come to an arrangement," I heard the landlord, Samuel Weinstein, who had an apartment himself on the ground floor, answer in a low, throaty voice.

I knew what he had in mind. Jay had told me the man had been pressuring him ever since Dalton had died unexpectedly—and maybe off and on before that. He wasn't that much different from Dalton. Forties and nondescript looking. Built well enough if a bit on the heavy side. Good looking but not strikingly so, like I liked them. A steady Joe. But he was pushing it with Jay if he wanted to replace Dalton. He might have a chance, but it was too soon. Jay was the romantic kind in contrast to my acceptance of "whatever feels good" and reality.

"Please, Mr. Weinstein—Sam—I just can't now."

I could see in my imagination, the landlord standing real close to Jay, maybe a hand on Jay's basket, pushing the issue.

"That's too bad," Weinstein said. "I could be a help to you. And I dropped by because I had a hookup for you that would give you rent money for at least this month."

"I don't do that," Jay said.

"Pity. There's a clothes designer coming in from London for a show at the Capitol Hilton. An old friend of mine. It would be just as an escort for him for the evening and then in his bed for the night. He's nothing to sneeze at, and it would be $1,500 for just the one night. Not interested, I can see. Well, think about it."

I could tell he was at the door of the apartment from the lower volume of his voice. Jay had answered him, but I couldn't hear what he said. Knowing Jay, though, and his approach to the lifestyle, I knew he'd passed on his regrets. Then I did hear him.

"But, like I said, it's just a matter of the estate being settled. It won't be long. We were legally married and there aren't any other relatives to contend. And I could do a third until then. Can we do it that way?"

"The rent isn't due for two more weeks," Weinstein answered. "You have time to consider my own proposal—and Christopher Manon isn't coming in until next weekend. So you have time to think about that too."

Christopher Manon, I thought. Not just a clothes designer, but a premier designer and owner of an exclusive line of men's wear. I'd die to be able to wear his clothes.

As I heard the door to the outer hallway close behind Weinstein, I made an instantaneous decision. The apartment had a service stairwell that opened from the kitchen. I launched myself into the stairwell and down the

41

three flights of stairs, around the side of the building, and made it back into the front hall as Weinstein was at the door to his apartment.

"I was upstairs and heard what you said to Jay Gold, Mr. Weinstein. I'm Cole Stevens, a friend of Jay's."

"Another one of those dancers over at the ballet?" he said, looking me up and down. I could tell by the gleam in his eyes that he liked what he saw. I was vain enough to know that he would. Jay and I were virtual twins in everything but some of our attitudes. Which might be helpful in this case.

"Yeah, well, then you know Jay Gold is in trouble with the rent," he said. "And I'm a candy man, but not without stipulations. If you're a good friend of his, you might help him see reality."

"I'm a good friend of his, Mr. Weinstein. And I want to see him be able to keep the apartment. I'd be willing to help in any way I can. And I don't have any of the reservations he has on how to get that done. Maybe rather than convince him of anything, I could show you how much a friend of his I am."

He gave me another hard look, and then his face went into a broad-smile expression. "You want to come into my apartment? Maybe see my etchings?"

"Yes, I'd like that." We both knew what I had signaled and what his response meant.

He fucked me on the foot of his bed missionary style, and I gave him a good time, with us sucking each other off in a 69 position before I opened my legs to him, begged him to cock me, and told him what he wanted to hear about how good he was, how big his cock was, how much I was enjoying him plowing me. And, as a matter of fact, he wasn't half bad, especially if I didn't zero in on the face; he'd kept his body in reasonable shape and he'd had a shower.

Afterward, over a beer for him and ice water for me at his kitchen table, before he bent me over that and

42

took me from the rear again, we set up appointments for two more sessions. This was to cover the shortfall in Jay's rent for the coming month. Then I maneuvered him into asking me to take the one-night gig with Christopher Manon the next Saturday night.

"I know you offered it to Jay, but there's not that much difference between us physically. And there's a whole lot of difference between how we'll take casual cock. You've seen what I can do now. Do you think your friend will find a timid and not fully willing Jay more fun to fuck than me?"

"Point taken," Weinstein said with a smile and an intimate search with the hand, which I let him know was appreciated. It wasn't fully appreciated, of course, but the things we do for friends. I planned to get full appreciation out of Christopher Manon, though.

I'd have to arrange for Jay to take my place in *Petite Mort* that night without telling him why I needed the night off, but that's why we had two casts—so that they could cover for each other, as needed. The ballet director liked to pair Jay and me in roles, not only because we were nearly twins in build and appearance, but also because we were so amenable to covering for each other—and we didn't put our claws out and try to belittle the other one for ascendance in the role. I wouldn't tell Jay why I needed the night off, and I'd use the money from the Manon escort service to cover another month of Jay's rent.

I got Weinstein to agree to say he'd take the one-third rent offer up front from Jay for the next five months. That way Jay would think we was getting what he offered, no strings attached, and, when Jay paid the back rent portion, Weinstein would come out ahead financially—although when the time came maybe I'd negotiate Weinstein down from that as well.

The cost would be out of my hide, but this was what friends were for, I knew Jay wouldn't agree to it if he knew what the real deal was, and I didn't mind the casual sex all that much.

Weinstein's cock certainly wasn't a particularly difficult chore to take, and from what I remembered of Christopher Manon's suave looks in the press photos I'd seen, he'd be my type. I didn't often get paid when a guy who aroused me took me to dinner and spiked me afterward.

\* \* \* \*

My adventure with Manon started on Saturday morning, when his driver picked me up at Weinstein's apartment, where I'd writhed half the night away with Weinstein doing pushups on my body. Where that might tire out most guys, the night with my legs open to Weinstein only had me keyed up—and interested in moving up in partners. Weinstein was OK, but he was no Adonis. It was only up from there.

Manon's limo driver, Ropo, on the other hand, was just what my appetite was whetted for. He was a six-foot-four, tank of a big black bull, with a bald head and the face of a prize-fighter thug. He was ugly as sin in the face but divine in muscular, athletic body elsewhere. He was dressed in the black livery of a hired limousine driver, which fit him like a glove.

As I came down the steps of the apartment house and slid into the cavernous back of the limo that was to take me to a spa for grooming for the night's festivities, I felt both randy and playful and brushed my hand along the bulge of his crotch as he opened the limo door for me and I slid by and into the back of the limousine. I smiled at him to let him know that hadn't been an accident and felt a little lurch of my own as he jerked and his eyes slitted at the passing attention.

He poked his head into the car to make sure I knew where we were going. "I'm drivin' you to Mr.

Manon's store for a tuxedo fitting for t'night first. Then to the Bethesda spa for treatments for a workover. Back to the store after lunch for the tux. Pickin' up Mr. Manon early evening for the dinner at the Hilton."

"Sounds good. Doesn't seem to fill the day, though," I answered, with a saucy smile. "We'll have to see what we can do to fill in the extra time."

"I's don't know about there bein' extra time," Ropo answered. I could see in his face, though, that he was thinking about that extra time himself. He had a funny accent. I couldn't place it but it didn't seem to be from D.C. There almost was a bit of British in it—but something more guttural, primitive than that.

"You do know, don't you, Ropo, that I'm Mr. Manon's date for the evening and night—that he's going to fuck me? That I let men fuck me? You might be interested to know that I'm partial to big black bulls and that I can't get enough of it. You, for instance. If you swing that way, I wouldn't mind being fucked by you."

"Wouldn't know anything about that, Mr. Stevens," he said. He'd pulled his head out of the back of the car, but his voice sounded strained. "Best get you to the clothes shop now."

I was in seventh heaven at the Christopher Manon downtown store, where instructions had been left for me to be given not only a tux but all of the sexy underwear, shoes, and socks that went with it plus a change of casual clothes and a pair of silky sleeping shorts.

"Mr. Manon is fanatical about style," the fitter offered, "and the men around him must be dressed to the nines—in Christopher Manon clothes."

That was quite all right with me. I did wonder what the man was thinking when he was outfitting me for the slinky sleepy shorts, though.

I made a point of trying it all on in full sight of Ropo, who was standing like a good soldier off to the side and, I guess, doing bodyguard duty. I made sure to get a good look at his crotch from time to time, and yes, I could tell he was hard. So, he was a player.

When I was finished there and we were walking out to the car, he stopped me with a big mitt latching onto my elbow. He turned me and said, "I called and had the spa appointment changed to the afternoon. If you were serious—"

"Is there someplace you can take me where we can fuck?"

There was. The store had a garage behind it for the store employees and to serve the apartments above. Ropo told me that the two-story penthouse apartment was reserved for Christopher Manon when he came to town. It's where we would be returning tonight. The space for the limo was way in back in the shadows, with blank cinderblock wall on three sides. The limo itself had tinted windows. The only clue that anything was going on in the limo was if it was being rocked on its springs.

And, every part of Ropo's body being as magnificent as I supposed, the limo did indeed get rocked hard on its springs.

There were miles of legroom in the back of the limo and a plush seat a passenger could be swallowed up in. There were clothes strewn all over the floor in the back, as, now fully into the tryst, Ropo quickly pawed me naked and I managed to strip him of his shoes, trousers, and briefs—all Christopher Manon labeled, I noted— before kneeling between his spread legs and starting to work his cock and balls with my mouth. I had unbuttoned his jacket to find he was bare underneath and that his chest was bulging with muscles and huge nipples, standing at attention.

To assure him I was no novice, I showed him my trick of rolling a Trojan Magnum on his stiff rod with my mouth. This put him over the edge and ended the foreplay before I was really ready to receive the cock. But the pain and effort of getting it inside was half the pain-pleasure of

46

being fucked by a big black bull. The other half was experiencing the depth he could reach, how vigorously—and long long—he could pump—and how much cum he could produce when he finally had me pinned under him, shot off all over my face, and then made me clean him with my mouth.

He sat back in the middle of the seat while, initially, I sat on his cock, facing him and saddled in his lap, my arms around his neck and kissing him on the mouth with no care that his mug was ugly when the rest of his body was so beautiful. He allowed me to control the rising and falling until we both knew I was fully open to him. And then he took over, pulling my legs up into the seat until they were bent at the knees, with my toes buried in where the seat back met the seat cushion.

"Crouch up," he growled, and when I pulled my buttocks up, maintaining my balance with my feet wedged into the seat crack and my arms around his neck, he took over the pumping, thrusting up, ever faster and deeper into me with his monster cock.

He had the stamina to go on forever. I was the one who's leg muscles gave out first. I also was the one who had come first, up his bare belly. When my legs gave out and I sank to the quick on his cock, he changed my position, pushing my back down toward the floor, supported by his legs, and my legs up his torso, the toes just touching the ceiling of the limo. Grabbing my waist in both sides, he pulled my ass channel on and off his cock, while I groaned and moaned, and he whispered how much he liked being inside me.

We finished with me pinned down by him, stretched along the backseat, and him poised over me, holding and stroking his cock until he'd come in prodigious spouts on my face and then had me clean the cock with my mouth again. I was beginning to wonder if I could apply for a staff job doing this for him.

The spa visit was anticlimactic after that fucking, with every inch of me being massaged and pampered. I left wondering why they'd even bothered to put a clear coat on my nails and also wondering if the ballet makeup director would let me keep the brighter blond highlights they'd put in my washed, cut, and styled hair. They'd even trimmed my bush and shaved the down off my chest. My pits were bare. I, apparently, only now was worthy of being dined, entertained, and fucked by Christopher Manon.

Ropo delivered me to Christopher Manon's penthouse apartment after we'd picked up my clothes at the store downstairs, saying I could dress—I'd already been showered, enemaed, and toweled dry at the spa—and wait there for Manon to return home and dress himself. We'd leave for the evening's events from here, in a limo driven by Ropo.

"Do we have time for another—?" I asked at the apartment door.

"I don't know when Mr. Manon will be back. And he'll probably call me to be driven back here, and I'll have to be ready to do that immediately."

"Well, don't worry," I said. "I won't tell Mr. Manon what we did."

"He won't care. In fact, he asked me to give him a report if I had you before he did."

I blushed and meekly entered the apartment. I had nothing in sophistication over these men. But then I turned and started to ask him another question. He anticipated it and cut me off, though.

"I've already tweeted him that he will have a fine evening and night," Ropo said. "You should know that we share. And, oh, by the way, I'd suggest the sleeping shorts for now and changing into the tux later when Mr. Manon tells you you can—unless you hadn't figured out why you were given an enema at the spa." And then, with a rare grin running across a customarily blank and guarded face, he turned, and went down the stairs, the athlete in him scorning the elevator.

I was trembling and my butt was twitching. By "share" did he mean they doubled another guy? I'd done that before, but I'd had no idea that was a possibility now. All of a sudden I felt like I might be fully earning that $1,500 I was being paid. Well, I was being paid more than that if I didn't have to return the clothes I'd been outfitted for downstairs.

Then my thoughts went to Jay. I had come on to Ropo, but what if I hadn't? What if he'd taken his slice anyway? How would Jay have reacted to that? I could enjoy it, but I wasn't Jay. Had I maybe done an even bigger favor for my friend by stepping in for him than I'd thought? Did it matter whether I enjoyed this kind of sex or not, or did it matter more that Jay was being saved from something he wasn't in tune with?

* * * *

I entered the apartment on the top floor, which seemed to be one large room, with all glass walls toward the street and sides of the building. And there were deep terraces beyond the glass walls at the sides. Areas were delineated by furnishings as living room, dining area, and kitchen, but no walls between them. There was a kitchen bar between the appliances and the dining area. It took me a minute to find the winding staircase that went down to the level under this one. The place was deserted.

The staircase took me down to the bedroom level, which contained more living space than the upper level. I found four bedrooms, each with a bath, and a study or office. There were suitcases and clothes stacked around in two of the bedrooms. The master bedroom obviously was Manon's. But the other one? Ropo's?

Had Ropo come from London with Manon? that would explain the strange accent. Maybe he was from

London too—but obviously not native British. Maybe Nigerian? He wasn't chocolate brown like blacks I knew in the D.C. area. He was jet black. So, maybe African by way of London. A lot of D.C. blacks I fucked had jet black cocks, but lighter-colored bodies. With Ropo, it was all black cock color—and a very memorable cock, if I might say—like a thick sausage, uncut.

If Ropo had come with Manon and was staying here as well, that would indicate a closer relationship than normal for employer and driver. Ropo had said the two shared. A chill of anticipation went down my back.

I picked out one of the other bedrooms and unloaded the clothes I'd been given downstairs.

At nearly 5:00 p.m., I was sitting on a living room sofa facing north and picking out monuments over near the Washington Mall through the plateglass window. As suggested, I was wearing only the cobalt-blue silk sleeping shorts, which fit me, but were designed to ride low on the hips and high above the knees.

I turned my head toward the door to the apartment when the lock was turned and it opened and then I sucked in breath as Christopher Manon entered. He was all that his press photographs promised: tall; slender; perfectly proportioned; gray hair; slight beard; everything perfectly trimmed; elegantly dressed; carrying himself like the model that he obviously had been throughout his life.

He smiled, said hello, and noted in a honey-toned voice, "You must be my date for tonight. Cole Stevens, is it? I'm Christopher Manon." A patrician English accent. The type that was used in TV commercials to assure buyers that the product was both sophisticated and worked a charm.

You most certainly are, I thought, and stood up from the sofa, as he moved across the room toward me, giving me an appraising scrutiny as he moved, his smile indicating that he liked what he saw—which I assumed he would. As a modern ballet dancer, I kept myself finely honed. It was quite an effort to do so.

"I see you've settled in. I hope you like the clothes that were picked out for you."

"Yes, thanks, I did . . . I do," I answered.

"And Ropo tells me he fucked you in the back of the limousine and that you're quite a good lay."

I didn't know what to say to that, so I remained silent, slightly off kilter. Manon didn't seem to notice or to care that I hadn't responded, though. He continued speaking in a matter-of-fact tone.

"It's been a busy day so far. We'll have to be on our way at seven. But we have time for a drink. I'm having red wine. What would you like?"

"Just sparkling water, if you have it," I answered. "If not, just ice water, thank you."

"Ah, I do suppose that a dancer is like a model—that you have to continually watch your figure."

He said that while he was in the kitchen getting the drinks. When he came out, he handed me a glass of sparkling water, took a sip of his wine, and sat down close beside me on the sofa.

"And I could continually watch your figure as well. Very good shape you're in, I'm happy to say. Do you mind if a check what I'm paying for?"

"No, of course not," I answered in a breathy voice. It was so matter of fact. I'd never actually taken the role of call boy or paid escort, although I'd occasionally been paid for sex. I wondered if the john was always so straightforward and bald in these sorts of arrangements. Once again, I tried to see Jay in this position—and couldn't. I could see him bolting for the door. This was especially so because, with the wine glass in one hand, Manon had the other high up the inside of one of the legs of my sleeping shorts, weighing my balls and fondling my engorging cock.

"Nice, very nice," he said. He leaned his face over into mine and, getting the message, I moved my lips to meet his. The red wine was luscious on his lips. I regretted that I hadn't asked for that myself. It didn't really matter; I was getting the essence of the taste of it now. The kiss otherwise was very nice too. Slow and sensual, his tongue parting my lips but then only invading a fraction of an inch, flicking a bit, promising more. His hand was stroking my cock, which was filling out fast to his touch.

But then he had pulled away, sat up, and took another swig of his wine. I let my body, twisted on the sofa, recline back on the arm of the sofa.

He sat there, making small talk, asking me about the ballet and how it was like working there and whether I'd ever modeled before—and whether I acted the escort often, being visibly pleased to hear that I was new to it. Just a normal conversation, if you didn't take into account that he was slowly jacking me off inside the silk sleeping shorts.

When I came close to coming, I told him I would if he didn't stop. "I want you to," he said, simply, and then when, with a jerk and a sigh, I did, he continued stroking me, slathering my staff with my own cum and giving it slippery strokes. But it was a signal, I guess for his next question. "Did you bring the medical certificate?"

"Yes, it's on the dining room table," I answered. Weinstein had made me get a complete checkup, saying that Manon would want to bareback.

He sat there, looking down at me for maybe a full minute, both of us holding place other than his hand that still was stroking my cock inside the sleeping shorts. He had a thumb on the bulb and I was producing precum again, which he was spreading around on the cock head. The front of the silky shorts was slick and wet with cum.

"You look so innocent, so inviting, lying there like that," he said.

"I can be anything you want," I answered.

Letting loose of my cock, he put his wine glass down and stood. "I'm going downstairs and shower and get naked. When I come back I'll take you for a spin. We have time before we have to be ready for the program. Ropo said you were cleaned out at the spa. Correct?"

Still matter-of-fact, almost clinical. "Yes."

When he was gone, I sat up and drained his wine glass, looking hungrily at the kitchen counter to see of the bottle was out and to gauge if I could sneak a refill before Manon got back. He was going to fuck me before the program and then, undoubtedly, again afterward. He was going to make me work for the $1,500.

An hour and forty-five minutes before pickup now, I thought. But I was wrong about fucking me twice.

I was lying across the cushions of the sofa when he came back, my back against the arm, my legs bent and spread, my feet on the seat of the sofa. I gasped when he came back, fully naked. His body was beautiful. Not beautiful in the powerful, primitive way Ropo's was, but like a classic Italian statue. Perfectly formed on a tall, thin frame. Full chest, but narrow hips. A dick that wasn't thick, but was impossibly long. And half erect.

He caught me eyeing his cock. "I was thinking about you," he said in the smooth voice of his. "And what position to ride you in the first time."

He looked at his now-empty wine glass and gave a little laugh, but rather than refill it, he came down on top of me between my legs. I hadn't seen the velvet handcuffs before then, but I felt his hands gliding up my arms, forcing my arms over my head, and then snapping on the cuffs around my wrist, the lead going around a sturdy floor-to-ceiling pole lamp column next to the sofa arm so that my arms were immobilized above my head.

Then he began eating up time by exploring every inch of my body with his mouth and hands, gliding over every curve, exploring every crevice—until he had me moaning and begging for his cock.

When he entered me, I was well open to him, having been prepared with his fingers and tongue. He fucked me slow and deep for well over a half an hour before he released his seed inside me. When he was finished, we now were late and had to scramble to shower and dress in our tux.

I wasn't given a moment to contemplate how long and completely I'd been taken.

What would Jay have done in this situation? Of course, once I'd been bound to the pole lamp, there wasn't much I could do—other than come for the man two more times.

\* \* \* \*

Christopher Manon was every inch the suave English gentleman and impressive celebrity as we exited the limousine, driven by a uniformed Ropo, by the red carpet outside the entrance of the Capitol Hilton. The hotel fronted on 16th Street, just two blocks up and within sight of the north portico of the White House. And he didn't have me slinking about in the shadows. He handed me out of the limo and had an arm around my shoulder as we strutted into the Hilton and over to the elevators leading to the ballroom, where a raised walk had been erected for the models who would be showing his fall collection.

I guess when you are a men's clothes designer of international reputation, being overtly gay is fully acceptable to the public. At no time before in my life was I so openly presented as the male date of a male celebrity.

He was not only personable to everyone about him throughout the fashion show and then at the dinner afterward but he was closely attentive to me, as well. It was as if I was some treasure perched on a pedestal and that he was courting me. No one would have known that just a couple of hours earlier he was fucking me on a sofa in his Washington apartment—or that he planned to resume doing so after all of the partying was over.

He introduced me to other celebrities, making no bones about saying I was a principal dancer at the Washington Ballet—and I was surprised at how many people this seemed to impress—and he was continually whispering to me who this or that was and little vignettes of his working relations and of the triumphs and travails of putting together his fall fashion collection. In public, he treated me like a friend and date on the same level as he was and with as much reason to be there as he had. He had treated me with respect on the sofa, but at no time had there been a misunderstanding of our respective positions—he on top and me on bottom—or that I was there to serve his pleasure and that a mere finger touch on my inner thigh was to be responded to by my opening my legs to his cock.

Whenever he got the chance, he'd point out to others that the tux I was wearing was also from the fall collection, and he'd fish for and always received compliments on how well I looked in it. It was as if we were a standing couple, not that we'd only met that afternoon and that I was mostly here to give him sexual release at a price—a full-service escort; a male prostitute.

By the time we got back to the apartment, I'd forgotten that I wasn't Cinderella and that Manon wasn't Prince Charming. I was quickly brought back down to earth on that score, though.

"Shall we cap the evening with a drink?" he asked when we entered the top level of the penthouse apartment. "And this time I think you need champagne, not just sparkling water. You'll exercise it off. You did very well tonight."

I accepted the champagne, and we stood at the wall of glass, looking in the direction of the lit-up Capitol building and monuments on the Mall, making small talk about the evening's events. He seemed to be completely relaxed. I was increasingly keyed up, as I knew that this was the point at which he'd bed me again. The afternoon session had been exhausting but fully satisfying. My mind was running wild on what he would do with me tonight. As wild as the possibilities that I entertained, though, they came nowhere close to reality.

"It's time to go downstairs," he said as he took my empty champagne glass from my hand and placed it, with his, on the kitchen counter. "You will be in my bed tonight."

It wasn't lost on me that he hadn't said I would sleep in his bed that night. I presumed I wouldn't be getting much sleep in that bed. He was right.

I stopped dead still in shock when we entered the master bedroom, Manon behind me and with a possessive arm around my chest. The bed already was occupied. Ropo, naked, stretched out, and working his cock with a beefy hand, was reclined there, facing the door.

"I believe Ropo told you earlier that we liked to share," Manon murmured, as he hands started unbuttoning, unfastening, and unzipping my tux.

My clothes were neatly folded on one chair, and Manon was sitting in another one, facing the bed, only the fly to his tux open and his cock exposed and hard to his stroking touch as Ropo placed me on all fours on the bed and mounted on and crouched over me, fucked me hard. At some point I collapsed underneath him and he rolled me onto my side, facing him, my thigh over his, and his cock buried in my channel and thrusting, thrusting, thrusting.

I watched—while being fucked by Ropo in this position—Manon slowly disrobe; place the pieces of his tux in the closet and drawers, as appropriate; climb up on the bed behind me; grab my hip with a hand; and start working his long cock in above Ropo's in my channel, as I writhed, groaned, and gasped.

56

They worked me together, bareback, and came inside me almost simultaneously. Then, sandwiching me between them, their arms entwined and binding me to the bed, they both drifted off into a sleep of light snoring. It took me longer to go to sleep. And I didn't sleep for long, as they, in turn, woke during the night, and individually fucked me again.

In the morning, I was awakened by Ropo, standing in the doorway to the bedroom, in his chauffeur's uniform, and holding two cups of coffee. One was for me, and while I drank it, he told me that Manon was already up and out; that he, Ropo, had a pay envelope for me; and that he would drive me home.

"Can you drop me off at the Washington Ballet instead," I said. "I have a performance to give this afternoon." I tried to be as nonchalant as he was being. It was just a day and night of escort and prostitution work. I wouldn't put any more thought or concern into what had happened over the last twenty-four hours than Christopher Manon and his chauffeur had. It was just a successful doing of a favor for a friend, substituting for what it didn't bother me to do but that probably would have devastated him.

I put it all out of my mind—or convinced myself I had—until the middle of the performance of *Petite Mort* that day, when, in a moment out of the spotlight on stage, I looked out into the audience and found Christopher Manon there.

I received a dozen red roses in the dressing room after the performance. I didn't have to guess who they were from. And then there was Ropo at the door, saying, "Mr. Manon be out in the car. He wants that you come to the apartment with him. He will make it worth your while." I didn't take it as a request. I didn't need for it to be a request.

It was just Manon and me in the bed; me on my belly, arms over my head and cuffed to the headboard;

and him saddled on my hips and fucking me slow and deep.

Afterward, as I lay in his arms, he murmured, "I wanted to see you—to be inside you—one more time. I only wish that—"

"No you don't," I interrupted—gently, not angrily. "Commitment and permanence aren't in either one of our natures," I continued, guessing rightly what he was going to say. "You've been straightforward and honest with me to this point. Don't tell me you want a more permanent arrangement. You don't, and neither do I. This is fine—this is glorious—but it's only for now."

"I suppose you're right," he acknowledged. "But I'll pay you for this, for today."

"You don't have to," I said. "This was as much for me as for you. I probably should be paying you."

This made him laugh, but I could tell that he appreciated it. He probably had been only on the paying end of everything in life for some time.

"Nonetheless, I'll pay you for your time. And I'd like to engage you the next time I come to Washington. Is that too much commitment for you?"

"No, I answered," pleased in my turn. "I would like that."

"There's something else I'd like," Manon said. "You were a real hit, wearing my tux last night. And you're in perfect shape for a model. I want to contract you as a model for my shows on this side of the Atlantic."

"I have a job," I answered—somewhat with regret, because the offer certainly was enticing.

"It wouldn't take much of your time. You could easily juggle the two. You do that now with another dancer, Jay Gold, I understand. I could sign him as a model too and you two could trade off in both jobs."

"Jay? You know of Jay?"

"Yes, of course. He was who Sam first told me about as an escort. I was given a file on him—and then on you. There seemed to be little difference between the two of you."

Once more my thought went back to Jay. No, Manon wouldn't find us at all alike. First, Jay would not have fallen in with Manon's and Ropo's attentions as I had. And if he'd succumbed to Manon's charm and talents, he would want the commitment that neither Manon nor I required. I didn't tell this to Manon, though. Both he and Jay had escaped that discovery.

After we had both showered and were dressing, Manon stuffing banknotes in my pocket over my weak objections, he said, "Ropo will drive you home."

"Thank you," I answered. "If you don't mind, though, he won't be back too quickly."

Understanding, Manon gave me a small smile and said merely, "Yes, of course."

\* \* \* \*

When I next called on Jay at his apartment, I found his door open, and so I walked in. I heard the sound of sex coming from one of the bedrooms and was drawn there—to find Samuel Weinstein on his back on the bed, naked, and Jay, also naked, saddled on the older man's hips, facing his head, and riding Samuel's cock.

Jay's expression was dreamy eyed, and I had to conclude that in the week I'd been working on being Christopher Manon's escort, Jay had overcome his grief at the passing of Dalton and decided that Weinstein could be his next sugar daddy. This no doubt was all laid out by Weinstein as the best opportunity for Jay and Weinstein had promised some sense of permanence in the arrangement.

I must admit that it neatly solved the rent problem—except that Weinstein may now be making money from all sides of the situation, including, from what I'd gathered, the previous weekend pimp service for

Manon. I didn't mind Jay turning to Weinstein as a replacement for Dalton, but I wanted to make sure that Weinstein's cut out of either of us was pared down to something fair.

I knew of one way to declare to Weinstein that I was watching and expecting a recount. I stripped off my clothes, mounted the bed and Weinstein's chest, in front of Jay, and presented my cock to Weinstein for sucking. He was happy to comply.

Behind me, Jay covered my pec with his hands, and I turned my face to him for a kiss. We didn't fuck, but we did kiss and hug.

It was all going to work out. I had carried through with a solution that benefited us all—and especially my friend Jay. I was glad to do it. That's what friends do for each other.

# I'm So Sexy

I can feel the eyes on me as I follow the student guide along the catwalk skimming the tops of labs on one side and looking out into a campus quad through a massive glass window on the other. Nice little piece of ass, walking in a saucy way, knowing I'm behind him, watching his little butt twitch in the tight trousers as he walks along, pointing to this and that with little flourishes, batting his eyelashes at me when he turns to speak to me. Eyes raise to us as we pass and then stop and stare—both women and men. More women than men, but it's the men I scrutinize for the tell-tale signs of interest—speculative interest in me. I am used to it; it isn't something I do; it's something I am. I don't deny it, and, at the same time, I don't deny I use it.

I like to fuck. I don't see it as my fault that I'm packaged to find it easy to do that—for men to readily accommodate me.

I can feel the student guide, Tim, tremble as I touch him on the arm to stop his progress so that he can explain to me what is going on in one of the labs below. He turns, sweeps strands of straight, golden-blond-dyed hair out of his face, and smiles a shy smile for me. I can tell from that and his trembling that I can have him. In fact, just from the way he made sure I knew he was twenty, a college senior, I knew he was available.

He wouldn't be my first choice, really. But I'm just visiting and he is obviously available and willing. I'm not sure I feel energetic enough to put the effort into acquiring better.

I've found I can have almost any man—and woman too, if I was so inclined—with them pursing me rather than the other way around. It's just the way it is. A science colleague and lover once told me that, in addition to the look of me, it was pheromones—something I exuded that made others want me. I scoffed, but he claimed to be serious, and it certainly worked with him.

Tim answers with surprise. "I understand you've devised the Tristan Variation, which uses. . . ." Rather than listen to him rattle off what I already knew so well, being the "Tristan" of that variation, I concentrate on his expression, which is as much one of admiration—almost worship—as surprise. He seems to realize that I'm not really listening to what he says but am concentrating on him—personally. I give him that special smile, and he melts into the walkway. This is going to be very easy. I hadn't wanted him at the start; he was a bit too effeminate for me. Now, feeling myself harden, I do.

"Yes, we experiment with that too at Arizona," I say. "I just wasn't familiar with that brand of equipment being used for the research here."

"I thought you—that Arizona—were far ahead of us on that process, Professor Tristan," he murmurs, still a bit breathless because I've left my fingers on his forearm, burning my brand into his flesh, testing on whether he will withdraw. He doesn't.

I know it's a question on why I'm interviewing for a post here. I'm king of the labs at Arizona—their current hope for a Nobel Prize. They give me everything. They even pimp for me, knowing that my needs are nearly insatiable. Why would I ever leave there? "One can stay in one place too long," I say. "Life can get too complicated, too much of a rut. I'm not much for long-term commitment."

Just the once, I'm signaling. There's no chance of something building from it. Take it or leave it, little boy. If you're good with a one-time fuck, I'm your man. This. This is at the center of why I am looking beyond Arizona. The increasing lack of understanding there that I really do want someone fresh each time—and preferably someone unused or only slightly so, someone innocent to how totally I will use him.

"Perhaps after the tour, we could go for coffee," he ventures. ". . . I'd like to hear more about the program at Arizona."

Home free. "Perhaps a drink at my hotel instead."

I feel him shudder as he nervously brushes down the front of his trousers, trying to hide the bulge we both know is there—the trousers I know I'm going to pull down those long, long legs of his along with his bikini briefs when I pull him up off his knees after he's sucked me ready.

That's after I've had my fill of fondling his curves and listening to his intake of breath while we're kissing. When I reach around with both hands, separate his bare butt cheeks, and penetrate and open him with fingers of both hands as I hold him close in a deep kiss, he sinks to the floor in front of me and takes my cock in his mouth. Who knew a young man so innocent and fresh looking could give such expert head? He can deep-throat it all, and that's saying a lot. It's not the first time I think he was assigned as my student guide as a recruitment ploy. It would be hard for my reputation not to precede me.

I presume the powers that be here—whoever was assigned to pimp for me—assumed I would be impressed with experience and mastering when, in fact, I would prefer innocence, albeit acquiescence, to what I do with the gift.

63

I lift him up and turn him toward the bed. Trembling and emitting little burbling sounds, he positions himself—one knee on the bed, the other foot on the floor, thighs spread, arms stiff arming the bedspread, the material bunched up in his fists, now emitting mewing sounds—as I roll on a Trojan Magnum.

I reach up and brush his hair to one side, exposing his neck, a throbbing vein. He's open to me in more ways than one. If I were a vampire, I believe he still would receive me.

He gasps, groans, and tightens up at the entry, but I hold there a few seconds to permit him to adjust before I reach around to take one pectoral in each hand, thrum his nipples with my thumbs, press my lips to the throbbing vein, and thrust with my hips.

"Oh, daddy, daddy. Yes, daddy, yes."

He doesn't have any idea yet what "daddy" has in store for him. We've already established he's not my guide for the next day, which is good, because he isn't going to be in any condition to be able to guide anyone tomorrow.

\* \* \* \*

I "get" it when Aaron mentions knowing Joseph Cleese, husband of one of the deans at Arizona, as Aaron is the husband of the dean I am scheduled to meet with informally over dinner at her house this evening. I should have gotten it when he met me at the door of his columned colonial house a block from the campus in some form of loose-fitting silk lounge suit and said, "I'm afraid Janet can't join us. Some sort of mishap at a lab at the college. She said we should go ahead with the dinner, though, and she'd be along when she could be. You do have to eat somewhere, and Cook has it prepared. Janet says she'll talk with you tomorrow if she doesn't make it back soon."

If he knows and talks with Joseph, I wonder if he volunteered to face the required "dinner with a faculty member" duty alone rather than just having Janet call and cancel. I would suppose so. He has dressed the part. A willowy, flowing movement, well-preserved academic type in ochre-colored silk, letting off a sensuous slithering sound with each tightly orchestrated movement. Brazilian? Argentine? Had I heard that he had married Janet to get into the country? It didn't matter. Not young by any means, but well preserved, both hard and soft bodied, each where it counted. Younger than Janet, though—and, for me, much more appealing on the eyes.

Candlelight on the table. Smoothing out any wrinkles. A sensual, knowing smile.

Referencing Joseph Cleese says it all. The young, boy toy husband of the dean of the college at Arizona, initially my tennis partner and subsequently much more than that to me. But not the best recruitment move in anticipation of my decision for a change. Under these circumstances, I would have fucked Aaron anyway, given the opportunity, without the reference to Joseph. I was in the mood for something more substantial than the student guide, something more Latin. The Latins are fiery and uninhibited. And Aaron obviously wants it; He's boldly feeling me up under the table and giving me the eyes of want before we've finished dessert.

But it reminds me that it's the students and the boy toy Josephs of Arizona—the possessiveness of and battles between them—that have me shopping for another post—less stress; fewer complications. Being reminded of that doesn't mean I'm not going to fuck Aaron, though.

As a one-time taking, he will do just fine.

Since I didn't hide knowing Joseph and, by extension, what Joseph would say about me and because I am calmly letting Aaron fondle me under the table, he becomes bolder in what he could offer in the way of recruitment incentive. It hasn't taken me long to understand that Janet not being here is no accident—and that the recruitment pitch is coming from Aaron, not her, by design.

Janet is putting her best case forward, and that's Aaron, not her.

"I know that Joseph makes what you like available for you in Phoenix," he says. "I'm the head of student housing here, and I'm in a position to broker privileges with fresh underclassmen wanting favorable housing and willing to be available for the first time to get a good room."

"That's interesting," I respond. It isn't interesting in the way Aaron probably thinks I mean, though. I had never gotten a man under me, and opening his legs, through bribery or the hint of privilege to be gained by him. And Joseph went out of bounds if he left the impression with Aaron that he procured any tail for me.

In a guest room, because he "just couldn't do it in the bed he shares with Janet," Aaron wants to ride me cowboy style, and I let him. Before this he gives me an expert blow job. I get that he's not faking what I can take from him. His BJ is as good, if not better, than the student guide's was. Does this college have a class in it? First time I've had a man fuck me in foreplay with his armpits, hiding my cock under his arm on either side while he's nibbling on my nipples and fucking me with the movement of his arm. Raising his dark eyes, with the long, curly eyelashes, and staring into my face with lustful eyes; murmuring what must be dirty words in Spanish. Or is that Portuguese? Who the shit cares? Either sounds sexy when my cock is being rubbed in his armpits—and then between his thighs before I manage to get around to holing it.

I let him think he's in charge. Rising over me, marveling at the size of me. Wondering out loud if he can take me in the ass, when both of us know he could sheath a Volkswagen bus. Making gasping sounds about size when I produce the Trojan Magnum, insisting on rolling it on my cock himself, making a big scene of wetting the sheathed shaft down with his mouth. Sucking me inside his ass. Milking me dry with shimmering channel muscles. Oh, yes, he's done this before. He's done this frequently. And, yes, he'd be a good ride if I signed on here. Hard to beat a South American for enthusiasm, openness, and inventiveness. Riding, riding, riding me. Sucking every bit of cum out of me.

A good fuck, of course, but not what's fully arousing to me.

Sitting afterward at his kitchen table, him just in sleeping shorts; me naked and sprawling off the seat of the chair, because "I want to see your beautiful body move, your lovely big cock rise again."

So, we're going to do it again. I'm game, but I look at my watch. Janet is taking her sweet time. I get it already—what I can have by transferring to here. It's not their fault that they've misjudged what I prefer.

Drinking coffee—black and strong—and a good cognac. His hand stroking me under the table.

Fucking him belly down from behind on the kitchen table, while he laughs and wiggles his ass, muttering guttural words in Spanish or Portuguese, until I've given it all to him, scaring him with what "all of it" means, settling down to a rhythm of long, deep slides, listening to him gasp and moan. His passage shimmering, grabbing and releasing. Me getting as much pleasure as he is. A slow build to a mutual explosion.

"Oh baby, baby. Yes, baby, yes."

Asserting that he's the daddy, having more than ten years on me. But he's playing the sub role expertly.

"You're so sexy," he continuously moans as I plow his ass. As if I didn't know that already.

Barely dressed again and leaving when his wife's car pulls into the driveway, with Janet giving a cheery wave with the driver's-side window down. Aaron standing at the door, barefoot and still only in his sleeping shorts.

OK, I get it about Janet's willingness to share. Preplanned. Has Aaron called Janet while I was showering and dressing and told her it was safe to come home? This is what I can have if I sign a contract?

Only it's what I already have at Arizona. It's why I'm leaving Arizona. Still, Aaron certainly has a talented mouth and ass. I must be on the lookout for South American tail.

\* \* \* \*

Paul Compton, my age, my handsome face, my perfect physique, and the chair of the department at his young age for reasons that go beyond academic smarts, closes and locks the door behind me when I arrive for my interview. The shade over the window in the door to the corridor comes down. No attempt whatsoever to hide the maneuver. Stays very close to me as I enter the office. A fiery redhead, with the mane of a lion. A pullover sweater as tight across his chest as it can be, just as are the faded jeans—both easily shucked, though, I learn.

To think a dean would dress like this, you have to know Paul. I'm not fooled, however. I know he has dressed like this just for me. I'm sure he has nothing on underneath the jeans, something that it would have been nice to have someone bet me on, as he doesn't—which would be clear to anyone following the line and curves of the bulge. No surprises here. This is vintage Paul Compton. We have history from graduate school. That history not being the success with me that Paul probably thinks it was, him having been aggressive and wanting to talk of "forevers," both of which rang "walk away" bells for me.

"We can talk later," he says in a husky voice. Couldn't be clearer. He's only gotten better with age.

But then, so have I.

I pull the sweater over his head and rub his quarter-sized aureoles with my perpetually five-o'clock-shadow cheeks. He groans, and the nipples stand at instant attention, filling out, and begging to be sucked. I suck them, one after the other. We're standing in the middle of the room, swaying against each other. Moaning, he reaches down and unzips me and moves a hand into the slit. "Oh, fuck, Mr. Sexy. You remember me, don't you? Drop dead sexy and ready for it. Don't make me wait, Mr. Sexy. I want you inside me." He begins to climb me with his legs but changes his mind and maneuvers me toward a chair.

He fucks himself on my staff in the desk chair, Paul naked, me fully clothed except for my shirt unbuttoned for his hands to roam and my fly unzipped for him to ride my cock, facing me, as I sit in the chair and he straddles me, I valiantly try to get all of his aureoles in my mouth, one after the other. Sucking and fucking, the nipples needing to be teethed and sucked.

On my back on the desk, leveraging off my heels on the floor. Paul saddled on my cock, riding me hard, as I palm his pecs, thrumming and pinching the nipples, and counterpunch in long, deep thrusts. Another power bottom; wanting the cock, wanting me working it inside him, but wanting to think he's the one in control.

I know that would be an unending battle if I came to work in his department, the struggle for control in the question of who is controlling the fuck.

"Yes, you stud, you stud. Fuck me, yes, fuck me. Work those nubs."

As if whatever I do is at his command. Can he ever get enough?

That's the interview. Of course he offers me the position—me knowing the position entails more than a teaching spot; he's making quite clear he wants a submissive top—as, dressed once more, he lifts the shade and unlocks and opens the door to the outer corridor.

I say, my eyes on the lines and curves of his bulge, that I'm certainly considering it. And I am, in fact, wondering what he's doing for dinner—and who's doing him afterward. I wouldn't mind showing him what I've learned since graduate school, what I can do on top. And in command.

He says, "I'll enjoy having you work under me. I think you'll enjoy it too."

We both laugh when I counter, "Don't you mean me working on top of you," but I can see that the smile on his face doesn't reach to the eyes.

Still, he's more of a challenge for control than I've encountered from anyone before. He's fucked me balls-aching dry. I'd almost forgotten that about him. Voracious.

\* \* \* \*

Dean Raffer, tall, elegant, impeccably groomed and dressed, flashes me a brilliant smile as I'm ushered into his office and sit in a chair facing his desk. He stands and comes around the desk, sitting almost sideways on the desk in front of me, the heel of one spit-polished tasseled loafer on the carpet, the other leg bent and dangling. Showing me a slim profile with a good chest—his studied "best side." His crotch is puffed out in the tailored slacks. He's hard—I could tell when he was watching me enter the room that he would be—and he wanted me to know it.

Reaching over and grasping my knee with his manicured hand, the fingers long and strong. "We would love to have you on the faculty here, Robert. We could have ever so much fun."

Talking to my basket, not to my eyes, lips parted and tongue darting out. So sure of himself; sure all of the other recruitment efforts have settled it and he's just in to establish that his needs are part of the deal.

As I rise from his grip, I tell him I'm strongly considering it—but I'm not. I'm already thinking about the next college where I can interview. This is just the sort of stress and complicated life that is prompting me to leave Arizona. I can't help it if I am the way I am—not that I really want to help it, mind you. I'm just too sexy for false humility.

"What do you have on for dinner tonight?" he asks. "We could—"

"Alas I have plans," I answer, trying to show regret in my eyes, but the plane schedules back to Arizona already going through my head. If I call ahead, I know Joseph will drop everything and meet my plane. But it will cost me. Such is the burden of the world's sexiest man.

# Inevitable Case

I picked my way through piles of corrugated tin, broken toilets, and lawnmower parts and came to a halt when I saw the blue uniforms and the wheel-less old Lincoln Town Car, with the smashed-in engine compartment, sitting on concrete blocks. Mullins had said it was an Inevitable Case when he'd called me, but I'd never get used to seeing the various ways that could play out. What we referred to as an Inevitable Case was a street whore or hustler some john or pimp had taken for that final ride.

The back door of the Town Car was open and I could see the body—small, slim, and folded over in a near-fetal position, knees on the floor of the car in front of the backseat, chest pushed up against the partition wall to the driver's compartment, the red sash around the neck, angrily contrasting with the supple, creamy skin. Golden curls drooping down over the side of the face. Even from here I could see that it was a young Caucasian, probably male. At least I'd been told on the phone that it was a male, connected with a series of cases we were pursuing.

When I got closer to the car, Mullins and Paxton looked up and gave me a slight grimace. I didn't know who any of the young, uniformed cops were who were milling about the scene—more cops than were necessary,

72

certainly. Sightseers just like the people gathered at the entrance to the junk yard. No doubt they were from the local Bronx precinct. Mullins and Paxton I knew because they were my men. We all were Central Headquarters Vice Homicide, the only such specialized unit in the city. The case had already been bucked up to us because of the red sash. It was becoming a city-wide signature, as was the victim also IDing as a young prostitute.

Flat chested. That was where the "probably male" had come from. No one had messed with the body to be positive about that. The side of his chest was hidden by the fold of his arm. If there'd been tits in evidence, protruding beyond the curve of the arm, it could have been a young, slim female, of which there were plenty walking the streets of the city. Now that I was closer, I could see his shorts and briefs down around his ankles and the T-shirt—a familiar one, but it probably was a popular design—puddled on the floor of the Town Car.

The perpetrator had been sitting on the seat, with the rent-boy riding him and facing the front seat. The red sash probably had started as just a breath-control kink and turned into something terminal. You'd think these young street whores would take notice of what little we put out on the street about this—be careful of red scarves and of johns interested in breath control.

"Any ID on him?" I asked Paxton.

"Left him his wallet, in his shorts, Mike. Name on the NYU student card is Sean Parks."

I grunted. "Leaving ID follows the pattern. Thumbing his nose at us. Didn't care that we knew who the vic was in short order. Probably meant he was picking them at random, not providing a pattern of mutual contact. Time of death?"

"The ME hasn't arrived yet," Mullins answered. "Apparently it was a busy night in the Bronx."

I leaned into the backseat and reached over and brushed the curls of the hair away—and my hand immediately began to tremble. It couldn't be. But of course it was. I took a moment to take deep breaths. Mullins and Paxton couldn't see how this had undone me.

Either his name wasn't really Sean Parks, or I had been duped. I knew him as Spencer Prentice. Same initials, though. And same angelic face and smooth, perfectly formed body. And if he really was a student at NYU, he must only be taking a class every other week. He was into—had been into—so much other shit. Including this. I had warned him several times about this. But, like all barely legal youths, he thought he was invincible. Well, now he was marked up as just another inevitable.

I swallowed hard twice and came out of the car, putting on my "just another day" face, even though the inside of me was jumping up and down and wanting to keen a death dirge.

"Anything unusual found?"

"Pretty much clean as a whistle, as usual," Mullins said. "I'm sure the ME will find he used a condom, and the body and the car surfaces have been rubbed down with cleaning solvent. True to pattern. But, what the fuck, why is a junk yard left without any security like this? No dogs even, and the fence is a joke."

"It's Pedersen's Junk Yard," I said. "It's one of those last stops for junk. Pretty much anything no one could possibly do anything with anymore. I was raised just a couple of blocks from here. Me and my brother used to use this as a fantasy land playground during off hours. So nothing unusual found at all?"

"Nothing other than this rosary," Paxton said, holding up a string of beads. "At the base of the partition, by the body. But it could have been put there by anyone at any time, I suppose."

I froze. I could feel myself starting to hyperventilate, but I had to keep it together. None of the cops here could know what I was feeling. "Here," I said, pulling an evidence bag out of my pocket, "Put it in here and I'll get it into the evidence file. But I bet you're right—that it's not connected with this. Our man hasn't been that sloppy before."

"Do you think it belongs to the rent-boy? Do you think he was Catholic?" Mullins asked.

"Hell if I know," I answered. "We'll have to check that out." What was screaming through my head, though, was a response that hell, no, he wasn't Catholic. Spencer's religion had never gone beyond himself—which was the root of what had gotten him here. If he believed in any ism, it would be narcissism.

I stuck my hands in my pockets so the guys couldn't see that they were trembling. It was hot as hell out here. I had left my coat and tie in the car and was just in my short sleeves—which alone marked what we were doing here as reality and not a TV show, where the cops chasing the criminals through the alleys all wore tailored and pressed suits—and still I was sweating like a pig. Of course, I was sweating more than the other guys were, which I hoped they weren't noticing. I had to get out of here. I leaned back into the backseat as if to check something and laid a hand on Spencer's shoulder, closed my eyes, and mouthed an abbreviated prayer.

He may not have been Catholic, but I was. An Irish Kavanagh through and through. Feeling guilty went with the religion, and, God, did I not feel guilty now? Spencer, of course, was beyond feelings of guilt.

I had told him it would end like this if he didn't rein it in, but, of course, he hadn't believed me. Had I believed it really would happen to him? If I could say yes to that, why hadn't I tried harder to prevent it?

"It's hot as hell out here," I said, coming up out of the car. "No reason for all of us to wait out the ME. I'll go back to headquarters and start the file work."

I knew that neither Paxton or Mullins would object to that. The choice of standing out under the sun in the middle of a smelly junkyard and fighting off the flies was a thousand times more agreeable to both of them than filling out paperwork.

I drove the three blocks to Saint Barnabas Catholic Church, went into the church gift shop, and bought a rosary that, luckily, was identical to the one Paxton had handed me. Neither he nor Mullins would have any idea I had pulled a switch. I put it in another evidence bag. I'd sanitize it before I checked it into the evidence file, though. No use getting some Saint Barnabas parishioner who liked to finger merchandise she didn't buy involved in this. It would just be another teaser the red sash killer had cleaned any possible prints from. Mullins and Paxton both had been wearing evidence gloves, and I had put a pair on before approaching the car. I had to just hope that the first cops on the scene had been as careful.

I had no idea what I'd do with the rosary that had actually come out of the Town Car. I would think about that later. In the end, I knew I would send it to a private lab for fingerprinting. I knew I couldn't go without knowing.

When I went back to the car after leaving the gift shop, I sat there for a good twenty minutes, taking deep breaths and trembling, with tears rolling down my cheeks.

It wasn't just Spencer I was hyperventilating and crying for.

\* \* \* \*

Both the Central Headquarters Vice Homicide unit and my apartment, if you could call essentially one room, a bedroom only large enough for a double, and a bath an apartment, were located in the South Central district of Manhattan, just to the east of the Avenue of the Americas. But I usually went for coffee on the west side the avenue, just inside the Chelsea district. Chelsea was more eclectic than the surrounding districts and open to various lifestyles, which seemed to accommodate each other amicably. I went to the same café in Chelsea most of the time to rub elbows with another lifestyle than my presumed one without running much of a risk of being tagged with it. No one at work knew of my inclinations. I could hang with the NYPD boys as much as anyone and spent a lot of time in the gym with them being just another one of them. None of my compatriots came over into Chelsea for their coffee fix or knew that I did. I could sip and ogle in comfort there in my completely different world.

And there was a lot to ogle. I didn't touch. At least not the clientele. Despite being another world than South Central, it still was too close to home. There was a barista, though, who I struck up an acquaintance with over time. A short, slim-bodied blond, with curly hair, an angelic smile, a sassy nature, and a mouth that spieled light sarcasm and increasingly pointed innuendo the longer I came in and saddled up to the counter for my "just black and strong."

After a few months, he was Spencer and I was Mike—and we both knew, since I didn't retreat from his innuendo, that we both were likeminded and interested.

I would have hit on him, but I was afraid I'd break him—that I couldn't control myself in using him. It was a David and Goliath thing. I didn't have much question that he was gay. He didn't try to hide it much. But I had him by at least eight inches and surely weighed twice as much as he did, though I wasn't a fatty. Four days a week working hard in the gym and my active and athletic work style pounding the streets kept me in top shape—as did the need to pass the regular exams. Vice homicide was an elite unit.

Then came the day, a slow day at the café, and one where I'd come in late and a little bummed out from the case I was working on and one that was nearing the end of Spencer's shift. I certainly hadn't planned it. I'd never been in this late before, and I'd never thought of when

Spencer got off work. Maybe it was my late presence that prompted him, but the proposition was his, not mine. I don't know as I would have ever done more than have looked and jawed suggestively. I had gotten a rush out going just that far that kept me coming into the coffee bar.

Leaning over the counter, he whispered to me, with a smile that reached right up to his blue eyes, "You want to fuck me, don't you?"

Replacing my first shocked look with a steady gaze, I told him the truth. "Yeah, of course I do. I've wanted to since the first day I walked in here. But we don't have to—"

"I'm off in ten minutes. I live nearby, although it's not much. If you have something close that's better, neutral ground—"

"I'll spring for a hotel, if you know of an acceptable one nearby."

"I don't know about acceptable, but there are several within a couple of blocks that rent by the hour and where I'm known and there won't be any hassle."

That was the first inkling I had that Spencer was a rent-boy on the side. I probably should have put on the brakes then—I was hitting entirely too close to my own food bowl in Vice—but no part of my body would have agreed to that at the time.

"I'll supply the rubbers," he said. "Can I hope that you'll need a Magnum?"

"As a matter of fact I do," I answered. And that wasn't a lie. But it was part of the problem. I wasn't afraid he wasn't old enough; he had to be to work as a barista, and I'd checked through the restaurant records registered with City Hall until I'd proved that—showing I was interested in him for some time. But, age aside, he was such a small guy that I'd been afraid all along that I'd split him. But if he was a rent-boy, he must have managed that before I came along.

"But doesn't it worry you—put you off—that I need a maxi rubber?" I asked, not being able to ignore the concern.

"Don't worry about me," he'd whispered in the dimly lit and dingy hotel room, the curtains billowing at the window open to the orange-to-red flashing of a neon sign, as he crouched, raised on his knees, at the foot of the bed, facing me, naked, as I was. I had found that the best of the rent-boys could gauge the wants and capacities of their johns, and Spencer was among the very best of rent-boys. I needn't have worried. He was so trained to the life that he'd been reamed to take it.

He had one hand around the back of my neck—we had just been kissing—and the other one was between us, on my cock, having just smoothed the Trojan Magnum on my erect and throbbing staff. He somehow divined that I wanted to come into him quietly and deeply, to hold his small, smooth body close in my bear hug, and for him to moan deeply for me as I took him slowly at first, but rising to a crescendo of thrusts.

"Don't worry about me," he repeated. "I can handle it." He arched back then, pressing his shoulders into the surface of the mattress, and raised one of his ankles to my shoulder. He nudged my left hand with his right foot, and, taking the hint, I grasped his ankle and raised and held his other leg out. The bulb of my cock was pressed at his entrance. He had nearly melted when he found I had a thick Prince Albert cock ring in the bulb and he claimed to be delighted at the sound and feel of it clicking against his teeth when he knelt on the floor before me and sucked me off as soon as we had entered the room.

"Fuck me. Fuck me deep, Mike," he murmured.

At first I didn't think that was going to be possible. But then it was. He was every inch the experienced rent-boy. He opened to me and I penetrated a couple of inches, holding while both of us gasped and moaned.

"Deep, deep," he pleaded and then arched his back and groaned as I gave it all to him. The next twenty minutes we moved in concert, like a well-oiled machine, our murmurings, gasps, groans, and moans drowned out by the sound of the street traffic three stories below the open window. Slow at first and then faster and faster; me doing all the plowing at first, but, gradually, Spencer moving his hips in counter punches to my deep thrusts so that we were working together. Holding him close to my chest, his face at the level of my chest and nipples, with Spencer giving me attention there as I plowed him.

"I wanted you from the first day you entered the coffee bar," he whispered.

"I wanted you before I even met you," I countered, "when I was just imagining the perfect lay."

All too soon he was becoming vocal, arching his neck back, panting and yelping to the ceiling; shuddering and ejaculating between our bodies from his hard, but small, boyish cock. His coming brought on mine, and I barely had time to pull out of him, jerk off the condom, heed his "On my face; come on my face," plea, and scramble up on the bed on my knees before I jacked all over his smooth cheeks, and he was raising his face, taking my cock in his mouth, and cleaning me off.

"Why didn't you do this to me the first day you bellied up to the counter?" he asked.

"I was afraid you couldn't manage, that I'd split you in two," I murmured as we lay stretched out against each other on the bed. "You're so small, delicate looking, but a body of steel in the clutches."

"And you're such a thug," Spencer answered. "But I think you can tell I like thugs. If I'd known about the cock ring I would have jumped your bones weeks ago. Such a big, hairy, muscular brute. Just what I like. Mafia? I've imagined you in the Mafia."

"No, not Mafia," I answered. "Probably worse in your estimation." But I didn't tell him I was a vice cop. He didn't ask. He was busy rummaging around in the pockets of his jeans, which were entangled with the bed sheets.

"What you are doing? I don't sign autographs."

"You could, you know," he said. "You're that good at it."

"I bet you say that to all of your johns."

"Yes, I do. But I don't say that to all of the men I chose to fuck for free. And that includes you. Here, this is what I was looking for. I want you to do me again."

He was holding up a condom. I wasn't usually ready to perform this soon again, but Spencer was everything I wanted in a lay, and I was already literally up for him again.

"You have more of those in your pocket?" I asked.

"Certainly."

"Enough, do you think?"

"I hope not. You can bareback me, you know. I get checked regularly."

"I think not," I answered, although later I could have kicked myself for not having engaged in that ultimate intimacy with him.

I rolled him over onto his back and came with him, on top of him, but taking most of my weight on my knees wedged between his thighs and my forearms on either side of him. He raised his buttocks to me at the perfect angle for my entry, and, crowned once more, I slid inside him and fucked him deep and slow again.

We came to the hotel three times more in the next four weeks. He asked no more about me than he already knew—not even where I lived. I wanted to make love to him in a more uplifting place than this fleabag hotel, but I had a strict policy of not going to where they lived or letting them know where I lived. That he did it for me was marked by my not having sex with anyone else during that period. I usually spiked a guy twice a week, rarely the same guy twice in succession, and in New York, I always had opportunities. I went to two gyms—twice a week to the gym with the guys I worked with, but then twice a week to a different, more discreet gym, where I presented well enough on the exercise floor that I never had to leave alone—or could manage my business right there in the showers, sauna, or changing cubicles.

But Spencer was the kind of lay that put me off anyone else.

We could have gone on like that for some time, I suppose, if I hadn't pulled vice operation duties one evening. I did what I could to avoid that special duty, as I always was afraid that I'd open my car window on a sting to some sweet young thing I'd done in the gym shower. And that's exactly what happened that night.

We were raiding the streets of the nearby Garment district one night, when I rolled down my window and the young guy peering in and opening with, "Is there anything I can do for you, handsome?" turned out to be Spencer.

"You?" he then said. "This is a cop car, isn't it? I knew I should've stayed back on the curb."

"Get in, Spencer," I growled. "Fast. Fewer who see us the better."

"You are a cop, aren't you, Mike." And then, when I didn't deny that, he said, with a sigh, "You're right. That's worse than Mafia."

"Just get in the goddamn car, Spencer. You need to be off the street tonight." It was a "bring 'em in en mass" night, with the focus on this district.

We were both silent as I drove off, and then in circles in central Manhattan, not sure where to go. I should have taken him back to the fleabag hotel in Chelsea, but my homing instinct took me back to my own place in South Central. I'd never brought a lay home before. I had a strict policy about that. I have no idea what I was thinking.

He said nothing the entire time. He just sat up against the passenger door with his hand to the side of his face, turned away from me.

I had cooled down when I entered the parking garage. "OK, here's the deal, Spencer. You have to stay off the street tonight. I can take you back to where you live or wherever as long as you pledge not to go back in the Garment district tonight. Or I can take you upstairs, to my apartment, fuck the stuffing out of you, and pay you something so that your night isn't a financial bust."

"You don't have to pay me nothin'," he muttered.

When we got up to the seventh floor and entered my apartment, we both could hear the heavy breathing and groans coming from my bedroom.

"Shit," I said.

"You runnin' a brothel from here?" Spencer asked, smiling wickedly.

To wipe the grin off his face, I fucked him on my kitchen table, him belly down on the table, and me hunched over him, with one leg on the ground and the other one raised so that my foot was on a kitchen chair, to give me extra leverage in the thrusts. His leg was trapped over mine, opening his buttocks wide to me, and I held his wrists with one beefy hand and trapped his arms behind his back. His wrists were bound over his head by the set of handcuffs he'd seen me carrying and insisted on trying out.

I fucked him hard, and he claimed to be loving it.

I was still covering his back and panting after the finish when a twinky young Hispanic poured out my bedroom, buckling his pants, with a T-shirt over his shoulder. He stopped, wild-eyed when he saw Spencer and me—and especially when he saw the handcuffs in use. His hands went to his neck, which he rubbed hard, twisting his neck this way and that, and then, suddenly, he bolted for the apartment door and was gone.

Spencer and I had our pants back on and were sitting at the kitchen table, when my brother, Liam, sauntered out of the room. He was dressed in black trousers and a black, silky shirt, and he was adjusting his clerical collar. Seeing us, he just smiled. I had the impression that he gave Spencer a bigger smile than he did me.

"*Father* William," I said in a stern voice, emphasizing the "father," "I think I've told you I didn't like you using my apartment for your special sessions." I always used the long form of Liam's name, his church name, when I wanted him to know I was serious about something.

"Your apartment was close by, and the young man was in special need," Liam answered breezily. "Who is this beautiful angel gracing your kitchen?"

"None of your—" I started to say, but Spencer, wide-eyed and mesmerized answered for himself.

"I'm Spencer. Spencer Prentice. I work at the Escafe coffee bar off the Avenue of the Americas in Chelsea."

This was more information than Spencer had ever given me.

"Don't even start, Liam," I growled. "He's off limits. I doubt he's even a Catholic. You're not a Catholic, are you, Spence?"

"I could be," Spencer said in a small voice, turning his face to me only briefly before turning back to goggle at Liam. It wasn't just that Liam was a priest, I didn't think. He'd also gotten the looks and dancer's body that had been denied to the big lug that was me at birth.

"Uh, forgot something," Liam said, as he turned and reentered the bedroom. When he came back out, he had a red sash, which he wrapped around his thin waist and tucked in. "I spread the bed back to where it's more presentable than I found it," he said. "You going to take young Spencer back there now and fuck him silly, Mike?"

"Get out," I growled. "More none of your business, bro." I knew I was doing a lot of growling, but Liam got under my hide. He always had. Everyone thought he was so good. I was the only one who could see the truth.

"Can I sit in the corner and watch?" he said. "I'll be very quiet."

"I said it's time to leave, *Father* William," I answered.

He laughed and left. Spencer's eyes followed him all the way out of the apartment. Then he turned to me, and said, his voice incredulous. "He really a Catholic priest?"

"Yes, he's really a Catholic priest."

"He really your brother?"

"That too, regrettably."

"He's hot."

"He's a priest. Hot shouldn't come into the conversation."

"And you're really a vice cop?"

"Not exactly. I'm a vice homicide cop. Just on loan to street vice for the night."

"And a vice cop sampling the goods should come into a conversation?"

"I don't always have to have a conversation with the guy I fuck. You and I don't talk much, do we?"

"He's hot and you're cool," Spencer said, his eyes shining and glassy. "I've been fucked by vice cops before but I've never been fucked by a Catholic priest."

"Neither have I, Spencer, Neither have I. Now do you want me to take you somewhere?"

"Yes, into your bedroom," Spencer said. "I'm hornier than hell."

"So am I, Spencer. So am I."

We were both at the top of our arousal meter. I fucked Spencer harder than I'd ever fucked him before, and when I was afraid he'd break, he egged me on. He didn't break. And he claimed to love what I could do with four sets of handcuffs.

* * * *

I returned to the Vice Homicide unit before Paxton and Mullins got back after the discovery of Spencer's body in the Bronx junkyard. That gave me time to package up the original rosary found at the scene and send it off to the lab at my former precinct in the Bronx. They were used to doing analysis favors for me both because I got along with them famously and cultivated their goodwill and because the Vice Homicide lab was notoriously uncooperative. I was head of the unit, so all paperwork on lab results would come to me.

When Mullins and Paxton rolled in, a good three hours later, I was on the phone to our own lab—which already had a tech unit out at Spencer's apartment taking fingerprints. I had escaped a bullet, I realized, by never having gone to wherever he lived. But right now I was hassling the head of our lab enough to make him dig in his heels and balk at my demands to fingerprint the rosary I had bought and wiped clean chop chop.

"I can get more cooperation out of the South Central general lab," I said into the phone loud enough for the guys to hear me as they entered the office, to which the lab chief did what I wanted—told me to use the South Central general lab then.

"No cooperation from our own lab," I said to Mullins and Paxton as they settled into their desks. "So I'm sending this rosary you found to South Central."

"Works for me," Paxton said.

By sending the rosaries separately to two labs outside of Vice Homicide, I retained control over which rosary to put into evidence. Paperwork by the Vice Homicide lab would automatically go into the evidence file. I would personally receive the results from outside labs and could suppress one and accept the other without an anomaly showing in the case record. I had to enter anything coming from outside labs to the case file myself.

"The ME kept you waiting for hours, did she?" I asked them.

"No. She arrived soon after you left," Mullins said. "We got a lead on where the victim worked and went over there. A coffee joint called Escafe. Not far from here. In Chelsea." They both rolled their eyes at the mention of Chelsea. We all knew what kind of guy could be found there—and we all joked about it. "Like we thought, he moonlighted as a rent-boy. I wouldn't be surprised if everyone working in that place rented by the blow job after hours."

"Anything they can tell you about who he had been seeing there?" I asked, trying to make my voice seem casual.

"Not much. A couple of the workers said Parks had been gaga over a customer lately. A big bruiser. But nobody could say much about the guy."

"Parks?" I asked. But I immediately saw my mistake. Their Parks was my Prentice. I rushed on. "Maybe we should have the beat cops out there check in every once in a while with the staff to see if the guy comes back."

"Yeah, I'll take care of that," Mullins said.

Sounded just fine to me. I'd be finding myself another place to get coffee. I'd never go near Escafe again.

"What do you suppose this is for?" Paxton asked, holding up an evidence bag with the red sash in it that Spencer had been strangled with. "I thought it was a scarf, but it seems to be some sort of sash instead."

"Beats me," I answered, keeping my voice from cracking. "Send it along to South Central analysis. I'm sure the killer was careful enough not to leave prints, but maybe the lab can say what the sash was for."

Of course, even I could say what the sash was for. It was worn by a popular order of Catholic priests in the New York metropolitan area. The last time I'd seen one like that, my brother had wound such a sash around his waist after I'd caught him fucking Spencer. And that was the last day I'd seen Spencer alive.

* * * *

Mullins had been morose all morning at the unit as we suddenly were up to our keisters in what we had already started to call the Red Scarf Murders and, when he'd complained about the "fuckin' Inevitable Cases," I'd sent him into a foul mood by pointing out that whore and street rent-boy murder cases were likely to predominate in a special Vice Homicide unit. He was relatively new to the unit, but that this hadn't dawned on him before was an index to how bright he was. No one beat him in tenacity and willingness to wear out the shoe leather, though.

The third young, small rent-boy had been found in and around the Bronx area strangled in flagrante delicto with a red scarf or sash. It was only later that we changed "red scarf" to "red sash," as the signature—which we took as a mocking of us—quickly narrowed down. It was later yet that we were to identify a red sash with an order of Catholic priests in and around the New York metropolitan area.

I made the connection faster than the other guys. But I kept it to myself. It haunted me from the last moment I saw Spencer alive, which was later in the day that we met together in the precinct and decided, finally, that we had a serial killer on our hands.

I left the precinct early, the meeting and the intensive planning we had done on how to proceed—knowing that the serial killer had given us very little to go on—having worn me out and left me with a headache.

I heard them immediately when I entered my apartment. Liam was using my bedroom again as a convenient love shack, isolated away from his life as a priest at the Saint Barnabas Catholic Church in the Bronx, not more than two blocks from where we'd both grown up—to pursue entirely different professions, if twins in our sexual preferences.

The door to the bedroom was ajar and I couldn't help myself from walking over and peering into the room. Liam, naked and lithe in contrast to my rugby-player build, was on his back on the bed. Spencer, also naked, small, willowy, blond, perfectly formed, was riding Liam's cock. He was saddled on the rod, which I knew to be longer if not as thick as mine, and facing away from Liam's head, his hands gripping Liam's bent- and spread-legs kneecaps. Liam had the ends of the red sash to his priest's vestments fisted and the sash itself looped over Spencer's throat. Liam was using the sash like reins to guide Spencer back and forward on his cock. The two were so engrossed in their grunting sex ride that they couldn't have been aware of me standing at the door.

The red sash wasn't being used for breath play, but the effect was close enough.

I didn't stand there long, but broke away with a low groan of despair and disgust, trudged to the refrigerator, and pulled out two beers. I was on my third before they were done, and Spencer, tucking his T-shirt into his shorts, came out into the room.

To his credit, his initial glance at me was one of embarrassment and guilt. He quickly covered that with an expression of nonchalance. He said nothing to me, but turned and went to the door to the outside corridor. He turned back, though, when I called out his name.

There was so much I could say to him, not the least that I didn't consider him just a sexual-release toy—that I felt so much more deeply for him—but I was so keyed up and trying so hard to hold my emotions in check and not to lash out that I simply said, "You have to be careful out there, Spencer. And you have to tell the other young guys to do the same. There's a serial killer out there preying on guys just like you. There have been three murders in the Bronx in the last week."

I didn't mention the red sash part. I should have. But I just couldn't. Not because of Spencer but because of . . . I found I could not let myself even start to form the implications.

"I don't go to the Bronx," Spencer responded. His mouth formed a word to say something else, but he didn't say anything. Giving me a hurt look, he turned again and was gone. In his wake, my brain was screaming out the word "inevitable."

I would have given anything to know what he wanted to say to me but didn't. It was the last time I saw him alive. I certainly had more to say to him than I did. Things might have gone differently if I'd told him I was falling in love with him.

I had more to say to Liam when he emerged from the bedroom, adjusting his clerical collar and his sash. I had no trouble unleashing my anger on my brother.

"He was off limits. Surely you knew that," I yelled at Liam.

"Why, just because you were nailing him yourself?"

"Because he means more to me than that," I retorted. "You've done this before. You've always wanted to take what I had."

"He came after me," Liam said. "I didn't see your brand on him."

"Came after you? He found where you lived and worked? He came out to the Bronx, to Saint Barnabas?"

"He told me where he worked and he did so in a way that I knew he was propositioning me."

"So, you came into Manhattan and went after him. Even knowing he was with me. Get out, Liam. And watch your back, man. I don't know what you're into, but—"

"What I'm into? What do you mean? You've always known I fuck men."

I wanted to tell him, to unleash my suspicion. And God knows I was mad enough at him to let it all out. But I just couldn't. Still, I was working up to it and had muttered, "You need to watch yourself from me," when he exited the apartment and shut the door between us. Even when I'd said it, I knew he'd misinterpret my meaning. I hadn't spoken as a brother; I'd spoken as a cop.

\* \* \* \*

Neither Paxton nor Mullins were in the office when I came in, which was strange but was just as well. I'd stopped in the mailroom on my way up and found that both of the rosaries were back from their separate labs. I entered; sat at my desk; put both reports, with rosary attached in an evidence baggie, in front of me; and went through my opening-up ceremony in slow motion. I didn't want to look at each report but I knew it would be best if I did and made whatever switch was necessary before the other guys arrived—from wherever they were. They both usually arrived at work before I did.

With trembling hands, I opened the most definite report envelope—the one from the South Central lab, where I'd sent the rosary I'd bought. I knew what the report would say, and that's what it did say—that the rosary had been cleaned of any prints—but in opening it first, I could hold off my fears from looking at the other report for a bit longer.

Spencer entered my mind again. Spencer folded up, naked, in the backseat of the Lincoln Town Car in Pedersen's Junk Yard in the Bronx, the red, choking sash, around his throat. The last thing Spencer had said to me was "I don't go to the Bronx."

But Spencer did go to the Bronx—or was taken, supposedly willingly to the Bronx. What could have been in the Bronx to lure him there? I couldn't think of it being anything other than Liam. Liam lived at the rectory of the Saint Barnabas Catholic Church. Just a few blocks from Pedersen's Junk Yard. Not that far from either of the

91

three other places the bodies of young, small rent-boys had been found: in an abandoned building, in a park, in an alley behind a liquor store.

"He came after me." That's what Liam had said. I couldn't get the implications out of my mind.

My hand wavered over the closed envelope attached to the rosary found at Spencer's murder scene, the rosary I'd sent to the Bronx lab. My hand was trembling; I was having trouble opening the envelope, and then I heard them, talking excitedly in echoey voices as they mounted the stairway outside the door to the Vice Homicide unit—Mullins and Paxton.

Quickly, I opened the center drawer to my desk and swept both evidence bags in, shutting the drawer as the two entered the office.

"What's up, guys?" I asked. "You're late."

"No, you're late, Kavanagh," Mullins shot back. "We've been downstairs at booking. We caught a break in the Red Sash Case."

My heart rose to my throat. Paxton took up the discussion.

"Bronx precinct caught a guy practically in the act. Would you believe it's a Catholic priest?"

The heart in my throat started throbbing.

"Well, a defrocked one," Mullins cut in. "A stripped priest living on probation in the rectory of that Catholic church not far from that junk yard where we found number four."

"Saint Barnabas?" I asked, barely able to get the words out. My heart had receded a bit from the "defrocked" information, but not much.

"Yeah, guy named Hubert. Was calling himself Father Hugh, but the charge sheet says Hubert Hastings. A record for pedophilia, and the church cut him out of his priest role but is letting him live at that church while he's on probation."

I was in control enough now to discuss the circumstances of the arrest, but just briefly. The guys wanted coffee.

"Want us to fill your cup?" Mullins asked as they turned toward the door. The break room, where the coffee urn lived, was down a flight.

"Naw, thanks, I'll get a cup later," I said. I, in fact, was badly in need of coffee just then, but handing my cup to them would have shown them how badly my hand was trembling.

As soon as they were through the door, I slid the desk drawer open and took out the lab report on the rosary I'd sent to the Bronx. Hubert Hastings. The prints had been identified from his incarceration for pedophilia four years earlier. He'd been in prison up to a few months ago—landing back in the Bronx before the serial murders had started.

My ragged breathing made me aware of how long I'd been holding my breath. Home free. Or was I. Were we? What did this actually close out about where Liam stood?

I had no idea—and probably wouldn't until time had gone by without another red sash-signature murder. I'd be on pins and needles for months.

Whatever, it would never bring Spencer back to me.

# Thirty-Year Anniversary

(Requested by dmmc)

The young black bull was seated on the bench press in the dim light of the after-hours gym, back pressed to the reclining back support, hands gripping the narrow hips of the smaller, older man flexibly draped above him, facing away from him, and pulling the thin, wiry frame of the sub off and on his monster cock. Who would have known, the black bull wondered, that such a small frame, with such narrow hips, could sheath such a long, thick cock? Or sheath it so willingly, expertly. And open right up for him.

"I call this the figurehead fuck position," Damont said in a gravelly voice, as he grunted at the effort to pull the older, but in-great-shape man's ass on and off the cock. The guy had been fully submissive, eyes downcast, a slight smile on his face when Damont had tried out innuendo and then moved to suggestive comments, and, finally, to a direct statement that Damont was going to fuck him. The man had signaled yes to everything. And he'd opened his small ass right up to take the cock.

"Not many can do this. Such a small body and yet I can get deep inside you. You're remarkably flexible for your age. How old did you say you were?"

"Thirty-five," Aaron, small, hirsute, but perfectly proportioned of stature, answered with a groan. "Oh God, oh Jesuzzz, you're so big, so long. Deep, shit you're giving it to me deep."

"I could pull back if—" Damont, a massively built black bull of twenty-two, the gym's trainer, answered with slight concern. He was still in awe at how well and hungrily the man had taken the cock.

"No, no, keep at it. Deeper, bigger," came back the answer in a whimper. "I can take it."

Amazingly, Damont Jefferson, realized, Mr. Stein *could* take it. No one before had been able to take this position this long. Aaron's ankles were hooked on Damont's shoulders, the flexible small Jew's fists were locked behind the black bull's thick neck. Aaron's tautly arched torso was cantilevered out over the end of the bench. And he was moving his pelvis, pushing back on Damont's thrusts to take more of the big black inside him with each stroke.

It was the fourth night Aaron Stein had come into the gym to work out until closing. Damont had picked him out of the crowd early because of the flexibility the man was showing—particularly for his age. Damont had guessed twenty-eight and thus was shocked to find, in the throes of a difficult fuck position, that Stein was thirty-five.

Damont didn't have that flexibility, although he had agility and grace for a man his size. He was a powerhouse of muscle, a walking advertisement for the gym and how it could develop a man's body—every muscle group bulging perfectly. But Damont liked complex fuck positions. From the first night Stein had come into the gym, Damont had had fantasies of bending the man into the shape of a pretzel and fucking the stuffing out of him. The small, but perfectly shaped man with the fascinating swirls of curly black hair on his body wasn't more than half Damont's size—in bulk and weight. Damont liked his submissives small and vulnerable to his strength and overpowering control.

They usually showed fear, though. This one was fearless—hungry to be used hard.

Stein had returned the looks and remarked more than once what a magnificent brute the black bull was, and so, when they were nearing the end of the fourth night exercise session, Damont boldly came over to Aaron and asked if the older man was interested in private one-on-one training after the gym closed. He was pleased when Aaron jumped at the offer.

He pressed his advantage, putting his mouth close to Aaron's ear and his hands on Aaron's bare belly, both of them having been working out wearing just a jock and athletic shorts, and pulling Aaron's buttocks into his crotch to let the small man know what he would be risking. "I'm also gonna see what challenging positions I can put your beautiful little body in and fuck your lights out."

"That's the training I was hoping to get," Aaron answered. "You're the black bull I wanted handling me as soon as I first walked into this gym. I hope you're this big when it counts."

"Been had by black bulls before, have you? How many?"

"I've lost count. They're my fetish. The heavier hung the better. I can tell you're hung."

"So you don't want me to be gentle?"

"I want your worst."

It had started like it would be a regular training session, Aaron reclining on the backrest of the weight bench, his feet firmly planted on the floor on either side, a heavy barbell over his head. Damont was straddling his body, spotting him in the lift, his hands fisting Aaron's wrists.

Aaron started it, leaning his head forward and mouthing Damont's engorging cock through the material of the athletic shorts and jock pouch. Quickly Damont had both off and had returned to position, still fisting Aaron's wrists, working at timing the thrusts of his cock down Aaron's throat with Aaron's lifting of the bar bell. This had led to Damont's testing of Aaron's flexibility on the bench with the figurehead fuck position, which the thirteen-years-older submissive was managing with aplomb.

As they stood, both naked, at the gym's bar, gulping Gatorade and recovering, Damont asked, "You some kind of gymnast or something? I've seen that in you when you were working out in earlier sessions. And you handled the figurehead position better than a guy half your age could."

"Through college, yes. Tried out for the Olympics, but didn't quite make it. Couldn't give it up. Guess I'll have to give it up one of these days, though. I'm getting too old for this."

"Not that anyone would notice. God, you're flexible and have a sweet ass. Gotta have you again tonight. You tried out for the Olympics of taking black bull cock? If so, you're a winner."

"No, that's for the Guinness Book of Records." The little guy wasn't the least bit shy about lying under black guys.

"You do a lot of this?" Aaron asked. "Big stud like you. Often fuck a man as old as I am? I see you with the younger guys."

"You got the body and the flexibility I like. It's all in the moment. You ain't too old in this moment. Look, you got me hot and bothered again."

"I can't believe I took one that big, You got to be at least ten by two."

"Yeah, somethin' like that," Damont answered, not bothering to hide his pride. "You an expert in getting measurements on them? That a magic number for you? Biggest you've taken?"

"I've taken a whole foot of it."

Damont whistled. "A black man?"

"Yes, always black men."

"I believe it. I guess I should feel lucky to take on such a connoisseur of black cock."

"The luck is all mine—in hooking up with you."

Damont whistled in awe again. "I didn't hit bottom. And you didn't do more than whimper. Twelve inches, you say?"

"It was thin. You have the best combination. Taxing girth. I was in heaven. Couldn't do more than whimper. God, I can't believe a young super stud like you would do an older guy like me."

"And you took it like a champ. And I'm gonna give it to you again now."

"Thought you'd never ask—no, not ask, declare. I want a man who just takes what he wants. Got another position like that one? This is supposed to be a special training session."

"What were your specialties in college gymnastics?"

"You mean beside black bulls? I've been hooked on guys like you since I was younger than you. My specialties were the parallel bars and the rings."

Damont grinned.

They were on the double parallel bars, upper and lower bars. Aaron's pelvis was straddling the upper bars, his ankles wrapped around the bars on either side to give him stability. His torso was arched downward between the bars, his fists gripping the lower bars on either side. Using extraordinary muscle power, Damont was stretched over Aaron's body, his fists gripping the high bars on either side, the pads of his feet pressed into the high bars on either side below, with Damont doing pushups on top of Aaron, his cock buried in Aaron's ass.

After a brief rest, Damont showed Aaron how he could do him on the rings.

Aaron's face turned to Damont's for a deep kiss as they were cooling down, Damont's cock going flaccid inside Aaron's ass—but not withering, a cock that never could be described as withering, Damont whispered, a note of awe in his voice, "You could take this forever, couldn't you?"

Aaron wanted to cry out, no, as good as it is, I feel my age. I just don't want you to feel my age. I don't want to lose this before I have to. What he said was, "With you, I could do it forever."

In the shower, having soaped each other up, Damont was hard again—twenty-two and virile, he could get it up every ten minutes; he could produce buckets of cum. Aaron was pretty good in that department himself. Damont growled, "Reach for your ankles," and Aaron dutifully showed he could bend in a perfect jack knife and grasp his ankles. He groaned as Damont thrust inside his ass and began pumping hard again.

At the door to the gym, both dressed now and Damont locking up for the night. "I suppose it's a younger man tomorrow night," Aaron asked, his voice rueful.

"I don't do this regularly," Damont said, almost in a huff. "I'd get the boot here if I did much of this here. You just moved in a way that made me want to try demanding positions out. You performed like a champ."

"A thirty-five-year old champ," Aaron said. "You need a younger man."

"You keep saying that. We'd both like it better if you stopped saying that," Damont said. He too was concerned about the age difference, though, and was trying not to think about it. For now, this moment, this man's body and ass were perfect for him. And seeing what positions the man could take was arousing in its own right.

Damont couldn't remember the last time he'd fucked a guy four times in one night. And his dick was telling him that he could enjoy Aaron again right now, right here. Maybe a standing fuck in the middle of the street, with the small guy draped in front of him, his legs hooked on Damont's hips, his fists locked around Damont's neck, Damont crouching a bit to give him leverage for brutal, deep thrusts upward. And Aaron, despite his age, could take him like a champ in this position. He'd already shown that flexibility, that vigor, that willingness. The perfect sub for Damont. Now at this moment in time, regardless of the man's age.

"I almost wish—" Aaron started to say, but then stopped, in embarrassment. No, he thought, I won't say it. He deserves a younger man.

"I want to see you sometime, outside of the gym," Damont suddenly blurted out.

"I'd like that," Aaron answered, blushing. He deserves someone younger, he repeated in his mind, but I can't help being selfish. "Sometime would be nice."

"How about you coming to my place, now. I live nearby."

"Yes."

"I want to fuck you all night."

"Yes."

"You ever been fucked by one of your other black bulls in a standing fuck?"

"Yes."

"You could take it from a thick ten incher in a standing fuck?"

"I can certainly try. Oh, god, I want to try." Even if it's only for tonight, this is what I want, Aaron mused, as, putting a big, black mitt possessively on Aaron's butt, the black bull guided the trembling older man up the street.

Aaron wasn't trembling only in anticipation of having that black monster cock working inside him again tonight—although that certainly was a reason to tremble—but also because he was on the edge of what he could take. So far he had hidden well how taxing this had been for him—albeit heavenly taxing. He no longer was a twenty-year-old. He'd taken more than one black bull at the same time at twenty. Somehow he had to continue making Damont believe that he could take all that Damont could give him and meet it with flexibility, stamina, and willingness. The last of these he'd lose was willingness. He'd had no idea he could still attract a hung black bull at his age—if only for tonight. The black bull's sole interest seemed to be wholly in how many taxing fuck positions Aaron could endure him in. It was up to Aaron to accommodate him if he wanted continue to have a night he'd always remember.

\* \* \* \*

Damont knew what the luscious young piece wanted from him when the juicy blond asked to be spotted on the rings. At fifty-two, now owner of the gym, Damont had managed to keep his muscular hunkiness, although he was finding it hard now to maintain himself. He'd do so for as long as he could. Nobody would want to go to a gym owned by chief trainer who had a pot belly.

Young guys still flocked to the gym for the attention of the big black bull muscleman owner, though—to be touched and manipulated in exercise positions—and, they hoped, more than that.

The blond called Damont over to the rings, which he'd pulled himself up on, and had opened his legs and encased Damont's hips with them, when Damont came up close behind him and put his hands on the young man's waist to hold him steady before pulling away to watch the young man perform on the rings. For a moment, prolonged by the young man holding tight with his thighs, Damont's crotch was pressed to the young man's buttocks. Damont was hard. They both knew that Damont was hard—physically wanting it as much as the blond obviously did.

The guy was a great-looking piece and had that gymnast's flexibility Damont had always liked—and the guy clearly wanted him. The young man was trembling as he felt the strength of Damont's mammoth cock pressed into his butt.

Damont knew that he either had to step back to make the blond stop trembling at the contact so he could do his rings routine or pull the guy down, take him back to Damont's office, and fuck the stuffing out of him on the daybed Damont kept there. He didn't have the slightest doubt which of these the blond wanted—that he could give the submissive guy ten thick inches and he'd be back for more.

Damont held for the longest moment, his thoughts going back thirty years to the night he'd fucked the small, hirsute Aaron Stein six times in athletic positions. When he'd fucked Aaron on the rings, they'd started in this position—except that both had been naked and hard and Damont's ten, thick inches had moved up into Aaron's channel as soon as Damont had positioned himself close in back of Aaron. They'd already fucked twice and Aaron's hole was custom reamed to Damont's demanding dimensions.

Aaron had taken him fully twice. Aaron would keep on taking him as long as Damont could manage a hard on.

Aaron, gripping the rings overhead, had encased Damont's hips with his thighs, just as this young blond was doing, but, further, he had crossed his calves under Damont's buttocks, locking his ankles, holding Damont's cock buried deep inside him. Damont had lifted his own hands, grabbing for the rings, his hands closing in over the smaller ones of Aaron. And then, lifting his feet off the floor, he had swung them both, back and forth, and higher and higher, pumping for an ever-wider arc of swing while the motion caused him to rhythmically pump Aaron's hungry ass with his huge cock.

Damont could have this young blond the same way. He knew it; the blond knew it. The gym had just closed. They were alone. The blond wanted Damont to fuck him, Damont wanted to fuck the blond. He wanted to see how flexible the young honey was, how many taxing fuck positions he could endure.

At fifty-two Damont's tastes in sex hadn't changed all that much in the last thirty years. And he was still a hunk. And young men still came to the gym wanting to be taxingly fucked by the big black bull with the ten thick inches.

\* \* \* \*

"Sorry I'm late. I had to stop at the store for a couple of things." If Damont was feeling guilty, Aaron didn't tune into that—not even when he saw that Damont was carrying a large bouquet of flowers and something in a small plastic bag.

"Flowers. You brought me flowers," Aaron said, pleased, but also a bit apprehensive. "No problem with being late. There's a lasagna in the oven, but it will keep."

"Good, because I don't think we'll get to it for a while." Damont's voice was gravelly. Aaron recognized the sign of that and he began to pant lightly and felt himself going hard. At sixty-five, Aaron could still go hard for Damont.

"Here. Give me the flowers. The stems should be cut and I need them to get into water."

"Just a minute for that," Damont said, crossing to the kitchen counter, sweeping Aaron into his arms, and giving him a deep kiss. In the process, he knocked Aaron's cane onto the floor from where it had been hanging from its handle on the edge of the kitchen island counter. Aaron had needed to use a cane since the automobile accident five years earlier. The leg was more numb now than painful, but it had caused Aaron to stop his years-long rigorous exercise regime in an attempt to keep himself desirable for Damont. He'd never become comfortable with being able to keep up with what Damont wanted from him.

Aaron was putting on a few pounds now, although he had exchanged hard exercise for hard dieting, but a little thickish around the middle now, he was still looking better than a sixty-five-year-old had the right to look. His catering business had done real well. He'd helped Damont buy the gym. Aaron suspected that Damont stayed with him because of that, although Damont continually denied that and declared that he still found Aaron fascinating sexually after all of these years.

"You give the absolute best blow jobs," Damont would say at this time, to which Aaron would answer, "You have a lot of experience with that to do the comparison, I'm sure. I know from personal experience what happens at that gym of yours." This would make Damont clam right up.

And when Aaron pointed out that he now was sixty-five and, with the added disability of the bum leg, "We can't fuck on the trapeze anymore, and I know how you like that," Damont would counter with "Don't forget that I'm fifty-two now myself. Trapezes are out of my life too."

But when they had this standard exchange tonight, Damont's thoughts guilty went back to the young blond on the rings earlier that evening—how good he smelled, how well his slim waist fit between Damont's beefy hands, how hard he'd made Damont. How much the sweet young thing had wanted his butt cheeks split by the cock.

How much he wanted to swing with Damont on the rings, the cock finding new depth with each upswing of the arc.

"Here, let me do that," he said, reaching over for the flowers. He just managed to stop himself from saying that Aaron was hacking the stems mercilessly by not being able to hold his hand steady. The essential tremors that had set in in the last two years, making Aaron's hands tremble almost uncontrollably when he was nervous, were doing a real number now.

Aaron obviously was very nervous about something. Was it because Damont was late in getting home? Was it because Aaron thought the flowers reflected something Damont felt guilty for this evening?

"You know why I brought the flowers, don't you?" he abruptly said.

"No, no I don't," Aaron said, his eyes downcast. "But you don't have to tell me why. It doesn't matter. You're here. That's all that matters. You've stuck with me. I don't care what you have to do to keep yourself satisfied."

"For thirty years," Damont said. It was almost a whisper. His voice was husky. "We've been stuck with each other for thirty years, Aaron. That's what the flowers are for. It's our anniversary. It was thirty years ago today when we first fucked that evening in the gym—and then in my apartment, with me moving in with you the next day. It's our anniversary. That's the why of the flowers. In appreciation for thirty great years. And you haven't asked what's in the bag."

"What's in the bag?" Aaron asked in a choked voice.

Damont pulled the box out of the bag—a box of Trojan Magnum condoms. "It took me a while, standing at the counter, to decide how big a box we'd need for tonight."

They stood in the center of the living room, pulling at each other's clothes and kissing before Aaron managed to get on his knees in front of Damont and show that he still could give the best blow job Damont had ever had.

And then Damont showed he still had remarkable recovery powers at fifty-two and both showed that age and infirmity had not stolen their ability to do a standing fuck in the middle of the living room. And later, the lasagna already cold in the oven, Aaron showed that a bum leg was fine running up Damont's meaty torso, ankle hooked on Damont's shoulder. And that his other leg was still flexible enough to just sit straight out and up from his hip as Damont held it wide at the ankle to widen access in Aaron's ass to a cock that hadn't lost a millimeter in length or girth, as Damont drilled him hard and deep. Damont was putting all of the desire into the pumping that he had fantasized to do with the young blond on the rings earlier in the evening.

He was dreaming, yes, of fucking an athletic young man in taxing positions. He could do nothing about his fetish for this but to resist it and, successfully, to put Aaron's face on all of the bodies of the men he fucked in his dreams—as he strongly resisted doing earlier in the evening or he might have given in and given the young blond the cocking he do obviously had wanted.

The truth of it, though, was that there had never been another man since that night thirty years ago with Aaron. Whenever there had been the temptation, Damont had done the comparisons, and Aaron had always come up the winner—with so much going for him beyond the sex.

Damont lowered his face to Aaron's as he drove his dick hard inside the older man. Putting his forehead against Aaron's, he watched the expressions of ecstasy that his pumping, long, hard, wide, inside Aaron's channel was bringing to the older man's face. It was all worth it— all of the other denial of desires so hard to control—to be rewarded with those expressions.

The two men could still bring gushes of cum out of each other, and as long as that was the case . . . well, for an eternity after that as well.

"One thing about the Trojan Magnums, though," Damont whispered when they were done and after Damont had told Aaron what the next fuck position was. "It's our last box. If the only way I can prove to you that there's no one else and won't be is to go natural, that's what we'll do. It will be more enjoyable anyway."

Aaron sighed. That was the best anniversary present. At last he believed.

# Hanging off the Appalachian Trail

(At the request of R. P.)

Rocko stood aside, stripping his hands of the rubber gloves, and watched as Howard Holt released the young, slender black man from the chains that had had him suspended from the ceiling. He gingerly lifted the college student, Ray Taylor, and lowered him onto a nearby cot before he could sink fully to the stone floor in the playroom of the basement of Holt's Victorian mansion on the hill above the Blue Ridge Mountains town of Buena Vista, Virginia.

The late twenties black bull stud, Rocko, readjusted the black leather harness crisscrossing his bare, muscled chest. He turned to the stainless steel cart beside him and tidied up the tit clamps, stainless steel pinchers, flogger, short whip, electric zapper, ball weights, enema bag, and leg extenders laying on the cart. He had used them all in the last hour. Mr. Holt liked everything tidy after a session.

He was just the muscle behind the session. Howard Holt had guided him in every maneuver. His routine had been much the same the previous night, with Holt himself, Rocko's employer at the service garage where Rocko was an auto mechanic. Holt was Buena Vista's leading businessman, and by his own command, he'd already experienced all that the young college student of tonight had been subjected to. The leggy black youth, Ray Taylor, was a student at the Mormon-owned college in town, Southern Virginia University, played basketball, and was studying drama.

He was at least dabbling with the idea of experimenting with sex with other male students at the college. There wasn't the slightest doubt, gauged by his reaction to tonight's playtime, that the student had never had anything as exciting and testing applied to him before in his life, though.

Ray Taylor had been working part time in Holt's landscaping business, and although Holt had noticed the perfectly formed, tall young man doing hard manual work in yards, his specific prurient interest had been in whether the young man aroused Rocko—which he did. This was the first time that Howard had brought a Southern Virginia University student down into his basement for him to watch Rocko work over—and Ray had local family to boot. Holt usually took Rocko to nearby colleges—Virginia Tech, in Blacksburg, or Radford or Longwood in the towns by those names—to pick out a young man who turned Rocko on and who was found to be actively gay and in need of money. And a young man who was cocky and thought he was invincible. He certainly had to think that he could withstand anything that was done to him.

Ray was neither cocky nor did he believe he was invincible. But he was curious and really needed the money. He had come to Holt. His car needed new tires. He'd heard what Holt got off on—watching Rocko put a young man through the paces and do Holt likewise, both men being aroused by the session with the college student. Holt was fifty-five, still in good condition, but tired of and too old now to meet black studs casually who would beat and torture an ejaculation out of him.

So, he'd hired one of his garage mechanics, who was into the BDSM lifestyle, to take care of his particular needs. Holt's needs included being humiliated, manhandled, and worn out sexually by a big-cocked black bull.

Rocko had suggested it wasn't a good idea to do a local guy like Ray, even if he said he was willing to do it for the $500 he needed for new tires. Invariably, the guy didn't really know what it entailed, how cruelly Rocko would use him before he and Holt were keyed up enough for the fun of Rocko doing Holt. And who knows what havoc could be let loose if a local unsatisfied customer spoke out.

When they went further afield, they could bring the guy up into the mountains in the night, blindfolded and bound on the floor of the backseat of the car and could return his bruised and moaning body to "wherever" before the break of day. The guy would have no idea where he had been taken. But Ray knew where he'd be taken hard by Rocko. And he'd know Rocko did it even though Rocko would wear a black mask over his leather pants and chest strappings. And Ray would know that Holt had orchestrated it all.

More often than that, a drifter going through town would pole dance at the local gay dive for a beer and change and Rocko would give him a sample in the bar's back room of what he'd have to do for $500. Rocko's sample rarely matched how taxed the young guy ultimately was, although they occasionally surfaced a pro in the art who went the distance and still was able to walk away from it. Then in a few days the drifter would have moved on.

"Carry him upstairs to the bedroom," Rocko commanded, still in his dominant role.

"Yes, sire," Holt responded as he gathered the exhausted and broken Ray in his arms and moved toward the stairs to the upper levels. In the world outside this house, Holt was a king in Buena Vista—and he didn't even deign to speak to the auto mechanic, Rocko, when he visited the service garage he owned—among his other many holdings in town. But inside the house, when they were doing a session, Rocko was god and Holt was subservient. That was the way Holt wanted it. Certain relationships and routines were necessary to make Holt hard and cause him to gush.

Holt was hard as a rock now, as he carried the lightly moaning Ray up the stairs. Rocko had tortured the young black student's body with clips and ball weights and flesh clamps and no end of body teasers before he had flogged, whipped, zapped, and used a progression of every longer and thicker dildos to open the young man up—the latter a mercy, really, because Rocko was built very big. And, finally, Rocko had mercilessly fucked Ray from behind, while the young man was still bound. Holt had watched it all, licking his lips, and savoring the similar treatment he had experienced at Rocko's hands the previous evening.

Holt lowered Ray's body to a bed in an upstairs bedroom and cuffed the young man's wrists to the rungs of the brass headboard overhead before withdrawing, going down on his haunches on the wooden floorboards across the room to watch, as Rocko stripped off his pants, climbed onto the bed, rolled Ray's body onto his side, raised Ray's left leg, worked his hard cock into the channel that had been prepared by the graduated dildos, and started to fuck Ray again.

Ray had come a bit alive as Rocko worked his bulb beyond the rim and then gasped, groaned, and jerked as Rocko penetrated hard fast and deep, but then he settled down to light panting and moaning as Rocko plowed him for a second time. The ass play before that had well prepared the virgin to anal penetration well by the ten incher.

Although Ray moaned and whimpered through the ball gag he'd been wearing most of the evening, he was too spent and beaten down to resist the assault. He had assured Holt beforehand that he'd been anally fucked before, but Rocko was to assure Holt that that wasn't the case.

The one thing that was sure was that Ray needed that $500 for a set of tires for his ride and was so desperate for them that he was willing to do anything for the money. Rocko had done everything and then some with Ray's body, and Holt had watched it all and was so keyed up that he was down on his haunches across the room, moaning and whimpering along with Ray.

Rocko pulled out of Ray's ass, turned full frontal to Holt on the floor and growled, "I'm about to cum. Crawl to me and take my wad."

Licking his lips and panting hard, Holt slithered across the floor to the bed. Rocko lifted Holt's head up by the hair and positioned Holt's face in front of his throbbing cock. Holt took the cock in his mouth, and Rocko creamed his tonsils.

"Truss him up and put him in the back of the car," Rocko commanded. Holt scurried to bind Ray's wrists and ankles. He took up the clothes, now folded, that Ray had worn to the house and made sure that Ray, glassy-eyed but still barely with them, could see him stuff six hundred-dollar bills in the pocket of his jeans—it always was a good idea to overpay them a bit. Throwing the bound black college student's body over his shoulder and shoving the pile of clothes and a pair of sneakers under his arm, Holt trundled Ray out to the Lincoln Town Car and dumped his trussed body on the floor of the backseat. Later Rocko would drive him away in the still-dark of the morning and dump him and his clothes someplace close to his dorm at the university. It was up to Ray to get back to his dorm and come up with an excuse on why he'd been gone all night.

But before driving Ray anywhere, Holt returned to the upstairs bedroom, where Rocko, recharged, had a small whip in hand, made Holt go down on all fours on the bare wood floor, mounted him, and flogged him on the back, buttocks, and thighs as he fucked Holt hard.

Holt was hard and throbbing when Rocko turned him onto his side, bound his wrists and ankles, and then worked Holt's cock with his hand for nearly another hour, bringing Holt close to an ejaculation, but then backing him off, edging him, when he was about to come. Finally, complaining pleadingly of his aching balls, Holt was allowed to come.

Unbinding only his wrists, Rocko left the room and the house without a look back, one more task to do—dispensing with Ray—before going home for a couple of hours of shuteye before he had to appear for work at the garage in the morning.

Howard Holt loved every minute of the session he had set up and paid for. But if he saw either Ray or Rocko the next day, he'd do no more than give them a terse nod and walk on by. He would walk down the hill to the service garage at some point during the day to retrieve the Lincoln Town Car that Rocko would have washed and detailed for him.

At some point he'd ask Rocko if he'd liked doing Ray. If so, Ray could earn some more money—if he hadn't been scared off of what he had to do to earn it.

* * * *

Holt was standing at the beaded curtain to the back room in the bar he owned at the lower end of Buena Vista, watching Rocko put a blond Lynchburg College student through his paces before a more intense session up at the house later in the evening. The naked young man was stretched out on his belly on a padded massage table. His wrists were cuffed at the front edges of the table and his legs were spread by an extender cuffed at his ankles. Rocko, naked except for the leather chest harness and black half mask, was on his knees, straddling the young man's hips.

The student was writhing under Rocko as Rocko tickled him mercifully. Holt watched, licking his lips, knowing what came next, as suddenly Rocko reached between the young man's thighs, grabbed his nuts and began to squeeze and twist them. The writhing increased, the young man screaming ineffectually through his ball gag, his eyes bugging out. Holt began to pant, this being some of his own favorite play, imagining that it was him under Rocko, receiving this attention. Knowing that later that night, after the young man was completely spent from Rocko's play in the basement room of the house, it would be Holt.

The young man jerked, spasmed, and groaned deeply as Rocko positioned himself above him, fists down on either side of the blond's shoulders, split the young man's butt cheeks with a mammoth black bull's cock, and started to pump.

Holt lost interest at this point. It was one thing when the play culminated in this for him, but, in watching another man being sub fucked, the fun for Holt stopped with the torture play.

He moved back into the barroom and stood at the bar, ordering a beer from Manuel, the bartender on duty.

The gay part of the tavern wasn't large—just an entrance foyer, where a bouncer ascertained that the patron really wanted to be there; this barroom with a long bar, a few tables, and a small stage with a dancing pole; and a couple of multipurpose back rooms with toys, beds, and special equipment. The Lynchburg College student had been made to dance the pole until Rocko got in the mood and took him to the back. There had been few patrons present then. It was the middle of the afternoon, and this pretty much was a night-time club. The student was doing this willingly—but probably, like most, not having fully understood what "this" was. College students always needed money, were willing to try anything, and thought they were invincible.

After Rocko got through with them, most of them were subdued and broken. They certainly were broken in. If they tried to fight him, they were broken down.

The gay part of the tavern was on the back of the building, entered in back, in a corner of the parking lot and through the fenced-off area where the trash bins were kept. It didn't look like the entrance to anything and that's how the small gay community in the area liked it. The girly bar was on the street side and was much larger and covered with neon signs. There was a lot of business in this area of the state for that part of the club.

Howard Holt, mostly taken at face value as a white, good-old-Southern-boy, who had accumulated a lot of lucrative businesses and who spent enough time in the gym to look very good as a fifty-five-year-old extrovert glad-hander, hid his true sexual desires well. Very few in town would take him as a pain-loving gay sub who melted at big black bull cock and maximum body testing and humiliation. As long as he kept the gas station, car garage, and small grocery store open in Buena Vista and the residents didn't have to come down in the east from the Blue Ridge to Lynchburg or to the west to Lexington to get the necessities of life, any other businesses he ran were overlooked or quickly forgiven.

Most of those who knew he spent time at Stella's assumed he camped out in the girly bar in front, not in the gay bar behind, which few knew about. They assumed Stella was a wife who had died long ago or one who had walked off and left him, not willing to put up longer with his orneriness or the mistresses a successful businessman in central Virginia was assumed to have. They wouldn't have guessed that he'd never married, because he was stuck on men. And not just any men. His choice was big black bulls who would tax his body mercilessly and entertain him by letting him watch what they could do with young college students—and then, usually, as the spent young man hung there and watched, do him as well in the same way.

Even those few men and drifters who saw Holt in the gay bar assumed he was a power top. Few of them related him to Rocko, who they correctly sensed was a cruel sadist who could split them asunder and who they studiously avoided. They were aware what he did in the back room with the pole dancer talent Holt brought to the club, but they either assumed Holt didn't realize that was going on or, at best, ignored it, because word got around and hopeful young twinks did turn up looking for what Rocko gave them.

Holt was on his second beer when Rocko reentered the barroom from the back, dressed in shorts and a T, ordered and received a beer, and sat at one of the nearby tables.

Holt was talking with Manuel, the bartender, who had no other business to take care of at the moment.

"You been up on the Appalachian Trail yet this season, Mr. H?" Manuel asked, making small talk. "I know you like to hike up there."

"It helps keep me in shape."

Manuel took a moment to appreciate the shape Holt was in. He was older, but Manuel liked them mature. They had more experience. And Holt was one well-built older man. Manuel was a power bottom and he, like most, figured Holt as a power top. He'd really like to get Holt on top of him, but he assumed that the man was so steeped in the South that he wouldn't go with blacks or Hispanics. He was friendly enough with Manuel, though, so that was good enough. Good jobs were hard for a Hispanic to come by in this town other than cleaning toilets and picking fruit in orchards and here there were enough cruising power tops drifting through the bar to keep Manuel sexually satisfied.

"I'm going up tomorrow, as a matter of fact. I plan to hike north to The Priest and back," Holt added. The Priest was one of the higher mountains on the eastern edge of the Blue Ridge range between Lynchburg and Charlottesville down in the Piedmont.

"Should be nice," Manuel said. "If I was off, I'd like to go with you." It was a half hint, which Holt didn't take. Holt could have given him the day off. They could have hiked north, gone off the trail a couple of times, and Holt could have fucked him on the mountainside by streams. It was a dream of Manuel's, although Holt never seemed to bite.

The barroom had been mostly deserted as the two chatted. It was this fact that made Holt aware of the two men—both black—who had entered the bar and took up position very close to Holt on each side as he and Manuel had been engaged in bantering talk.

Holt liked to talk with Manuel. Holt had dreams of the well-built Hispanic trussing his body up and abusing and using him mercilessly. He had an obsession about whether there was any black in Manuel's blood and how big his dick was. He'd known Hispanics with black blood who had big cocks that were jet black in contrast to the dusky skin otherwise, the focus of attention going directly to the cock. Holt had dreams of Manuel's jet-black cock waving as, Holt strung up to the ceiling, Manuel danced around his body, flagellating him with a hand whip. If he'd had any hint that the Manuel of reality matched up with the Manuel of Holt's fantasy, he'd be asking Manuel to join him on the hike tomorrow—and they'd never get half way to The Priest. They'd be off the trail with Manuel abusing a gush of cum out of Hold's body.

Holt knew both of the men who had come in and hemmed him in at the bar—they were regulars here and were a couple. Holt and many others knew them as Mutt and Jeff. The tall, older—in his late thirties—thinner of the two was Buck Taylor. The squat one—in his late twenties—was Alfonse Jackson. Both were construction workers. Both were well-muscled. Holt had it on good authority that Taylor was a pure top, with an extraordinarily long dick as the major attraction to features that were on the ugly, gangling side. Alfonse, the smaller, chunkier, and better looking of the two had a high, squeaky voice and was known as a flip flopper. It was supposed that he stuck with Taylor mainly for the length of his cock, reputed to be an eleven incher.

The two muscled in so close on either side of Holt, ordering their beers in harmony, Taylor's voice a bass and Alfonse's a high soprano, that Holt knew they were there for him. He also figured he knew why they were visiting.

"What were you up to last night, Howie?" Taylor opened up.

"At home, alone—probably while the two of you were screwing at the back of your truck," Holt answered in a calm, "we're all just friends here" voice.

"Sure about the alone part?" Taylor persisted. "Sure you weren't up to the rumors on you?"

"What rumors would that be?"

"I had occasion to visit my nephew, Ray, at his dorm this morning. He was supposed to go out on a mowing job with me. But he wasn't up to it. I had to take him to a clinic. He said he was riding his motorbike yesterday up on the Blue Ridge Parkway and went over the edge. Managed to walk out but had wound up in a briar bush. The welts and such I saw on his body don't come from no briar bush, though. I've heard what goes on in your house up there. You do somethin' to my boy last night?"

"No, I didn't. I don't do that stuff," Holt answered, trying to put some indignation in his voice. And, indeed, he didn't. Someone else did that. That someone else did it to Holt too, and Holt got off in gushers in having it done to him. Tense up to this point, Holt relaxed. It may not have looked like he was out of the woods on this, but he now knew that Ray hadn't talked—hadn't told his uncle what had really happened to him. Taylor suspected that it was Holt who did it, but Ray knew better. He knew he was worked over by a black bull and Holt had done no more to him than watch—and had stuffed money in the pocket to his pants.

Ray was good enough with it. Holt would use Ray again. Ray surely wanted more work done on the jalopy he drove.

"Sorry to say, but Alphonse here and I would like you take a little ride with us, Howie. Just come along nice now."

Holt looked over at Rocko at the table. The big black, having heard it all, looked ready to spring. Holt gave him a negative shake of the head. He didn't want the possible involvement of Rocko to get into these two dummies' minds at all. Instead, he nodded to Manuel, who pulled a shotgun out from behind the bar.

"I think one beer is enough for you boys today," Manuel said, "and I'm sorry to report that the bar is closing early today."

Taking the point, Taylor gave Holt a piercing look and simply said, "Later, then."

The two men left the bar without a fuss. When Holt was ready to leave, both Rocko and Manuel were at the edge of the fence at the parking lot to make sure that Holt's Town Car was clear and that Holt got to it safely.

Holt kept thinking of the Taylor-Jackson pair in the vein of a harmless Mutt and Jeff and thus didn't give them much of a thought at all. He kept his mind on what was coming later that night.

The blond Lynchburg College student performed well for Rocko in the stocks that night, kneeling on a pad, his neck and wrists trapped in the holes of a wooden stock contraption, his ankles cuffed to a leg extender, his cock and balls extended painfully by heavy weights, and Rocko tickling him mercilessly before mounting his ass and whipping his back, buttocks, and thighs while fucking him deep and hard.

Holt appreciated the identical treatment later even more, as the blond student, totally exhausted, hung from an X frame and watched through slitted, half-glazed eyes while Rocko repeated the session on Holt.

\* \* \* \*

They let him get almost to The Priest on the Appalachian Trail, well away from Buena Vista and any other sign of civilization, before the black duo of Taylor and Jackson swarmed over Holt from both sides of the trail. He put up quite a fight and was nearly the match of the two of them together. Taylor had to knock him out with a well-placed slam of a rubber dildo.

When Holt came to, he already was spread-eagled, naked, with both arms and legs stretched to his sides, between two trees at the top of a rock outcropping, suspended over a drop off into a parallel mountain range on the western side of the Blue Ridge. There was nothing but forested mountaintops to seen in any direction, and there was no telling how far down the mountainside they were from either the Blue Ridge Parkway or the Appalachian Trail. Holt wouldn't have bothered to yell for help even if he could. In the event, the ball gag would muffle any screaming he might do.

His arms were stretched and tied off by rope to two trees at either side of the flat rock he was suspended over. His legs, similarly stretched and roped off to the trees were almost painfully extended. Other than his hiking boots, he was stripped down. Mutt and Jeff were busy wrapping the base of his cock and balls in the end of the rope, which they then would lead off to another tree in front him, pulling his genitals up and stretching them.

They'd already hung heavy weights on his ball sac that would fight to pull his balls down.

As soon as he came to, Holt began to writhe. Taylor and Jackson laughed cruelly. Unbeknownst to them, though, Holt was in seventh heaven. He shot off in Jackson's face, as the squat man knelt before him working on the knots of the rope encasing Holt's cock. It wouldn't, by any means, be Holt's only ejaculation of the ordeal.

Jackson didn't find that funny and had words with Taylor, who thought it was a riot. Angry, Jackson picked out a dildo from a bag Taylor was unloading, moved to behind where Holt was strung up, and shoved the rubber dick up Holt's ass. The man was almost lifted off his feet, his eyes rolled up into his head, and he groaned in ecstasy. Leaving the dildo nearly all the way up Holt's channel, Jackson came back around, stripping off his shirt, to show a stocky but well-developed chest and six pack. Taylor already had his T-shirt off, showing an equally muscled torso, the result for both of them from several year's work in heavy construction.

It was about then that Ray, called by Taylor to come up on the parkway after they'd first subdued Holt, arrived, leaving his motorbike on the parkway and following his phone GPS down to the coordinates Taylor gave him.

"What?" he exclaimed. "No, don't. He didn't do—"

"Shut up and stand out of the way, Ray," his uncle commanded. "Just watch and enjoy getting some of your own back, but don't get involved in this."

Defeated and knowing that the revved-up duo wouldn't listen to anything he said, Ray sat down on a rock and watched the show unfold.

Jackson was already clipping on tit clamps connected with a chain and was rewarded with a grunt, and then with a deep groan when he reached down and crushed Holt's distended ball sac. Taking four clips up from what Taylor had poured from the sack of toys they had brought, Jackson clipped two to each ball sac, causing Holt to writhe to the extent he could, moan, and begin to pant hard.

He shot another load, and Jackson barely got out of the way of the arc.

Taylor was pushing a short, many leather-pronged whip into Jackson's hands and choosing something that looked like a feather duster for himself, and they both went to work, Jackson whipping Holt from behind, and Taylor tickling him with the feathers from in front.

Looking away from this, Ray spotted movement up the slope where the sweeping branches of a giant fir tree nearly met the tops of low bushes. Focusing on it, he realized he could see Rocko hiding in the foliage. He looked to see if he'd be missed, but Taylor and Jackson were preoccupied with getting water into a large enema bottle they'd brought and taunting Holt with what they were going to do to him with it.

Holt was panting noisily through his ball gag, Taylor and Jackson misinterpreting fear for what Holt anticipated as pleasure that he wished the two would hurry up with.

"How did you get here?" Ray asked in a whisper when he got to Rocko and was pulled down to where he was sitting between Rocko's thighs in an open space under the spread of the fir tree branches. Rocko had a sawed-off shotgun in one hand and pulled Ray's body into his with the other. He pointed the barrel of the shotgun up under Ray's chin and scrabbled to undo Ray's belt with the other hand.

"Hey, wait," Ray whispered. "I'm not part of this. My uncle called me up here. I didn't know they had Mr. Holt. He just told me to get my ass up here. I didn't tell them anything."

"I followed you up here," Rocko growled. "I saw you tooling out of town, and I took Mr. Holt's Town Car and followed you up here. I was following your ass too."

"You didn't know they were up here doing this to him?"

"No, I came up here to do the same thing to you." Rocko put the shot gun down long enough to secure Ray's wrists together behind his back with the belt. He nodded off to the side where coils of rope and a sack of toys were piled.

Ray moaned at the sight of them and with the thought that Rocko intended to do to him what his uncle was doing to Holt. "But we have to do something to save Mr. Holt," he murmured. It was the last thing he was able to say. Rocko had taken the bandana off the curly black hair head of the young black and gagged Ray's mouth with it.

"Mr. Holt's having the time of his life," Rocko growled. "He don't need no savin'. You and me are gonna watch him getting his rocks off again and again, and you and me are gonna have the time of your life too. If I see them doin' something life threatening to him, I'll pull this shotgun on them. Short of that, I don't think he'd appreciate me breakin' into his fun."

And, sure enough, out on the rock suspended over the cliff, enema water was streaming down Holt's thighs as Taylor gave the bottle, its neck jammed up Holt's ass, another hard squeeze. Jackson in front again doing a nut-crushing routine on Holt, who almost got him again with the strong arc of another ejaculation. Holt was having a jolt of surprise pleasure.

Rocko turned Ray, pulled him up on his knees, jerked his shorts and briefs down to his calves, pushed Ray's face into the dirt at the base of the bushes, mounted his ass, and began to cock pump him. He'd whipped off his belt as well and had that looped around Ray's throat, creating makeshift reins. He jerked back on the reins with every other thrust up the young man's channel. Ray gagged at each jerk from the cut in his air supply. The two settled into a rhythm of the fuck that permitted them both to watch what was happening to Holt through the foliage.

Holt was being fucked now too. Both of his assailants were naked and in full erection. The ropes on his arms had been relaxed, and Holt was bent forward at the waist. Jackson, the smaller cocked of the two black assailants was taking Holt's ass first, as Taylor crouched in front of Holt and fucked his throat.

By the time Jackson was finished and they'd exchanged positions, with Holt grunting and groaning deeply to find that Taylor indeed was the rumored eleven incher, Rocko was done ass fucking Ray too, and had pushed him over on his side, had a death grip on Ray's balls with one hand, and was rubbing the glans of Ray's cock with the other hand. Ray writhed at the crushing of his balls and groaned a strong ejaculation from the worrying of his bulb and Rocko's efforts to finger fuck his piss slit.

Taylor and Jackson picked up their toys, loaded them into a sack, and walked out of the woods, not freeing Holt and not seeing where Rocko and Ray were hidden.

"Where's Ray?" Jackson asked.

"Beats me," Taylor answered. "The kid probably doesn't have the stomach for this. But if Howie gets out of this, I'll bet he doesn't touch the kid again."

After they'd left, Rocko freed Ray and said, "Wait here. Don't you go anywhere or I'll come for you and it won't be pretty."

"Don't leave me," Ray whimpered.

"What?"

"I want you to fuck me again. I want, like Mr. Holt . . . the ropes . . . you said you were going to string me up like Mr. Holt is bound."

"You want that?"

"Yes," Ray admitted in a small voice.

"Oh for the love of Jesuzz," Rocko muttered. "Stay here. I'll be back." While he was telling Ray to stay there, he was tying the young man's ankles together with his belt. Ray's wrists were still tied behind his back with his own belt. There was little chance Ray was going anywhere before Rocko returned.

When he went down to Holt, he didn't free him immediately. He moved behind him, thrust his cock in Holt's now gaping hole, and fucked him in the ass as the two others had done, while Holt whimpered his appreciation through his ball gag. Then Rocko untied him, leaned over and whispered something to him as Holt collapsed on the rock, and came back to Ray.

It took him several minutes to string Ray up between two trees, but he only did the young student's arms, as, commanding Ray to climb his hips with his knees, Rocko fucked him from the front, his fists around Ray's throat, almost making him black out before releasing him to gasp for air and then choked him in cycles as the fuck continued.

Afterward, coiling up his rope and stuffing his bags of toys, Rocko said, "The Town Car is parked at the camp grounds for The Priest. We'll get that and come back for your bike."

"Where's Mr. Holt?"

"He's gone to the car. I told him where it is. I think you're going to have to drive."

Ray didn't ask why, but as they got close to the car, he could see why. The door to the backseat was open, giving Ray a view of the back interior that the smoked glass on the windows otherwise would have denied him. Holt was in back, seated, his legs raised to the side pillars on both sides, his feet inserted in the loops of the hand holds there.

Rocko would be getting in back and fucking Holt all the way back to Buena Vista.

"He's had quite a day. Keyed up tighter than I've ever seen him," Rocko said. "He'll want a serious session tonight."

"Is anyone else . . . ? Do you need anyone else?" Ray stammered out.

"If you think you can take it, I'm sure Mr. Holt will be happy if I do you too tonight."

"My uncle and his boyfriend?"

"I have a feeling they'll be hanging around in Mr. Holt's basement tonight too. We can make sure they don't see what I'm doing to you, though—which is about the same I'll do to them."

# Not in Kenya

"Is the prisoner here, in the examination room?" The doctor for the central jail in Nairobi and I were standing in a white-walled narrow corridor outside a door with a plastic folder attached to it to hold medical records.

"Yes, Inspector. His name is John. He's barely nineteen."

"How sure are you?"

"Very sure. I thought of calling you in immediately. He's been beaten rather badly and they used something thick . . . in addition. That's why I called you."

"What is he in for?"

"Soliciting on the street, of course. That's why it's so easy to identify them."

"So, you think?"

"Yes, of course. That's why I sent for you."

"Is that all he's here for?"

"His sheet says robbery as well. Will that make it easier?"

"It should."

The doctor ushered me into the room. "John, this is Inspector White. Inspector Cedric White. He's on loan from the British police. You can safely tell him everything."

I looked at the Kenyan prisoner, John, and then had to look away. The doctor had said he was nineteen, but he didn't look nearly that age. He was just wearing prison shorts and was barefoot. And I could see how he would have gotten in the position he was in. Other than a face that looked like hamburger now and bruises all of his willowy ebony torso, there was an androgynous beauty about him and I could easily see that he would be appealing to a certain kind of man. He was sitting on a cushion, but more on one thigh than the other and was fidgeting.

"I'm here to help you, if I can, John," I said, as I sat on what would have been the doctor's chair and the doctor closed the door to the examination room behind him. "What has happened to you?"

"Nothing. Just a misunderstanding."

"With other prisoners?" I asked.

He didn't answer. I could tell that he was withdrawing into himself.

"If you don't tell me what happened, I'll have to have you sent back," I said.

That got his attention. I could see the panic rising in him. I was about to lose him.

"I'm not from the Kenya police," I said. "The doctor sent for me because I'm not. He knows what's happened to you. You've been sexually assaulted, haven't you?"

Nothing for a moment and then a terse nod.

"It wasn't other prisoners, was it? It was your jailers."

A short pause and then, "They used their batons at first. At first." He looked away, tears in his eyes and then he looked back and said with ferocity in his voice, "You won't send me back there, will you? I can't go right back."

"No, that's why I'm here, John. I won't send you back. There's another jail. A better one. And I can put on your papers that you're in for robbery, not for anything else. If you can just not . . . while you're there. If you can hold yourself in check, they won't know, probably—we can hope—won't take advantage. Can you do that?"

Tears in his eyes, he nodded, and, putting a hand on my forearm now, murmured, "I'd do anything for you to help me. Anything."

And I could tell that he was serious, that he would do anything not to be sent back to the jailers here, even as bruised and sliced up as he was.

"If you're going to last the next two years, you need to stop saying that to just anyone, son," I said, as I stood and left the room. I didn't make it back to my office before I was being paged to go out immediately into the bush out near Embu on an emergency. Since I was here in an effort to mellow the Kenyan police out on their attitudes towards homosexuals, in which they were only parroting the national attitudes, homosexuality being illegal here still, I had to assume that something in this regard was going down. I decided to take one of the transport vans, as it was likely that some poor soul who had gotten himself into trouble needed to be removed from the scene to a more neutral corner.

\* \* \* \*

I was guided into my destination, the last building down a long, dusty track bordered by a line of African palm trees, by a filmy column of smoke. When I arrived at the smoldering building, only scorched walls now, not more than twenty by thirty feet, with what had been a palm-leaf roof, it was like I hadn't come a minute too soon.

Two local Kenyan police officers had a young man, just in sports briefs, on his knees between them and one of the local cops had a baton raised menacingly. They stopped and withdrew a couple of steps from the guy on his knees when I pulled to a stop near them.

I felt my body tense up as I got out of the van and approached them. The kneeling young man was maybe the most handsome and well-built Kenyan I'd ever seen—not tall and gangling, but well fed, though not overfed by any means. He had his wrists handcuffed behind his back.

"What do we have here?" I asked, as I approached.

"Another one of them," one of the policeman answered. "We were just ready to take him in."

I wasn't at all sure that taking him anywhere was what they had been planning to do next. With my mind on the young, beaten man I'd just left at the Nairobi jail infirmary, I wasn't at all sure I hadn't just interrupted another example of taking their time in taking him into custody. For all the belligerence these people seemed to have against gays, their violence toward them, as I had seen since I'd arrived here, certainly took on sexual overtones.

As politely as I could I maneuvered my body between the kneeling man and the policeman on one side and said, "Thank you. I'll take it from here. You may leave."

I must have spoken authoritatively and decisively enough, as the two backed off. I put my hand out to the one who looked like he was senior and said, "Handcuff key, please." I had guessed right. He meekly handed me the key. They walked way, muttering between each other—they no doubt had been told I wasn't to be messed up; I rather publicly was here to monitor a police force that had gotten a reputation for violence, especially against gays. I watched them mount their bicycles, and, with not more than two looks back each, they took to the dusty track that I'd come down.

"Now," I said, turning to the young man when I'd seen the last of the local policeman, "What's the story on this burnt building? Are you the neighborhood arsonist?"

The young man snorted, obviously able to appreciate my reference to the neighborhood, as this was the only building in evidence in any direction across a scrub plain. His response took me by surprise and not just by what he said.

"I hardly think so," he said, in refined English. "This was both my office and my home. I'm not the one who burned it down. They—the ones who burned it—were still here when those policemen arrived, but, naturally, I was the only one taken into custody."

"You speak beautiful English," I said in surprise. It wasn't the only thing about him that was beautiful and that was having its effect, as well.

"Educated at Oxford," he answered "I've only been home for six months."

That explained the robust body, I thought. He hadn't been home long enough for starvation to have had its effect. "So, what were you doing in that building to get it burned down?"

"My name is Raili Kimeu," he said. "I think we should start off being civilized."

"In which case, you can stand up," I responded.

"I like the view from here," he said, giving me a smile. I wasn't sure what he meant—then at least. His eyes were at my crotch level. This disturbed me a bit, as he was having a stirring effect on my crotch.

"My name is Cedric," I answered, and then, realizing that, considering the circumstance, I was being too familiar, I said. "Inspector Cedric White. I was sent here from Nairobi headquarters."

"To save me or to brutalize me for being homosexual?"

"Certainly not the latter. I haven't ascertained what you were being detained for yet, though. If you didn't burn this building down, who did, and why?"

"I returned from the UK to work for homosexual rights in Kenya," he answered. "It's primitive that loving your own gender is still outlawed here. I am—or was, at least—publishing a gay rights journal from here."

131

"Ah, I see. Well, what are we going to do with you? Did the policeman fill out any paperwork here—take down your name or anything—before I arrived?"

"Not that I saw. And you may do whatever you wish with me. Come closer."

"Excuse me?" I asked, apprehensive and shocked. Had he been able to read what had raced through my mind?

"Come closer. You don't know me, but I know you, although I had no idea you were a policeman. I've seen you at Alexander's. Were you doing undercover work there? If so, you were doing it very convincingly."

Ah, Alexander's. The underground gay bar I sneaked into in a basement in Nairobi when I couldn't take the isolation and denial any longer. And, no, if he'd seen me there he wouldn't think I was on any sort of sting operation. Compelled, I moved forward, to where I was standing close to where he still knelt, his hands cuffed behind his back.

I moaned as he rubbed his cheek along the erection line inside my trousers—an erection that had been caused by a combination of being keyed up in the previous interview with the assaulted rent-boy prisoner and the ebony beauty of this young man kneeling in only sports briefs. Obviously the house had started burning while he was asleep, and he had escaped the fire with no more than what he'd worn to bed.

"Unzip yourself and pull it out," he said in a hoarse voice. "Let me suck you off. I wanted to do that the first time I saw you at Alexander's. Then you can take me in on a charge of what I clearly am and do."

"Not here," I answered, my voice no more than a croak. "In the van, where we can't be seen as well."

I was in the driver's seat and he, still cuffed, in the passenger seat, when I unzipped my trousers and fished out my cock. I was in full erection and the only thing he said before leaning over and taking it in his mouth was, "It's so big. I knew it would be."

He blew me for several minutes to the sound of his sucking mouth on my cock and balls and my answering groans, as I palmed the back of his wooly haired head to encourage him to deep throat me.

When both my cock and my ears were throbbing, he pulled off and murmured, "Wouldn't we both be more comfortable in the passenger seat?"

He was fully naked, and I was still clothed, except for my unzipped fly and my open shirt, as he sat in my lap, my cock buried up his ass canal, him facing me, and, my lips teasing each of the nipples on his smooth, ebony, taunt-skin over well-developed muscle chest. I rocked him back and forth on my cock and lifted him and set him down with my hands on his thin waist to maximize the friction of my cock working deep inside him.

I hadn't come prepared, and everything he owned was smoldering in his house. Neither of us had mentioned a condom or stopped in the dance to the fuck long enough to mention it, so I was barebacking him with a maximum sensitivity quotient of bloated skin sliding on undulating channel walls.

"In the back of the van," I said, with a gasp. "You'll be more comfortable. The rhythm will be steadier. I should be able to reach deeper."

"If you reach deeper you'll bruise my tonsils," he said with a laugh, but he pulled off me and I opened the passenger door.

The floor of the van, behind the barred windows separating it from the driver's compartment, was hard, but there were pads on the benches on either side of the compartment. I laid him down full length on one pad and folded the other one over to put under the small of his back, raise his buttock, and create a straight angle for the slide of the cock in his ass.

There were plenty of anchors for chains, and there were multiple sets of handcuffs in the van, so there was no trouble cuffing his arms above him, running to opposite sides of the outer edges of the front compartment seat backs, nor was there a problem in spread-eagling and raising his legs to handcuff to anchors at the back corners of the interior compartment.

He arched his back as I knelt between his spread and bound-off legs, slid back inside him, and he cried out, "Oh, god, that is deeper."

I leaned my torso over his, anchoring my fists on either side of his stretched chest and raised his face to where he could lick my chest hair and suck and nibble on my nubs while, slow, at first, and ever faster, I pumped his channel.

When he arched his torso and head back as I was giving it to him hard, his mouth took in the dog tags that dangled from a chain on my neck and sucked and teethed them. As I tensed and ejaculated inside him, his was panting hard and I could hear the teeth tearing at the metal of the dog tags. He came up my belly in the wake of my last spurt of cum inside him.

\* \* \* \*

"I don't think this is either Nairobi police headquarters or the jail," Raili said as I brought the van to a stop.

Leaving him trussed in the back of the van, I'd driven to the first clothing store I could found and bought a shirt and a pair of shorts. It was an open-front store right on the road, selling mostly army surplus, and the clothes I'd bought probably had been Kenyan army issue. The bosomy, toothless women at the stall kept trying to tell me that the shirt and shorts would never fit me—and she smacked her lips like she was very glad that my body wouldn't fit into them, but I just ignored her, paid half of the marked price, which made her grin at her good fortune, and stopped a mile down the road to open up the back, unshackle Raili, let him dress, and then put him in the passenger seat, his ankles locked together by a pair of handcuffs.

He'd given me a half questioning look—he actually hadn't questioned much of what I'd said or done up to that point; there was no objection in him at all when I'd fucked him—and I merely said that I didn't think it was in his best interest to run off while we were driving back to Nairobi. I already had in mind what I wanted to do.

"It's not either of those," no, I answered. "This is my house."

"Going to fuck me some more before taking me to jail?" he asked. He turned his face to the window, giving my neat little government-issue bungalow scrutiny.

"I hope to fuck you some more," I answered quietly. "But I won't force you. If you don't want—"

"What does it matter?" he asked. "You're with the police. You'll fuck me if you want to, one way or the other."

"Was that what that was back in Embu?" I asked, keeping my voice low, calm. "You didn't fight me because I am a policeman?"

"No, I didn't fight you because I wanted you to fuck me—ever since I saw you at Alexander's. I didn't know you were a policeman then, though."

"And it's the police you feel you're fighting on the gay rights issue, isn't it?"

"Among others."

"Do you want to go into my house or not? If you go into my house I'm going to fuck you again."

\* \* \* \*

Raili was spread-eagled, belly down on my bed, arms and legs pulled to the four corners of the bed and

135

cuffed there. I stuffed several pillows under his belly, which pointed his deliciously mounded butt cheeks toward the ceiling. And I'd spent some time eating his ass out, pulling his cock and balls through his legs and sucking them, and milking his cock to an ejaculation while I lapped at his asshole.

He spent his time moaning, groaning, and egging me on, telling me of the pleasure I was bringing him—and begging to get on with the cocking phase. If he was pretending, he was a great actor. Once I got started, of course, it wouldn't matter that much if he was enjoying himself or not. I was besotted with him. I had to have him six ways from Sunday.

When his begging for the cock became really believable, I crouched over him from above, encircled his waist with an arm, mounted him and gave him the length and girth of me deep and hard. He murmured the pleasure of feeling my silky chest hair rub across his back. My dog tags dangled down to beside his face—I'd notice later that they were bent and had teeth marks of them—and he turned his head, took them into his mouth, and sucked and teethed them and pounded his ass to a bareback ejaculation. I had condoms in the nightstand now, but, after the session in the back of the van, it seem superfluous to use them.

Besides, he said it had been the first time he'd taken it skin on skin and he didn't really want it from me any other way again, the devil may care.

I felt every inch the devil. I was supposed to protect prisoners from police predators and the condemnation of the public. But then, he wasn't really a prisoner, other than the handcuffs, I wasn't denying I swung this way, and he gave every signal that he wanted it. Or was I reading this just to support what I'd wanted to do—and then done?

Other than sex talk, we didn't speak about anything in particular or meaningful until the second fucking after

I'd taken him to the kitchen and fed and watered him after the first time. I'd kept him handcuffed in some form throughout. I hadn't pitched him on what I had in mind yet.

I took him more intimately the next time on my bed. I fucked him in a side split, his wrists handcuffed together to the headboard and his ankles handcuffed together. My thighs split him, and I held him close to me, stretched along him from the back, our mouths meeting in a lingering kiss, and my dick slowly mining his ass.

"Can we dispense with these bindings now," I asked in a murmur after we'd both come. "You don't want to sleep bound like this, do you?"

"Yes, take them off. This key must go to one set," he answered, pushing a small key out of his mouth.

"You had a key all along," I said, surprised. "You could have taken the cuffs off any time back in the van."

"Yes. I got them out of your trouser pocket. I wasn't sure of you. But then, quickly, I was."

I freed his wrists and ankles. The binding hadn't been my idea—not from the first. Raili had demanded it. He'd said he didn't want me fucking him if he couldn't feel the pleasure of being incapacitated and taken advantage of by a police officer—just what I was here in Kenya to make sure a young man didn't have to feel.

"What now?" he asked of me in the gathering dark as I held him close, my dick going flaccid inside him, but still inside him. "Do we go to the police for booking now on the charge of being a homo and letting my house be burned down—and maybe assaulting a police officer?"

"I haven't arrested you . . . and we've already established that the handcuffs were *your* fetish, not mine. You have two choices. In the morning—I can't bear to let you out of my bed tonight—in the morning I can drive you anywhere you want in the area, let you off, and make any reference to arresting you disappear."

"Or?"

"Or you can stay with me and I'll help you with your gay rights journal."

"Help me with my journal? How? The printing press was destroyed? And why? It's against the law. You're a policeman."

"I'm a British policeman, not a Kenyan policeman, and I was sent here to try to help get rid of the effects of this antigay law. I'll help you, but I suggest some changes. Don't put the journal out in paper. Distribution is a high risk. Use the Internet like everyone else does. Run a Web site."

"A Web site? How could I manage that in Kenya?"

"By using the Kenyan government. We can put the site up under the government's nose—on a government server. I could make it one of my programs. I could say it's a homosexual sting operation and that I have all the manpower I needed to run it. No one would even look at it from the government standpoint. The only sticking point is that someone else would have to provide the changing content. I couldn't do that. I could run the Web site right from here, this house. Right under their noses. They'd never look for the source here. If you continued to do the content, though, you'd have to do it from here. And that would mean—"

"Yes."

"Yes what?" I asked.

"Yes, I'll happily stay here—in your bed—for as long as you want me."

I wondered if Raili always, for as long as we were together—would be able to get to the point faster and better than I did.

# After Poker

Mike clung to the arm of Larry, the older man he'd met just earlier in the day but who was everything to Mike at the moment, as, one of six men concentrating on their cards, a pall of smoke hovering over the table, Mike won another hand of poker. He hadn't even played much poker before now. And he'd never been in a place like this before now, either. The poker table was in the corner of a smoky, boisterous barroom with a small stage, where a young black man in a puffy-haired black wig, sparkly red bra, and gold lamé G-string was dancing a pole to music being piped in from somewhere and men were shuffle dancing with other men—and kissing and fondling each other.

Mike had been curious and he admitted readily to himself that he'd taken to the beach in the morning in a micobikini to test out the possibilities, but he'd never been where he was now. And he'd done what he'd done that afternoon for the first time. He almost connected winning at poker at this table with an affirmation of a new lifestyle. If he wasn't so sore, he'd be giddy. And if the man on the other side of him, a tall, muscular man in cowboy boots and shirt who'd said to call him Tex didn't keep pushing the toe of his cowboy boot up the hem of Mike's trousers and rubbing Mike's ankle under the table. It wasn't that

Mike was disgusted about that; it was more that it aroused him and worried him about whether he was going to be promiscuous now that he'd crossed through the beaded curtain. It made him snuggle closer to Larry.

Ashamedly, that made Mike think of big cocks. The cowboy obviously had one, as could be told by the faded denim of the area stretched over his cock that Mike had spied as the poker players settled at the table. Mike knew it was vacuous to obsess on big cocks, but he always had. He'd just never been in a situation before where anything could come of the obsession.

Larry, although not totally ignoring Mike, was sending most of his attention across the table to another older guy, probably in his late thirties, named Clinton, who was in a wheelchair and who had a twenty-something thin, almost effeminate and androgynous attendant flitting around in back of him. Clinton kept giving Larry looks that raised a sense of trespass on Mike, a sensation he couldn't figure out the source for.

But then he could. Larry had come to the beach that morning and settled his towel next to Mike. Although older, Larry was strikingly good looking and in great shape, and Mike was intrigued by the pattern of hair on the man's chest and trailing down to the waistband of his bathing suit, setting off fantasies in Mike's mind of where the hair went from there. Mike had come to Florida and onto the beach to build up the courage to hook up. He'd never done it before, and it had become an obsession that he'd never done it. Larry's bathing suit was a tight one, and as they talked, Mike could see that Larry increasingly was aroused. So was he, and he couldn't hide it.

"See that house over there?" Larry had said. "The three-story one with the red tile roof."

Mike did see it. Quite a mansion.

"That's mine. Would you like a tour?"

"Sure, that would be great."

"My bedroom is especially nice," Larry had said. "I'd like to fuck you. I'd be willing to pay. Say $100? You probably were hoping for a younger guy, weren't you? But I have experience a younger guy wouldn't have. And a younger guy isn't going to pay you for it."

Now that it was here, Mike was scared. He babbled out that he'd never done it before.

"$200 then," Larry had said, smiling and nearly licking his lips. "You came to the beach for this today, didn't you? I can tell from your behavior on the beach. I watched you for a while from my house before coming down here. You came here for a hookup, didn't you? You've decided you want to try it out, haven't you? I'll make it so that you'll want it again."

Mike couldn't say that Larry was wrong about why he'd come to the beach—why he'd come in a bathing suit that hid practically nothing, and why he'd walked the surf line, exhibiting himself.

In the master bedroom of Larry's beach house, Larry had taken it slow. Sensually, lying on top of Mike, front to front, kissing Mike and moving his pelvis, causing his dick to drag against Mike's belly and rub against Mike's dick. Mike had come then. He apologized in embarrassment, but Larry had just laughed, saying it was proof to him that Mike was a virgin and excited him even more.

"You're young and virile—a beautiful body. You'll be able to come again when I'm ready to take it from you."

Larry moved down Mike's body, kissing and nipping on the way, as Mike moaned and trembled. For the first time another man had his mouth on Mike's cock and then his balls and then, for several minutes, lapping at his asshole, enticing his channel to open up. Mike came again while Larry was deep-throating his cock and moving fingers in and out of Mike's channel. Then, reversed and hovering over him, Mike received his first taste of a man's

141

cock, gagging, but eager to experience and learn now that he actually was doing it.

The pain of the first penetration, Mike on his back at the foot of the bed, and Larry crouched over him, holding Mike's legs spread and raised, was initially almost unbearable. But Larry took this slow too, wedging the bulb of his cock just inside the entrance until Mike calmed down and opened to the inch-by-inch invasion, huffing and panting all the time, while Larry gave him words of encouragement, of how nice Mike's body was, and of gratefulness for letting Larry be first. When Larry had pulled Mike's legs in, fully bent against Larry's chest, as Larry covered Mike close from above and took the younger man's lips in his and simply rocked back and forth on top of Mike, sending his cock rubbing across Mike's prostate, Mike was sighing and in seventh heaven.

"Can you take more?" Larry murmured.

"Yes, fuck me, daddy, fuck me hard," Mike whimpered. These were words he'd practiced for this occasion, taken from all the porn movies he'd watched. He was here, he already was undone. It wasn't a time to be shy. Everyone had told him that the pleasure would increasingly overshadow the pain each time he took a cock.

Larry rose again, hooked Mike's legs around his waist, and pushed his cock in deep. Once Larry's cock was buried and his pumping attained a slow rhythm, Mike's awe and relief that it was done—that a man's cock had bottomed in him and he'd taken it—took over and he let the pleasure of it sweep over him. As he pumped the young man's channel, Larry was pumping Mike's cock with a fist as well, and Mike came again, up his belly. He just lay back then as Larry moved on, pumping faster and deeper, to his own ejaculation.

They had been right. There was less pain in the pleasure each successive time. Of course Mike had only known the one cock as yet, but he wasn't thinking at the moment of there being bigger cocks. He'd certainly thought about that when Larry stood before him naked, though. He'd initially been disappointed the cock wasn't bigger, even in full erection. He just didn't know then how talented Larry was in wielding it.

When Larry invited Mike to stay with him and go out with him that evening, Mike was pleased at the thought that he must have performed for the first time well enough. It was well enough that, in the sultry high hours of the afternoon, with the windows open to the beach and the sea and a ceiling fan wonk-wonking overhead, Larry coaxed Mike up on all fours on the bed, mounted him, and fucked him harder and faster than he had the first time. This time was more possessing, but it still was sensual, and Larry was all attention to Mike's needs and level of pleasure-pain—and applied massive amounts of lube.

Larry wanted to take the chance of barebacking a claimed virgin, though, so condoms weren't mentioned. Mike was too dumb on the subject to bring that topic up.

For the first time, Mike was being well taken care of. Larry was older than the men Mike had imagined he'd go with, but, with age, had come experience and the willingness to treat a virgin right.

Now, at the poker game, as the chips mounted up in front of Mike, Mike was obsessed with wondering who Larry would be taking home—or going home with. Mike was of two minds about continuing with Larry. He'd come to Florida and out on the beach today to rid himself of his male-male virginity, which he had. He wasn't all that excited with falling immediately into a relationship, especially with an older, rich man who was dominating. Mike was on a post-high school fling. He didn't plan on staying in Florida.

Larry's body was good, but Mike had seen men in the gym showers; he knew that Larry didn't have a cock to be especially proud of, and Mike's obsessions had all been for big cocks. He fully appreciated that a smaller cock was a good beginning, though.

He wanted a bigger cock—a much bigger cock—before going home, however.

He couldn't help looking to the other side at the Texan . . . at his lap below the glass-topped table. Now that was a huge bulge, made prominent by the area being more faded than the denim around it—evidence that the Texan rubbed himself there frequently. It was an image that Mike found arousing—he suffered the urge to be in a position to rub the guy's basket himself. The Texan gave him a wink and lifted his boot heel to Mike's crotch. Shuddering—not entirely unpleasantly—Mike moved in closer to Larry's side. But he also spread his legs and moved a hand under the top of the table to hold the Texan's pressuring boot heel to his crotch.

The other two men—in their late twenties—at the table obviously were a couple. They only had eyes for each other and they had their hands all over each other. Much of Mike's winnings at the table probably came from their inattention to the game. Both hunky blonds, they looked like they'd just come off the surfing beach. They did, though, both look close to aging out of that scene. They had identified themselves as Frank, the taller and more muscular and evident dominator of the pair, and Rich. Mike looked at them with pleasure—not just because they were both handsome and well-built all-American athlete types but also because they obviously were a satisfied couple. They gave Mike hope that he would fall into something like that in a decade—with someone of his own age. At least that's what he had always thought. Being initiated this afternoon by a rich, older man had also been arousing. This big Texan on the other side of him, the one with the big bulge in his crotch, was arousing too. Being aroused by so many possibilities was disturbing.

It was especially disturbing when the Texan, moving back to the table after getting another beer, put his mouth close to Mike's ear in passing when Larry was exchanging words with the guy in the wheelchair across the table, Clinton, and whispered, "If you can break away from the old guy afterward, go with me. I can show you a good time."

Mike blanched and then blushed. He gave no answer; he just pulled closer into Larry's side. But he felt himself go harder. The Texan felt it too, because he'd paused beside Mike, put his hand on Mike's crotch, squeezed the hardened tube he could feel inside, and gave a little laugh. He muttered, "You want me, yes you do. I can fuck you so you know you've been fucked."

With a trembling hand, Mike moved the Texan's hand away, and he concentrated on the short conversation between Larry and Clinton. A hunky, topless Hispanic waiter, wearing suspendered tight pants pushing a bulge at his crotch forward, was moving around behind those seated at the table, swapping out empty beer mugs for full ones, and Clinton's attendant was behind Clinton and rubbing his shoulders. The waiter paused behind Mike and put his hand on Mike's shoulder, which caused Mike to flinch, because he'd been looking at the attendant massaging Clinton's shoulders and thinking thoughts of Clinton being massaged elsewhere by the flighty attendant, who was more beautiful than handsome. The waiter leaned down and whispered in his ear, "You're a real cutie. The man you're with is too old for you. If you want a real man, look me up later."

What a wild, wooly new world this was for Mike.

To prevent the waiter from getting a false impression of the touch, Mike looked up and smiled at him. The waiter squeezed his shoulder and smiled back, but then he carried on with his waiter duties, making sure that he bumped Mike's arm with a bulbous butt cheek as he moved on.

Mike was beginning to hyperventilate. He was only eighteen, entirely out of his environment and depth, and had had his virginity fucked out of him just that afternoon. Still, he felt like a moth circling the flame. He had no interest in leaving the scent of musk and looks of lust surrounding him. If he'd been looking for a new lifestyle, he'd found it in spades.

In a louder voice than was necessary, Clinton was saying, "Then you are just five houses down from me on Beach Road." Mike assumed he was talking to Larry. "We'll have to get together for a barbecue . . . or something . . . one of these days. Time to go home now, though. Brad has the night off after he tucks me in. With my condition I stay on the first floor, so my bedroom is right off the patio to the ocean front. Love the sea breezes, so I keep the French doors open to the patio. I'll be alone all night."

Mike doubted he had any more trouble deciphering that invitation than Larry did. He wondered if Larry would bite. But he found he didn't care. He wasn't really up for more sex with Larry tonight or with becoming one of Larry's possessions before Mike had time to try out his new lifestyle with others.

If he was interested in more sex, which was more appealing to him in theory than actuality, he'd like to try out the Texan or the waiter.

Having plopped back in his chair across the table, the Texan had raised the heel of his boot back up between Mike's thighs and was grinding it into Mike's crotch.

"I'm in too," Larry was saying, as he stood up and started to leave. "You need a ride anywhere?" he turned to Mike and said.

That was a pretty obvious signal too, Mike knew. Their hookup was over. "Naw, I need to the walk. I'm not going far."

"Be careful walking alone, then," Larry said, smiling to show he wasn't all that serious. "You were the big winner tonight. You might be able to buy a car with that, if you don't get mugged."

146

"I'm in as well," the Texan said, as he stood up and up and up from the table. He had to be at least six six, Mike thought. And standing, his crotch was at Mike's eye level. And the bulge was bigger than ever—and obviously hard. This guy has got to be horse hung, Mike thought, and hard—hard for me. And he felt embarrassed again to be thinking of that.

"I'll walk you to wherever you're going," the Texan said, turning a smile on Mike.

"Uh, thanks. I can manage it alone," Mike answered. Now that it was an actual offer—and he knew the Texan wasn't just talking about walking him anywhere—that bulge in the Texan's jeans was scaring him.

Everyone was moving away from the table now. Even the Siamese twins, Frank and Rich, were standing up from the table, but, surprise surprise, they were moving in different directions, Frank toward the stage, where the young black transvestite was showing admirable flexibility on the pole, and Rich toward the long bar, running all the way down one side of the room.

"Gotta take a piss," the Texan said. "Anyone else want to go back with me?" He was giving Mike a meaningful look.

Mike indeed needed to piss, but there was no way that he was going to go into the back rooms area of a gay bar with the Texan. He realized that there was a gap between what he dreamed of and what he, in reality, was ready for.

* * * *

Mike walked north on Beach Street and turned west on 8th, headed into the darker and seedier part of town. He was staying in what almost was a flop house. It was all he could afford. This was a trip to the beach just for himself, coming out of high school. His parents hadn't approved, but they'd said nothing when he insisted he needed to do this, although of course he hadn't told them what exactly he thought he needed to accomplish on the trip. He was eighteen, his own man now. They were just pleased that he'd stuck with the academics and not completely obsessed himself with soccer. They couldn't deny that that obsession had gotten him a scholarship to college, though.

He hadn't realized how dark it could be at night a few blocks off Beach Road. He was apprehensive and a bit keyed up. He'd never drunk as much beer as he did tonight. But then he'd never been fucked before as he was that afternoon. Yes, a few mutual hand jobs and beating off together with a vid running. Even only slightly veiled offers from his soccer coach, who flashed him with a big cock occasionally. But never all the way, and it didn't really count, he didn't think, that, after the hints and flashing from his coach, he had to go off and beat himself off.

Of course now he was eighteen, no longer in high school, no longer a player for the soccer coach, and initiated.

The actual fucking with Larry had been better than he had imagined, and he knew this was a lifestyle for him from now on. He'd probably even go back in and visit his soccer coach after this trip and let the coach do to him what he wanted to do. The coach was cut and he was hung. Mike knew that from the showers and the flashings. He had to admit that he was thinking of his coach off and on while Larry was fucking him. Larry was experienced. But he wasn't hung.

If Larry had been hung like the soccer coach was, maybe Mike would have felt he'd done enough. But he wasn't.

As he walked, Mike's mind wandered to going into the high school gym after hours and finding only the soccer coach there, coming, naked, out of the showers, his manhood hanging low, but rising as he sees Mike standing there, also naked. Mike on his back on a massage table, the ankle of one leg hooked on the coach's shoulder and the coach holding the other, as he forces that big cock inside Mike's channel and Mike arching his back and panting hard. The feeling like Larry gave him in penetration, but taxing his walls to open to it more, digging deeper, more possessive in the stroking, more one with the soccer coach in the rhythm of the fuck, much, much more . . .

Were those footsteps behind him? Mike turned onto Main and then zagged onto 9th. The footsteps were still there.

"Dark out here, isn't it? Bet you are thinking now that you'd like to have someone walking with you."

The tall, muscular Texan, Tex. Mike murmured something as the Texan came up beside him, but even he didn't know what he was saying. He began to hyperventilate, though, as the Texan put a strong arm around him and virtually propelled him down the walk . . . and then into an alley.

The Texan grabbed Mike's crotch, and laughed, no doubt thinking Mike's hardness was for him rather than in fantasizing about the soccer coach. But then as the Texan rubbed Mike's crotch hard, and Mike shuddered, thinking of the Texan's boot grinding his crotch back at the poker table and Tex's whisper of the good time he could show Mike, and the image of the man's hard cock pushing against the faded material of his jeans, the hardness did turn to being for him.

"Hard for Mr. Big, ain't you," the Texan muttered.

Mike's answer was lost in a moan.

Tex pushed Mike up against a cinderblock wall in an alley so dark, that the darkness out on the street now seemed to be light. He had his hands all over Mike and was pulling Mike's T-shirt over his head. The Texan already had his cowboy shirt unbuttoned and pulled out of

149

his jeans. His chest was massive, his nipples taut in prominent, dark aureoles.

"You want me. We both know that," he growled. "Teasing me at the table like that. Once you'd held the heel of my boot to your crotch, the deal was set. You're a saucy little piece."

"Here, you can have the money," Mike said. "Just let me go." The "just let me go" was a bit half hearted, as Mike was thoroughly aroused at this rough treatment.

Tex laughed like he knew Mike was only struggling because he was innocent to this. "I don't want your money," he answered. "I want your mouth and your ass. And you want my dick."

He grabbed Mike's hand and shoved it between his legs. Mike whimpered at the massiveness of the bulge and at the realization that he could actually feel the line of the hard cock through the material. "This is for you. Nine inches of it," Tex said, proudly.

The Texan pushed Mike down on his knees, his heavy body still pressing Mike against the wall. His fly was open and his hard dick was out. Mike resisted but to no avail, as Tex got five inches of it stuffed into Mike's mouth. "You treat it right now, boy, and it will treat you right."

The shaft was huge in girth as well as length, and Mike's eyes watered and he gagged as Tex started to move it in and out of his mouth, penetrating ever deeper down his throat. The Texan held Mike's head between his hands, holding Mike prisoner in that position and guiding the pumping. They both settled down to a rhythm. Mike's moans of pleasure and the voluntary attention he gave the cock betrayed him.

Tex laughed. "I knew you wanted it." And, as embarrassed and disgusted as Mike was, he realized that he did want it—that he'd been fantasizing about it for years. What he had dreamed of in his imagination was here for him in the flesh. He settled down, palmed the

Texan's buttocks, and took over the rhythm of the slide of his mouth on the cock. Laughing, the Texan released his head and let Mike do the work for a couple of minutes.

Content that the fresh piece had surrendered to him, Tex pulled him up by the hair, reversed him to where he was facing the cinderblock wall. Mike's arms were being raised above his head, Tex's fists grabbing his wrists. "Hold them there and jut your butt out to me," Tex commanded. Tears in his eyes, Mike responded as directed. He didn't want this. He *did* want this.

"God, don't be hard with me," Mike whimpered.

"I'll be very good to you," Tex answered, and laughed. "You're getting it all, baby. Daddy's gonna give it all to you."

Tex pulled Mike's jeans down, leaving him only in his sneakers, and went for the crevice in his buttocks with his lips and tongue and latched onto Mike's cock and balls with one hand, while holding Mike's pelvis away from the wall with the other hand palming his belly.

Mike shot his load. Tex laughed. "Pretty boy really wants it."

The young man's eyes were watering and he was panting and groaning hard, his cheek plastered against the cool cinderblocks, one of his arms—with no objection from Tex—lowering so that he could fist and beat his cock, as the Texan slowly worked his mammoth cock inside Mike's ass and pumped him hard and deep. Mike ejaculated again. A weaker production, but an explosion of emotion anyway.

Tex pulled out, turned him, back to the wall, muttered "Climb my hips," which Mike dutifully did with his knees, and Tex penetrated and began pounding his ass. Mike settled in completely with the fuck, with Tex chortling when Mike set his own pelvis into motion to receive the thrusts of Tex's cock and moaned a "Yes, yes, fuck me, daddy. Go deep. Yes, again and again." Memories of the porn movies again and what Mike assumed the Texan wanted to hear—both anxious that Tex continue stroking him and disgusted with himself for wanting it.

When Tex wanted to kiss, Mike opened to him. When Tex pushed Mike's face down onto his chest, Mike sucked his nipples. Tex pounded and pounded, until . . .

He too ejaculated, in an arcing stream up Mike's belly, having pulled his dick out at the last second. Tex didn't use condoms either. Having shot off, though, he pushed his dick back in, through the lube of his cum and slow fucked Mike until, with a sigh, Mike came again in just an afterglow.

With a laugh, Tex let Mike sink to the ground. He presented his cock for cleaning, and Mike dutifully sucked it dry.

"You wanted it. Yeah, you wanted it bad," Tex muttered. Then, reaching down for Mike's jeans, he fished around in the pockets and pulled out the roll of bills Mike had won at poker.

"Guess I will relieve you of this after all." He zipped up and sauntered off to the mouth of the alley and was gone.

Mike huddled there, still panting hard and checking in with all of his body parts for an assessment of damage done by the brutal fuck of the horse-hung cock. He was ashamed to admit it, but admit it he did. That's the way he wanted to be fucked—and with a huge cock like that. That's what he'd look for in a hookup.

It was worth losing his poker winnings. He'd won in another sense. He could go home now. Soccer coach, here I come, he thought.

\* \* \* \*

"Stop fussing. You have the night off. Just go."

Brad, Clinton's attendant was fluttering around the bed. "Sure you'll be all right? The urinal jar is just there on the nightstand."

"Yes, of course," Clinton answered through clinched teeth. It wasn't really Brad he was irritated with. It was good that the urinal jar was nearby. What irritated him were these legs of his that just didn't work. And what irritated him the most was that it had interrupted an active sex life. Brad was no help with that beyond full-body massages and the occasional blow job.

Brad was very much a bottom—and his effeminacy and androgynous looks turned Clinton off anyway. He wanted a man—a man like Larry at poker tonight. Imagine that he lived just five doors away. Clinton had had to buy men from a local gay dating service to come in and service him. Just once he'd like the excitement of someone showing up unexpectedly and fucking his lights out. Someone strong and good looking. Larry was older than he was, but he looked fit. Clinton hoped Larry had taken the broad hints he'd laid down at poker. He'd been thrilled when Larry had let that young, sweet-looking piece who had been hanging onto him know they wouldn't be going home together. If he only had taken the hint.

"So, I'll be off then. You want the lights off or on?"

"Off, please." They went off and Clinton listened to Brad flit around the living area for a few minutes and then leave. He turned his face toward the open French doors, open out onto the patio and then the beach and the Atlantic Ocean. He could hear the relentless surf lapping up on the beach, and it lulled him to sleep.

The next he knew he was being blindfolded and gagged with a ball gag and his arms were being pulled up above his head. Velvet-lined handcuffs were attaching his wrists to the slats at the corners of the headboard. He was on his belly. He had no idea where his legs were. They

153

were useless to him. He couldn't feel them—hadn't felt them for years.

The man coming down on the bed on his knees beside him was turning Clinton's shoulders toward him. He knew it was a man, because the ball gag had come out, to be replaced by a hard cock filling his mouth and pushing toward the back of his throat. Clinton knew how to give head. He opened his mouth cavity to the cock, pulled back his teeth to give the cock depth, and made an O with his mouth. His lips closed tight over the cock. He didn't mind giving head at all. Larry had taken the hint. If only he could reach his own cock with a hand. He certainly had feeling in his body down to his cock and balls. His balls ached for attention.

And just as he was thinking this, his pelvis was turned on a hip, a hand closed over his cock and gave it a few pulls. Then it descended to his balls, laced fingers through them, and distended and squeezed them. Clinton moaned his pleasure and hummed on the man's cock, obviously, from the sound he heard, giving the man pleasure too.

The cock was so big. It was reaching for Clinton's tonsils. But Clinton didn't care. He knew, to the pleasure of his assailant, how to deep throat even a thick, long cock.

The fist returned to Clinton's cock, and just the thought of the sex he was having—and not having to pay for—keyed Clinton up to the point that he shot his load.

The man pulled his cock out of Clinton's mouth and put the ball gag back in. He pushed Clinton over on his stomach and then was below him, eating Clinton's ass out, while Clinton panted and moaned and groaned. The groaning increased as the mouth was replaced by a lubed finger, then greased fingers—two three, four—up to the knuckles. Fist fucking Clinton's ass up to the knuckles.

Would he go deeper? The whole fist? Clinton writhed from the waist up. Couldn't do it from the waist down, of course. He panted heavily, crying out for the stretching of his ass by knuckles to be replaced with a nice, big, juicy cock.

His wish was granted. He heard the snap of the condom being put in place and then he was covered close above by a heavy body. All muscle and vigor, pounding his ass with a cock almost as thick as the knuckle fuck had been—and much deeper inside him.

Clinton tried to talk, to scream, through the ball gag. He wanted something, something more.

As if understanding, the man pulled the ball gag out long enough for Clinton to mutter. "Yes, yes, fuck me. But I need to come again. My balls are aching. Can you—?"

The ball gag was replaced, but the man had understood. He pulled pillows over and stuffed them under Clinton's belly, pointing his ass toward the ceiling, but also pulling him up on his useless knees, lifting Clinton's pelvis off the bed so that his cock and balls could dangle. The man mounted Clinton again, covering him close, but now a hand went under his belly and milked Clinton's cock to another ejaculation.

Clinton was in heaven.

The snap of the condom again and then the man ejaculated, on Clinton's back. He left the bed and Clinton could hear him moving around the living areas. He returned after a half hour or so, though, and turned Clinton to his side, signaled another crowning with the snap of a condom, lifted up one of Clinton's numb legs, slid his cock inside Clinton again, and fucked him to another mutual ejaculation.

Exhausted, Clinton drifted off to sleep with the man still embracing him from behind and his cock going flaccid inside Clinton's channel. He was long and thick enough, though, that the cock didn't lose position inside Clinton.

When he was sure Clinton was asleep, the Hispanic waiter at the gay bar moved off the bed. He checked the pillow case full of loot he had pulled together from the living areas between fuckings. He was wearing skin-tight gloves that he wouldn't take off until he was well away from the house. He carefully removed the ball gag and blindfold from Clinton, waiting again for the man to settle down into deep sleep before slowly releasing him from the handcuffs. The waiter had brought all of these toys and probably would be needing them again—maybe even to come back here. The paralyzed man had seemed to enjoy the fucking so much that maybe he'd forget—or forgive—that he'd been robbed as well.

In any case, that wasn't Manuel's problem. He'd gotten what he'd come for multiple times. He hadn't done a crippled man before. It was kind of exhilarating. The man couldn't do anything but lie there and take it. His ass and cock and balls were just as sweet as if he could use his legs. It was fortuitous that the man had been so pointed at the poker table about where he lived, that doors would be open, and that he'd be alone and defenseless.

* * * *

Larry was standing, leaning back on his Lexus coup in Clinton's driveway, arms folded over his chest, when Brad came out of Clinton's house.

"Mr. Caldwell is in there, in bed, alone, if you—"

Larry interrupted Brad. "I didn't come for Clinton Caldwell. I came for you. Did you think I was signaling him back at the poker table? I guess, since you were standing just behind him, you might have thought that I was interested in him."

"You were signaling me?"

"Sure. You're cute and sweet and sexy."

If it hadn't been dark, Larry could have seen Brad blush. Brad wasn't exactly experienced. Most of his friends were girls and most of his activities were girlie. He might even have more girlfriends if he wasn't more beautiful than most of them were.

"You want to take a ride with me?"

Brad didn't know what to say. He'd planned to take in a late-night movie, alone, tonight and then work on the scrapbook of photos of his trip to Miami with some of the girls a few months ago. And then to bed with his Teddy bear.

"Have you had sex with a man before?" Larry asked, being persistent.

"Sex?" Brad asked, almost swallowing the words.

"You attend Clinton Caldwell, and he obviously has his needs and likes men. Do you jack him off when he wants it."

Brad looked away, but he did answer. "Sometimes."

"Do you give him blow jobs?"

Brad didn't answer, but he didn't say no. Larry didn't ask him if he rode Caldwell's cock, because it was obvious that they both were bottoms.

"Does he pay you extra for those services?"

"No." A pause and then and almost indignant, "But he pays me well."

"I'll give you $50 for a blow job if you'll come in my car with me."

Brad didn't answer; he was too busy examining the tops of his sandals.

"Get in the car, Brad," Larry said, opening the passenger door of the Lexus.

Brad hesitated, but only for a moment. He was accustomed to following orders. Larry drove only as far as the carport of his own house five doors up the beach. He held Brad's head between his hands as he sat in the driver's seat and Brad hunched over from the passenger seat and sucked his cock. Brad was good enough at it that it was clear he had done this for Clinton Caldwell often enough—and maybe for others, as well.

When he was done and had licked Larry's cock clean, he sat up and pressed his body against the passenger door. He undoubtedly knew what Larry was going to say next.

"You ever been fucked by a man? I want to fuck you. I'll give you another $50 to go with me now."

"Fucked. By a man?"

"Yes. Fucked in the ass. I bet you have a sweet little ass."

"No . . . no . . . never. Not that."

Larry whistled and smiled. Bonus day. Two virgins in one day. "But you've thought about it . . . wanted to do it. Right?"

Brad didn't answer. There suddenly was something on the glove-box door that he had to examine.

"I'll give you $150 more to be the first one to use your ass. I'm very good at it, I assure you. You'll be glad that I was first. You've just been shy and frightened about it. I'll handle you right."

Larry fucked Brad on a blanket on the beach below his house, just beyond the line where the lights of the house reached and far enough off the water and in between two beach dunes so that anyone strolling the water line this late wouldn't see them. Maybe hear them, but not see them.

Brad would have been a screamer at being spiked if Larry didn't keep a hand over his mouth most of the time. But Larry hadn't lied. He was good at taking a young man's virginity and was expert at making a complete job of it.

Brad was on his back, knees drawn up to his chest, butt turned up to the sky, with Larry covering him close, his cock inside Brad's ass channel, a hand over Brad's mouth, Brad's eyes wide with pleasure-pain, while Larry rocked their bodies, the bulb of his cock rubbing back and forth over Brad's prostate. Brad didn't hold out very long before he creamed Larry's belly.

Larry took his hand away from Brad's mouth and replaced it with his own mouth, Kissing Brad deeply through one, two, three ejaculations into Brad's channel. Larry didn't like using condoms on virgins and Brad hadn't mentioned the need for one.

Taking his mouth off Brad's and looking into Brad's still-wide and glazed eyes, Larry whispered, "Was that too painful for you?"

"Yes . . . no. I never imagined . . . fuck me again, daddy. Can you? . . . you're so big."

Larry knew he wasn't big at all and that, after him, Brad was likely to learn what big was. But Larry was experienced, and that was what Brad needed at this moment.

"Oh, yes, I certainly can fuck you again . . . and will." Brad had such a sweet ass. Men didn't just lose their virginity to another man and that was it. There were levels of initiation. A man's cherry could be popped in so many ways and on so many levels by another man. Taking Brad up the levels would be a distinct pleasure. Before the night was through, Larry would be on his back and Brad would be riding his cock and fucking himself. "Let's go into the house," he said, and then added, "What do you feel about being bound?"

And indeed he could take a malleable and willing Brad up several levels before the night was through . . . and did.

\* \* \* \*

The couple that had been plastered together at the table, hardly paying attention to the money they were losing to the ripe-looking strawberry blond youth clinging to Larry, parted not six feet from the poker table. Frank, the taller and more muscular of the almost-twin blonds moved to a seat just below the stage, where the former Nathan and current Natalie was displaying "her" wares in a sensuous winding around the pole to the increasingly insistent music of "Bolero." The thinner and shorter of the two, Rich, made a beeline for the bar, where there was barely enough space for him to fit between two big, black bulls, who watched him approach and licked their chops.

Natalie's eyes went straight to Frank as he came close and sat in front of the stage. If anything, Natalie's movement became more suggestive and just at this point she lost her bra, leaving her clothed only in the gold lamé of a G-string that, though she had melon breasts, made no effort to hide the line of a dick inside the pouch.

She slitted her eyes and blew Frank a kiss. He spread his legs, put a hand suggestively on his basket, and pulled out a fifty-dollar bill. The question in his eyes was met with a smile and a nod. She hadn't contracted with another customer for after the dance. Frank rose and leaned into the stage. Natalie's dance moved her toward the edge of the platform, and Frank tucked the fifty-dollar bill in the waistband of her G-string and he kissed a star tattoo on her thigh. The deal was sealed.

In Natalie's small dressing room, large enough however, to include a studio bed, which was the most necessary item in the room, Frank lay, naked, on his back, his arms crossed behind his neck, his shoulders and head raised enough for his lips to reach the rouged nipples of Natalie's pride and joy melons, while the dancer danced on his cock, riding him hard in gyrations that were a memorable part of her act. Doing a pole dance on Frank's hard pole.

Watching Frank follow Natalie back through the beaded curtains to the warren of rooms behind the barroom, Rich reached down and took the hand of Big Black Bull 1 from his thigh, but he made sure to check out the surprise and pleasure registered in the big black's face when he moved the hand to his crotch. Big Black Bull 2 already was holding Rich in his lap as he leaned against a bar stool. The man's cock was pressing into the cleavage of Rich's buttocks, and even though Rich had not hooked up with these particular men before, he could tell that BBB2 was both horse hung and ready for action. BBB2 was possessively holding Rich by the shoulders, signaling that Rich was trapped. Rich had no intention of trying to escape, though.

BBB2 pressed his lips to Rich's ear and said in a voice above a whisper, necessitated by the noise level of the music and crowd in the bar, "Can we buy you a drink, blondie?"

"Does it seem like I need a drink to let you two DP me?" Rich answered, in a voice loud enough for even BBB1 to hear. As he said this, he pressed his crotch into BBB1's rubbing hand, showing the big black that he too was hard, and reached out to BBB1's basket, letting his fingers trace the barely imprisoned cock all the way from bulb to balls, which proved to be a satisfyingly long journey.

Both BBBs smiled and snorted. "You think you can take us both?" BBB2 asked.

"We can certainly try. Are you, by any chance, into S&M too? You look the part." And indeed they did. Both were of the biker genre and hard into leather, wearing nothing on their muscular ebony torsos other than black leather harnesses with silver studs. And both were in tight black leather pants with drop crotches and black biker boots.

"What you see is what you get," BBB1 responded with a growl. "Scared?"

"Try me."

They did, hanging a naked Rich from the ceiling by his wrists in the behind the barroom room—the one with padded walls and a drain in the floor. They whipped him and flogged him, with him groaning deeply through a ball gag. They raised his legs straight out from his sides with

161

ropes tied to the side walls, and then BBB1 came close into him in front and BBB2 came close into him in back. They rolled his pelvis back for BBB2 to penetrate him from behind and then forward for BBB1 to work his cock in on top of BBB2's, and then they counter pumped him mercilessly.

Later that night—really early the next morning—Frank and Rich met at home. They lay side by side on their bed, with a gay porn movie running on the TV at the foot of the bed. As Frank traced Rich's welts with his fingers, they shared the arousing experiences they each had had, each having enjoyed his own separate fetish. Then, after kissing and fondling each other through a sex scene on the TV, they lay close beside each other, each blond jacking himself off as they worked to ejaculate in synch with each other and with the stars in the next sex scene.

* * * *

Hobbling bowlegged out of Larry's house shortly before dawn the next morning, Brad pulled up in the driveway at the edge of the carport, trying to decide whether he had time to go back to his own small apartment to change clothes or if he should just walk down the street to Mr. Caldwell's house.

He did neither.

Strong hands pulled him into the carport and fumbled with his clothes. Using Brad's own T-shirt and belt, Tex gagged his mouth with the T-shirt and bound his wrists with the belt and hung his raised arms on a hook pounded into the brick above his head.

During the night Larry had informed Brad that he was lucky in his initiation, as later he'd meet men with bigger cocks and crueler fuck techniques. He had been right, but neither Larry nor Brad would have guessed that

162

Brad would experience that as soon as he left Larry's house.

Hooking Brad's knees on his hips, Tex fucked him against the carport wall with a monster cock.

But Brad took it like a champ, and after taking him and pulling the gag out of his mouth, Tex muttered, "You wanted it, I could tell. I saw you eyeing me at the poker game." Brad couldn't claim this wasn't so. "Do you want me to let you go here or take you down to the beach and pound the shit out of you."

"The beach," Brad squeaked in a gaspy voice.

The sun was coming up when Tex had Brad on his knees, his cheek pushed into the sand, and his hands scrabbling at the sand above his head, while Tex crouched over his hips and pounded, pounded, pounded.

Brad was moving quickly up the levels, and that was so all right with him.

\* \* \* \*

Mike was nearly all the way back to his hotel room when he discovered he didn't have his room key. At first he thought he must have lost it in the alley where the Texan had accosted him, but then he distinctly remembered having put it on the poker table at the gay bar—and couldn't remember having picked it up again. There was nothing to do other than to go back to the bar. Maybe it would be closed, but he had to try. He couldn't count on the desk at the fleabag hotel to be manned this late—or for the desk clerk to believe that he was registered there even if the desk was open.

The bar was open, though, although the crowd had thinned out and the noise level had dropped a bunch of decibels. As Mike entered the barroom, he recognized one of the guys from the couple that had been all over each other during the poker game. He was standing at the beaded curtain to the back rooms and kissing a small black

163

guy, who confused Mike at first. He had on a red robe, but it was slitted all the way down to show both melon breasts and a small cock. It struck Mike as funny that the guy from the game, Frank was his name, Mike thought, could be kissing a transvestite later in the night that he'd been Siamese twins with someone else.

But it had been one hell of a night. And the night wasn't over yet, at least for Mike. He walked over toward the table where they'd played poker, but the table was cleared off. He turned to leave, dejected, when he heard a "Did you lose something? You were in the poker game earlier, weren't you?"

Mike turned to see that it was the Hispanic waiter from earlier in the evening who was talking to him. He'd just entered the door into the bar from the street.

"Yes, I think I left a hotel key here, but it isn't here now," Mike said.

"Yes you did. My name's Manuel. You're a cute little trick, aren't you?"

Mike didn't quite know what to say to that. Manuel was leering at him. It barely registered that the waiter said he knew a key had been left.

"It's in the office in back—the room key," Manuel said, with a smile. "Come on back and I'll get it for you. I wondered who you left with—the older guy you were plastered on or the tall Texan who had the hots for you?"

Mike blushed.

"Or did you take them together? Well, come along into the back rooms with me."

He took Mike by the wrist and there was little Mike could do but follow him. They didn't make it to the beaded curtain covering the door to the back, though. As they passed the bar, one of two big black studs in leather who were standing at the bar, put a hand out that was stronger than Manuel's was and displaced Manuel's hand on Mike's wrist.

"Well, aren't you a sweetie?" BBB2 said. "Saw you earlier and wanted to stand you a drink, but you left before we could do that. Pull on up to the bar. You can go to the back to be fucked by Manuel later."

"Barkeep, a beer for our new friend," BBB1 said, as he pulled Mike close into him. BBB2 quickly filled the gap on Mike's other side. Manuel shrugged and continued on through the beaded curtain.

Later, Mike hobbled back to his hotel, without the key. But, luckily someone was at the desk, the same guy who had checked Mike in, and he gave Mike no trouble in providing a duplicate key. He even asked, with a voice tone of hopefulness, if Mike needed company in his room. But Mike was exhausted, bruised, walking bowlegged, and with stinging welts crisscrossing his back and chest under his T-shirt.

It was all he could do to shower in lukewarm water and to fall, naked, on top of the coverlet on the bed. He went to sleep instantaneously.

He woke, groggily and too slowly to prevent being blindfolded, having a ball gag put into place, and his wrists cuffed above his head at the corners of the brass-rod headboard.

He was on his belly. Manuel, having let himself in the room with the key Mike hadn't retrieved at the bar, stuffed pillows under his midsection, climbed onto the bed, and straddled his hips. Mike's body pulsed slightly under him in a weak, completely ineffectual struggle to resist. Manuel ran his fingers along the welts on Mike's back, before plunging his cock between Mike's butt cheeks, the cock sliding right in to the hilt. He laughed, admonishing himself for thinking the eighteen-year-old soccer player honey he'd lusted after in the club was a neophyte. He didn't latch into Mike's passage still being reamed wide open from the doubling the black bulls had given him.

Exhausted, Mike lay there and moaned as the Hispanic hunk covered his body close from behind, latched onto the skin at the base of Mike's neck with his teeth, and pounded away at Mike's ass. After a few minutes of pumping, Mike couldn't resist moving his pelvis with the rhythm of the fuck and sighing and grunting through the ball gag. He went hard and even managed a weak ejaculation.

The hard cock and cum dribble didn't escape Manuel's notice, but, rather than chalking it up to the uncontrollable virility of a health, well-toned eighteen-year-old athlete, he muttered, "I knew you wanted it."

He ran an arm down under Mike's chest, arched the young man's back up toward him, and then put them both into a forward and back rocking motion, pulling his cock out just enough so that his bulb rubbed across Mike's prostate in the rocking motion. Mike moaned deeply and began to pant. Manuel took that as a signal of affirmation and wondered how many more ejaculations he could coax out of the young cutie tonight. He bet he could evoke more than that older man this guy had been draped over at the poker table had managed.

# The Oldest Ball "Kid"

I could tell that Kurt had shot his load, because the towel attendant jerked and sucked hard on the tongue I had in his mouth and the two of them groaned in unison. The German tennis pro and I were holding the towel guy between us on the bed in Kurt's hotel room. The towel attendant's butt was plastered to Kurt's lap, Kurt's sheathed cock up his channel. Kurt was on his back, the towel guy's right arm trapped under him, and Kurt had been holding the young man's right leg bent up into his chest. I was on my right side on the other side of the towel attendant, his left leg trapped under my legs, my right arm under his neck, pulling his face into mine for the deep kiss, while the towel attendant fucked himself on Kurt's cock by raising and lowering his pelvis. The young man's cock was encased in my left hand, and I let him do the sliding with the same movement he was fucking himself on Kurt's cock.

Kurt having gotten off in him, I curled my right arm up under the towel attendant, palmed his belly, pulled him off Kurt's dick, and turned his buttocks toward my crotch. Understanding what I was doing, Kurt grabbed the young man's left leg and pulled it up to Kurt's shoulder. The attendant was incredibly flexible. He also wasn't completely prepared for the girth of my cock—Kurt was

167

better looking than I was, but I had much the bigger cock—because when I slid my cock into the channel Kurt had just been in, the towel attendant lurched, gave a little cry that was stifled because I was still French kissing him, arched his back, bringing his buttocks farther up in an angle that gave me a deeper slide; and kissed me back with a vengeance. Kurt's hand on the young man's cock covered mine, and we jacked him off together. This didn't take long, and I was still fucking him in long, deep strokes when he spouted off.

I always liked playing tennis tournaments with Kurt Steiner, Germany's number three men's player, because he had no trouble picking up tricks like this willing and flexible young towel attendant—we never asked him his name—and was happy to share the young men with me.

I was in Washington, D.C., for the annual August Citi Bank tennis tournament, a 500-series lead up to the U.S. Open, and found myself booked in the same hotel as Kurt was. Most of the tennis players were booked in the Washington, D.C., Marriott Marquis. We'd both arrived the Saturday before the tournament started, both coming in time for the qualifying rounds that weekend if we weren't seeded. But we'd both been seeded, me above Kurt. I was the number three American men's player.

Kurt had magic seduction techniques, which is why I liked to hook up with him when we were at the same tournament. He had nasty tastes, including threesomes and the occasional double penetration, and, for some reason the young men rushed to him to sign up for that treatment. I came along for the easy fuck that someone else set up. Kurt pulled me into his trysts as often as he did because he liked my cock inside him for a finisher too. He was a perfectly built Nordic blond with movie star looks, so I enjoyed fucking him as much as I did the young men he procured to share with me.

I hadn't known we were both booked in the Marriott Marquis until we both found ourselves in the hotel's gym on Saturday evening. As we exercised we talked about the possibility of going out and finding a little guy to share, when the willowy red-headed hotel pool towel attendant just, almost literally, dropped in our laps.

In no time Kurt was fondling him in the shower. When I entered, proposed to the attendant that he come up to the hotel room of one of us and be shared, he seemed a bit hesitant, but his hesitancy started melting away when I came up behind him, pulled him into my body, while Kurt was kissing him and pulling on his cock and balls, and we had him in a sandwich.

When Kurt told him to go down on his knees in the shower, he went right down and gave us both an expert blow job. Kurt's offer of $500, which I knew I'd have to cover half of, for a trip upstairs was enough to seal the deal.

After I'd come, I slid down the bed to share the young man's cock with Kurt, who was already down there. The towel guy just moaned and jerked when he came with two tongues working the sides of his cock. He lay there panting and moaning as Kurt went off the bed, grabbed the young man's ankles, and pulled his butt to the foot of the bed. I turned off to the side to see what Kurt had in mind. The missionary position was what he had in mind for the young man, crouching close over his torso, with the towel attendant's legs running up Kurt's muscular chest and his ankles hooked on Kurt's shoulders. He was pounding inside the towel guy hard and chewing on the young man's nipples, to the cries of passion and grunting from the towel attendant, when I decided it was time to add a doggy position.

I came in behind Kurt, worked my cock inside his channel, and to the tune of groans and grunts, I pounded Kurt's ass while Kurt pounded the towel boy's ass.

Later, when it was just the two of us, lying side by side on Kurt's bed, his left hand pulling on my cock and my right hand pulling on his, he told me about a waiter down in the main restaurant who he knew he could snatch for us the next night.

"Probably not a good idea, Kurt," I said. "I've got to practice hard tomorrow. My opening round match on Monday is with the Spaniard, Emilio. This isn't the best exercise for toning up for a match."

"But this is the exercise I know you love, Cliff," Kurt said with a smile on his face. He moved over me, straddling my hips. I didn't fight him as he positioned my cock at his hole and started sliding down the shaft. For the next twenty minutes of Kurt bouncing on my cock until I had filled out the bulb of a condom, I didn't think about the tennis tournament we were about to enter at all.

* * * *

I didn't get back to my room until after 3:00 a.m. the next morning, and I wasn't sleeping before that time. I dragged up exhausted and inhaled everything on the buffet table in the breakfast room that I thought would bring me back to life. Although I'd arrived in Washington early for the tournament, I'd made it further into the rounds in Atlanta the week before, so I didn't really have recovery time between tournaments.

I was disgusted to watch Kurt bounce out of the hotel in tennis togs and a stack of rackets on his back while I was still waiting for a cup of coffee and assessing the aches and pains in my body. Now that I'd thought about it, though, he'd made me do the heavy lifting last night—take the brunt of muscle use. Before leaving the hotel he'd come to the door of the dining room and talked with a cute, young waiter who handed him a thermos jug. I wondered if that was the waiter he'd suggested we spike together tonight. If so, I would be missing a good time, I could tell. Had to do what I could to avoid that, though. I couldn't burn the candle at both ends and still do well in the tournament. I was here for the tournament, not to fuck with Kurt and friends.

Well, mostly for the tournament; a bit to fuck with Kurt and friends.

It was Sunday and my trainer and I had a practice court at the Fitzgerald tennis center between two and four. I got there twenty minutes early to find that Kurt Steiner had that court for the hour before me. The courts were separated by a line of trees, with benches between them, and I sat and watched, waiting for my trainer, Wally, to show up.

I'd never seen the guy Kurt was hitting with before. For a minute I thought it was the waiter I'd most recently seen him with, but that was nonsense. Just anyone couldn't waltz in here and practice hit with one of the guys in the tournament. The guy was young, dark haired, and deeply tanned, a real looker. Very young. He was also very good, especially for a guy who wasn't more than five foot eight. Height—and wing span—had become strategically important in tennis. He was meeting Kurt shot for shot, but I had the feeling that Kurt was holding back.

Kurt didn't usually hold back for anyone, which led me to speculate that he was cultivating the young man across the net from him. This led me to scrutinize the guy closer, as the young men Kurt cultivated often ended up riding my cock.

Wally hadn't shown up when Kurt and the young guy called it quits ten minutes before their time was up. Kurt said his good-byes to his hitting partner at the gate to the fence surrounding the court with a "See ya later, Gene. Owe you a drink . . . and more." I saw the good-looking young guy flash Kurt a smile, turn and see me, give me a brilliant smile too, and then saunter off toward the main stadium.

Kurt walked over to where I was sitting on the bench. "I don't know how you do it, Kurt," I said in greeting. "You were up and out before me and you still look fresh after a two-hour hitting session."

"I'm German—and good genes, I guess," Kurt answered. "Speaking of which, I assume you saw Gene hitting with me. A real nice piece, isn't he?"

"Yeah, he looks like something you'd go after—and get," I answered. "A little young to be on your team, though."

"Oh, he's on my team all right. And he's older than he looks—free game. He'd like to be on your team too. He knew who you were. He pointed you out sitting over here and said you were one of his favorite players. He's good, as you can see. But he'll never make it to pro. Not tall enough and he doesn't move fast enough. He can fix the latter but not the former. I think he knows he won't make it, which is why he stays around doing what he does."

"Doing what he does?"

"Yeah, didn't you catch what he was wearing? Possibly not. You haven't been in the stadium yet this year, have you?—and they've changed the uniform."

"Changed the uniform?"

"Yes. He's one of the ball kids. Probably the oldest of the ball kids."

"Ball kid? He looks too old to be a ball kid—and too big, too muscular."

"Nevertheless, that's what he is. There's no limit on age, although they usually take them no later than high school age. We had a forty-year-old woman doing it last year, though. Writing an article about it or something. But she's gone now. That would make Gene the oldest one this year."

"Are you sure he's beyond high school? Could be still in high school from the size of him."

"Oh, I'm sure. I made very sure he was eighteen last year. You didn't make the tournament last year, did you? I made certain he was eighteen then, which makes him nineteen this year."

"You made sure, because—?"

"Yes, I fucked him. He's a wildcat in bed. Gives about the best blow job I've had. And he fancies you. He fancies you big. He told me so just now. He wants—"

Kurt had a foot up on the bench beside me and a forearm resting on his thigh, his hand dropped down to his crotch. He was leaning in toward me. "There's room over behind the fenced in dumpster area, Cliff," he said with a hoarse voice.

"Uh, I gotta practice, Kurt. This is my practice time and I see Wally coming from over there. I think you got enough last night."

"I blew you; you didn't blow me. I don't think Gene has to be in the stadium chasing balls for a while. I could rustle him up. We could DP him over behind the dumpster. I'm sure he wouldn't mind. He didn't flinch when I mentioned that you and I might do him together. He has a hole that opens right up. Room for two."

"You got a one-track mind, Kurt. I'm surprised you're such a good tennis player," I said, standing and motioning to Wally. "It's time to get serious with this tournament."

"You'll have dinner with me in the hotel, though, won't you?" he asked. "Nothing too taxing about that, is there?"

Dinner wasn't taxing. It was what came afterward. We, of course, ate in the hotel dining room because that was where the small, more pretty than handsome, dark-haired waiter was working.

Just as I should have known, a couple of hours later on Sunday night, Kurt and I were in Kurt's hotel room working the waiter. I was on my back on the bed, with the waiter facing me and riding my cock when Kurt

173

got up on the bed below us; crouched in behind the waiter and over my legs; pushed the waiter's chest down onto mine; and told me to grab the young man's wrists and hold his arms over my head, which I did.

I knew when Kurt's cock penetrated the waiter's channel, both because the waiter began to groan and pant hard and because I could feel Kurt's cock press in over mine in the channel. As we'd done before, we began a counter stroking, with me thrusting up as Kurt pulled his cock out and then me pulling back as he thrust. Then in a position I'd never doubled in before, I went on my back; the waiter sat on my cock, faced away from me; I pulled his back into my chest; Kurt came in facing the waiter, the waiter's thighs draped over Kurt's thighs; Kurt speared him, sliding in on top of my cock; and we all went bouncing to town. That waiter was such a willowy little thing, almost lost when sandwiched between two muscular athletes like Kurt and me, but, boy could he take cock, and he had one wide hole—at least Kurt and I made it wide for him.

Kurt stayed with us on the bed for just that one ejaculation that night, but he watched as the waiter reversed on my cock, his chest pressed into my raised thighs, and rode me solo to another ejaculation.

Just like with the towel attendant, the waiter was never given a name. After he left the room, Kurt wanted me to stay longer and play, but, I hadn't intended to be doing this at all the night before my opening match. The Spaniard, Emilio, wasn't going to be a pushover. After several unsuccessful attempts at good night, topped by that blow job Kurt complained I hadn't given him the night before, I returned to my room for a fitful night of sleep.

This wasn't my regular routine going into paid match play.

* * * *

174

I won my first-round match over the Spaniard Emilio, but it wasn't easy and it wasn't pretty. Not only wasn't I rested enough for match play, but Gene, the oldest ball kid, worked my match. It kept running through my mind what Kurt had said the previous day on the practice court—that the luscious young man took cock, gave great blow jobs, and wanted my cock. More than that, Kurt had said the young guy was willing to take double penetration, which, with Kurt, made me feel all hot and bothered. It certainly drained my concentration on the tennis match I should have been concentrating on.

That he had a crush on me was obvious from the start. When he gave me balls for my serve, he didn't toss them to me like the other ball kids did; he brought them to me, put them in my hand, let his hand linger there a second or two longer than needed, and showed me puppy-dog eyes.

The first time he brought me my towel to towel off my sweat between points, he murmured, "Here's your towel, Mr. Samuel. You're doing great. Here, let me give you my balls." Beyond the fact that ball kids shouldn't be voicing favorites, they really shouldn't be speaking to the players at all. And he did it with fluttering eyelashes and with his hand brushing his crotch. I could see it because I was standing right next to him. But I had to assume that those in the stands—there weren't many in the stands; it was early rounds yet—couldn't see that he was giving me extra attention.

I growled at him just the once, saying "Mr. Samuel didn't come to the tournament. I'm Cliff."

He answered back, "I'm Gene. And I'm a big fan." Socializing and exchanges of given names just isn't done between players an ball kids. Well, normally.

It took three sets to take Emilio. I was much the better player—that was obvious. But he was much the fresher player. That was equally obvious. I let my guard down for just a couple of points in the second set, but those points made all the difference in losing the second set.

After the match, I opted to shower there at the venue. No other players seemed to be taking that option, though, so I had the locker room and the separated shower stalls area all to myself—or so I thought. Coming out of the shower, soap still in my eyes, I groped for the towel I'd hung on a hook. But it wasn't there.

"Here's your towel, Mr. . . . Cliff," I heard a voice say.

It was Gene, the oldest ball kid, of course, and he'd come in to shower as well. He just had a towel around his waist, and his body was beautiful. Nineteen-year-old fuck candy beautiful.

His eyes probably went bigger than mine in seeing the other's body—mine fully naked.

"God, you're big," Gene said. "Mr. Steiner said you were big."

"Gene," I said. "You're a ball kid. I . . . we . . . I can't be doing this."

"You're going hard," he said with a smile. "Look, I'm hard too." He whipped the towel off his body to show that he, indeed, was in full erection. "You like my balls? Would you like to play with my balls?"

"You're just a ball kid, Gene. I can't mess with one of the ball kids. I know you're old for it, but why do you go on with it?" The question didn't fit the context, but it had been working on my mind since the previous day.

"I like to be dominated," he answered, without hesitation. "When I'm on the court and some stud like you is snapping his fingers for the balls or a towel, it turns me on. And if it looks like I turn the stud athlete on, I let him fuck me. I beg him to fuck me. I'm begging you to fuck me. You won't be fucking a ball kid. I'm a man. I've been fucked before. Dominate me and use me hard. I'm not a child. I've been balling men for a couple of years.

176

You must know I want you to fuck me. I told Mr. Steiner that's what I wanted—even more than wanting him to fuck me. I told him he could tell you. I know you fuck other men. I've locked the locker room door from the inside. We have time."

"Gene. I came here to play tennis. You saw me out on the court today. I almost lost. And part of that was because of you—because of you moving around the court and looking oh so sexy."

"So, you do want to fuck me."

"Of course I want to fuck you. But I'm going back into the shower, and when I come out I want to be alone and the locker room door to be unlocked."

I went back under the water—cold water this time. I couldn't hide the raging hard on I had. I heard the moaning and turned to see Gene, on the floor like a snake, slithering toward me.

"Fuck me, daddy. Dominate me. Use me hard."

When he reached me, he grabbed both of my ankles in his hands and started licking my feet and toes. I lifted him up onto his knees, mounted his hips, pressed his check into the soapy water on the floor of the shower room, thrust hard inside him, managed—just—to pull out before I ejaculated—but not before he had by jacking his own cock, and in time for him to turn and take the wad on his face and then to clean my cock with his tongue and mouth.

"Take me home, daddy. Take me back to your hotel. Fuck me all night."

That's exactly what I did.

* * * *

Up to this tournament I'd never checked ahead on who I might have to face in subsequent rounds if I kept on winning, which I rarely did yet in my career past the third round. But I did almost always make the third round.

It was just a superstition with me, as it is with some other players.

I should have checked, though.

Of course the young Gene exhausted me Monday night. He was only five years younger than I was, but, in athletic sexual fuck positions—like the crab, with him on all fours suspended over my body, facing the ceiling; or the standing fuck, with me walking the room with him suspended in front of me and me bouncing him up and down on my cock, or just the strain of crouching high over him in a doggy fuck for a half hour or more at a time, or the sixty-nine full mutual blow job—five years of conditioning and the flexibility of youth can make a whole lot of difference.

He was insatiable and inventive and had all sorts of pretzel positions that challenged my muscles.

In my second-round match the next day, I lost miserably, grunting and groaning on the exhaustion and overuse of my muscles the night before. The player I lost to was Kurt Steiner.

He had the audacity to grin as we were shaking hands over the net at the end of a loss that made him look like a real tennis stud—on TV—and me like an unprepared dud and to say, "No hard feelings, I hope. Gene was worth it, wasn't he?"

Dolt that I was—having gone straight to the pro circuit rather than college—I didn't "get it" until that very minute. Kurt had used Gene—and the lay sessions before—as a distraction and as exhaustive activity for me going into the tournament. Kurt had looked ahead and seen that we might meet in the second round, and my ranking was nearly ten slots above his.

I could do no more than smile wanly and walk off the court while he was still acknowledging the applause of the tennis fans.

Gene hadn't worked as a ball kid that day. Checking with the office, I learned that he had only been

178

brought in to cover more sicknesses in the ranks of the ball kids. "He's really too old to be a ball kid anymore," the supervisor confided in me. "And he called in sick today too—said he'd strained a couple of muscles and was hobbling around. There's really a limit to the age where a ball kid's duties are manageable. Do you not agree?" She looked at me as if I was going to stand up for Gene's right to be the oldest ball kid alive.

But I didn't.

If I'd had any sense I would have written off using Kurt's procurer services during future tennis tournaments. But I didn't do that either. I didn't rise much further in the rankings, and I'm happy to say that Kurt didn't either, but I made a living at it.

And the sex on tour was great.

# Chameleon Love

*June, 1940, Blaye-et-Sainte-Luce, France*

Henri noticed how quiet the square was as he left the bakery shop with the piles of baguettes under his arm to be delivered around the village. Was this the day, he wondered. The Germans would enter the town to occupy it any day now. Their month-long movement was just about to reach the Bordeaux region, arriving in his own village on the southwest coast at the Gironde Estuary before the push into Bordeaux. The only saving grace was that they wouldn't billet many troops here, saving the bulk of them to occupy the far larger and better strategically placed Bordeaux.

Many of the villagers had already left, so he had just two deliveries to make—to the large, but deteriorating villa directly across the square and then to the house of the teacher, Samuel Levin, in the smaller house at the edge of the square. He would dither at the teacher's house until it was time to scrum with the village's rugby team out in the field to the west of the village. The first delivery was to his own house, where he lived with his grandfather, Ansel, a former, greatly revered town mayor, now almost immobilized by gout, and his maiden aunts, Suzanne and Marie. The Ballard family, once the richest and most prominent in the village, had fallen on bad times financially, with the deaths of Henri's parents in one of the plague-like influenza outbreaks that had passed through the village a decade earlier. The bread he was bringing to them from the baker was part of Henri's wages from working in the bakery in the morning.

After the delivery to his relatives, Henri crossed the still-ominously and atypically silent square to the house of the teacher to deliver his daily bread as recompense for the tuition for the baker's four children. As usual, the door to the small house was ajar, the first floor of the building being two schoolrooms. Henri mounted the stairs to the dwelling of the teacher above, and knocked on the door.

"Is that you, Henri? You alone?"

"Yes, teacher. As always."

"Enter."

Henri did so, leaving the bread on the counter in the kitchen, living, dining and nearly everything else room and then moved to the doorway to the back room—Samuel's bedroom.

Samuel, dark, hirsute, forties, and bearded, was Orthodox in appearance, other than the fact that he was naked and sitting on the side of his bed in full erection. He motioned Henri to come forward and kneel before him, which the young, perfectly formed and handsome man in his early twenties did, without hesitation. Henri knelt between Samuel's spread thighs, took the teacher's erect staff in his mouth, and gave it suck.

Later Henri became as naked as Samuel. Samuel was still sitting on the side of his bed. Henri's body was reclined toward the floor, supported by Samuel's legs, with Henri's legs wrapped around Samuel's gaunt torso, ankles crossed behind his back, while, gripping Henri's wrists, the strong Jew pulled Henri off and on his cock.

When ejaculation was achieved by them both, Henri was belly down on the arm of Samuel's reading chair in the corner of the bedroom, with Henri looking down on the side table where Samuel's wire-frame glasses rested on student papers he was correcting, and Samuel crouched over Henri's back and fucked him from behind and above.

When both were dressed, Samuel, as usual, walked Henri down to the front door to the house after Henri picked up the coins representing his payment from the kitchen counter where he had laid the baguettes. After surveying the supposedly empty square—but not too well—the teacher and village male prostitute kissed inside the shadows of the hallway—although not far enough inside. After drawing away from the kiss, Henri looked down, laughed, and pointed out that Samuel's trousers were not buttoned. Henri did the service for him.

What neither had noticed was that there was an open-roofed German military command car sitting at idle across the square, where the Wehrmacht Hauptmann—captain—sat in back waiting for the column of foot soldiers to arrive for the formal occupation of the village. Hauptmann Gerhard Rein watched the farewell of Samuel and Henri in Samuel's doorway, the buttoning of Henri's fly by Samuel not the least, with great interest and with pleasure that it would not require much effort to set up his routine while in this village.

It was known to only a small segment of the population of Blaye-et-Sainte-Luce—mostly those connected with the activity—that Henri, the greatly attractive young heir to the declining Ballard fortunes, was also the village male-on-male prostitute. All villages had them, of course. In many villages they were barely tolerated—but tolerated nonetheless because they were a necessity of life. Henri was from a tragic prominent family and was so likable—and of such a handsome countenance and sweet disposition—that even those who knew of his nefarious function in the village and were not connected with it tolerated it and accepted him. Those who would publicly disapprove were simply kept in the dark to ensure village stability.

For his part, Henri enjoyed doing what men wanted him to do, and he needed the extra money and services to keep his family fed. His grandfather could do nothing any more but dispense wisdom and affection. His aunts took in sewing, but that was hardly enough to keep the roof of the large villa from caving in on them. So Henri had his arrangements—the morning work at the baker and bread for the family for an occasional side fuck by the variety-loving baker. The coins from the teacher. Select meats from the village butcher. And so forth.

From the teacher's house Henri walked west of the village to the field where the town team practiced its rugby. Henri was a popular player there because, though smaller than most of the rest, he was strong, fast, clever on his feet. And he was good with his hands in finding and holding the ball. Even a few of the rugby players could attest to how good he was with his hands. The village butcher, Giles, a huge, muscular man, was both the team goalkeeper and its captain/coach. He was the power player on the team, defending the goal fiercely and well.

Following the practice, while the other teammates, muddied but highly pleased with the practice and each other, headed east toward the village, Giles placed an arm around Henri's shoulder, with the excuse of pulling him aside to give him some strategy pointers. The others looking in the direction they were headed, Giles marched Henri into a grove of trees next to the field. Neither noticed the military staff car that had been parked near the field, with Hauptmann Reins watching the practice—both the play and the obvious after play.

In the grove of trees, Henri lay on his back between the roots of a tree with his soccer shorts and cup off, his legs raised and spread, as Giles, shirt off and soccer shorts pinned down under his balls, knelt between Henri's thighs. Henri arched his back, panted, and cried out at the initial penetration as Giles' oversized cock entered his ass channel. As the bigger man began to pump Henri's ass, the younger, blond beauty slitted his eyes, licked his lips, and ran his hands over the bulges of the butcher's chest and biceps. There would be a fine cut of meat on the Ballard dining table tonight. And Henri wasn't the least bit embarrassed at how he was providing for his family. He enjoyed the attentions of men, and it was a precarious life for all in the village, especially with the uncertainty of the now-arrived German occupation.

Henri loved the fucking. He didn't have to love all of the men who provided it. But if he had to be a chameleon about showing his love for what they did to him, a chameleon he would be.

After Giles left him, Henri lay there for several more minutes, his legs spread, calming his breathing. Giles had the biggest, cruelest cock by far of all the men Henri took in the village. It took Henri a few minutes to recover.

In those few minutes, however, Hauptmann Reins appeared at the edge of the trees, and the eyes of the two met. Henri defensively reached for his soccer shorts to cover his privates, but neither of them was fooled about what had transpired there.

Henri's first response was feeling a chill of fear run up his spine. The Germans were reputed to be highly puritanical—to persecute any variant activity. Would Henri be sent to the camps he'd heard about on the first day of the German occupation?

But then Hauptmann Reins smiled broadly at Henri, and Henri understood that that was not to be his fate. He smiled back, tossed the soccer shorts off to the side again, spread his bent legs farther apart, rolled his hips up, fisted his cock with a hand, and gave the German captain a provocative look. If a chameleon he had to be a chameleon he would be.

The German army officer unbuttoned his trousers, pulled out a long, thin, erect cock, and approached and sank between Henri's thighs. As the cock made a long, cruel thrust up into Henri's channel and Reins closed his hands around Henri's throat and began to pump, Henri, the chameleon, arched his back; gagged, gasped, and groaned, as he knew the German would want to hear; and began to move his hips in the rhythm of the fuck. There must be some way he could gain advantage from this for himself and his family in the German occupation, he mused.

When Reins had ejaculated and was holding Henri close and breathing hard, his cock still buried deep inside Henri's channel, Henri whispered in the almost adequate German he'd learned thanks to his liaison with Samuel Levin, words to try to bind the German to him—words of loving the fuck, of wanting it again. Of how handsome and masterful the German officer was. Of how he melted to the attentions of a man in uniform.

Beaming not only because of how sweet and willing Henri's body had been, or even that the young man knew some German, but mostly because the sweet piece wanted to be fucked again immediately, seeming eager to have Reins plowing him again, Reins took as little time as he needed to comply.

He'd been of two minds—whether to use the public humiliation of this young man and the resulting punishment as an example to cow the people of this village into subjugation, or to use him and hold the vilification for later. The Frenchmen's succulence and willingness had determined that he would live a little longer.

* * * *

Henri's premonition of what was to come and an understanding of the high-stakes risks that now existed propelled him into motion as soon as he returned to the villa. Luckily, he got no argument from Suzanne and

185

Marie and stalwart support from Grandfather Ansell. Of course he didn't tell them the real reason this had to be—but they weren't stupid. They'd heard about other French villages the German had occupied. They could discern what some of the safer options were.

On his way back into the village, Henri had stopped at the stablery and hired a buggy, horses, and driver to appear at the back gate of the villa grounds. He had no trouble doing so, as the stable master, Pierre, was one of his men. He only had to promise two free lays, which he considered cheap, considering the short notice and how far up the coast the farm of the Ballard cousins was. The deal was struck on the spot with Henri giving the stable master a quick blow job.

While Marie packed trunks for herself and Suzanne, Henri and Suzanne scoured the house for valuables whose absence wouldn't be notice by first-time visitors and hid them away in the recess in the chimney in Suzanne's room that had been used for similar emergencies in the two hundred years the villa had stood here. There were more secrets in the house than just this hiding place.

The women had been gone none too soon when the knock on the door that Henri had anticipated came. Standing on the landing in front of the door, backed by two soldiers—one older and grizzly and one almost as young as Henri and wide-eyed and full of unspoken questions—was Hauptmann Gerhard Reins, eyes aglow from the servicing he'd received earlier in the day. Henri didn't regret having given into the man. He was maybe in his late thirties, ramrod straight and tall, on the thin side, but muscular, hair even blonder than Henri's—nearly pure white—and piercing, cruel pale-blue eyes. The mouth was set in a superior-attitude near-sneer, which contrasted with the older soldier behind him, whose sneer was knowing and demanding. When he was honest, Henri had to admit to himself that he preferred a demanding—and, yes, even a bit cruel—man. This soldier, at least, had been told of Reins' tryst with Henri, Henri was certain. And it was just as likely that he wanted to claim a share.

"We require billets," Reins declared. "Your house has been identified as the most appropriate one in the village. And I expect it to provide full amenities." The captain gave Henri a meaningful look.

Henri knew there were houses in better shape, but he had to admit that this villa was the most imposing one and with the most furnished bedrooms. This had been his premonition—that the German captain would come straight here for housing—and other benefits. The "other benefits" fit in with Henri's desperate plans, though.

Henri merely inclined his head in assent and acquiescence.

"This is Obersoldat Johan Mueller," Reins said, gesturing to the older solder, "and this is Soldat Hans Kant," he said, pointing to the younger and obviously junior—and certainly only nervous one—of the trio.

And then Reins said what Henri had been hoping for. "We do not pay for the use of the house, but we pay for the food, enough for everyone under the roof—and who will that be?"

"Just my grandfather and me," Henri answered. "He is old and hard of hearing and won't be in your way."

"Ah, good. And for the heat when it comes to need that, and do you have servants?"

"Just the cook and a day maid," Henri responded.

"And because of the special circumstances, I will pay extra for your exclusive services—for me and these two soldiers who will billet with me. Am I right that you receive payment for your services? That this is a function you serve in this village?"

The look was piercing. The younger soldier didn't seem to understand what was being said, but the older one certainly did. And now Henri was certain he knew the real reason his house had been chosen by the captain for billeting.

"Yes," he answered demurely, eyes downcast. "These are the services I provide."

"And to my two adjuncts too?"

"Yes, of course."

Then Henri looked up—his smile went behind the captain to the Obersoldat, Mueller, conveying his particular interest in the rougher of the three. "If you'll come upstairs with me, I'll show you to bedrooms. All are prepared"—and, indeed, part of the work of Suzanne and Marie's departure was to remake their rooms, both quite comfortable rooms dominated by four-poster beds with heavy, durable canopies and strong corner pillars. And with thick draperies on the windows and thick, sound-proof walls. To be sure they understood, Henri noted, as they mounted the sturdy staircase from the front foyer, "There are four bedrooms on the second level. The bedrooms on the third are not in use. Both the cook and my grandfather have rooms on the first floor in a wing beyond the kitchen, well away from the main house. The rooms on the second floor are for you, your two soldiers, and me. My room connects to yours, Captain. I hope this meets your needs."

The German captain quite explicitly said that it did. Perversely, Henri had assigned Reins to Suzanne's room, the one with the fireplace that hid the family's most precious possessions.

That night Reins showed his fetish streak. He had his two soldiers tie Henri's wrists to a corner of the frame of the canopy bed in his room, with him, naked, stretched below. The grizzly and wiry older solder, Mueller, held Henri on one side by puling Henri's leg up toward the headboard, while the younger, magnificently built private, Kant, did the same on the other. Kant wasn't just the one in the best muscular shape; he also was the lowest hung of the three. Reins stood, ramrod straight other than the forward jut of his pelvis, with his long, hard cock thrust upward, while, his two soldiers maneuvered Henri's rolled up hips in position and then, screwing his ass channel on Reins' cock, moved Henri back and forth on the shaft.

Knowing what he had to do and sensing even then that he needed to enlist the sympathy of at least one of the three, and the choice being obvious to him, as he could tell there would be no sympathy in any kind to expect from Mueller, he turned his face to that of the youngest soldier, and the two kissed deeply.

Later, as Mueller cruelly pistoned Henri from behind, bent over the side of the bed, Kant knelt in front of the still-reclining Reins—by his own choice—and sucked Reins to an ejaculation.

Before dismissing his attendants, Reins had them tie Henri, wrist and ankle, to the four strong posts of the bed. They tied him high off the bed, so that the droop in his buttocks surpassed six inches off the surface of the bed. Bursting one of the feather pillows open, the captain poured the feathers over Henri's body and blew and delicately pushed them along the surface of Henri's delicate skin to take pleasure in Henri's moans and begging for relief and in watching him struggle against his bonds and writhe in midair. When Henri was whimpering from exhaustion, Reins moved onto the bed, knelt between Henri's suspended thighs, grasped and spread Henri's buttocks with his hands, pulled Henri's puckered entrance onto the bulb of his cock—then deeper and deeper on the cock, as Henri writhed, arched his head back and marveled in words he knew the German wanted to hear of how deep the cock was reaching. Then Reins pulled Henri on and off his buried cock to a mutual ejaculation, and Henri's murmurs of maximum pleasure.

Guarding the tone of his voice and pulling a wan smile across his face, Henri told the sadist German captain that this masterful sex made him love Reins and wish for all of the inventive ways his body could be used to stimulate and serve the German's needs. He hoped that Reins' inventiveness would last him for some days to come.

That seemed to be enough for Reins' wants for the night, although in days and nights to come he was to devise many more unusual and decadent fetishes in the taking of Henri, much of which entailed the bondage of Henri and the use of the strength of the bed pillars and overhead canopy. All four men retired to their respective bedrooms.

To further Henri's own plans, he crept into Hans Kant's bedroom in the middle of the night; climbed under the covers with the young, hung, magnificently built German soldier; coaxed him to the hardest of woods with mouth play; straddled the young soldier's pelvis; and rode him for an hour, leaving the young soldier glassy-eyed and murmuring of awe, love, and devotion.

Hans' hands on Henri's waist were strong and calloused. He was a young stud, new enough to sex with men to be surprised and jerk and tremble when Henri, thoroughly experienced in the pleasures of men, surprised him with intimate touches—eating out Hans' ass as he writhed and luxuriated in the first such intimate service, taking the young man's balls in his mouth and humming, taking Hans almost to ejaculation by deep-throating the whimpering warrior's throbbing staff before mounting him, kissing and pinching Hans' nipples while rising and falling on the cock, nipping his nipples and his neck for the feel of his flinching and driving his cock deeper, begging constantly in broken German for the cock to dig deeper, reaching back and entering the young stud with a finger at the conclusion and rubbing Hans' prostate to make him explode deep in Henri's ass.

Other than one of the village priests, who was delicate and almost effeminate in sex even though he was on top, Henri was mostly fucked by older men. It was a thrill to have a younger, perfectly cut, vigorous, and virile man between his thighs. And even after an hour, it wasn't just the one fuck, with Henri riding Hans' thick cock. The young German soldier lost his shyness and, after a short recovery, took control and rode Henri—and then rode Henri again—and again.

The German was fast and furious with fire-off power; Henri more controlled. Hans was kneeling over Henri's prone body, his knees separating Henri's bent legs as he released a bucket of cum across Henri's heaving chest. Learning fast, the blond god rubbed the bulb of his bubbling cock over and over again on one of Henri's cum-slicked nipples while taking Henri's cock in his other hand and pumping him. Seeing through the slit in the draperies that it nearly was dawn, Henri gave the German his seed, arcing it up to mingle his cum with the young soldier's on his chest.

Hans' breathy whispers of devotions, in which Henri discerned the word *Liebchen*—lover—assured Henri that he had won one ally in the cruel triumvirate.

\* \* \* \*

The days stretched into weeks, and it wasn't hard for Henri to make clear to the men he normally serviced and received favors from that he now was exclusively taken—and by the enemy. This was ominously so, though. The first thing he noticed was that the house of the Jewish teacher, Samuel Levin, was closed up, the windows boarded up, but with scorch marks on the bricks around them to indicate that there had been a fire.

It was Ansel who told Henri of the village gossip that Samuel had been taken away in the night and torches thrown through his windows that caused fires that the neighbors put out after Samuel had been dragged away. Henri had known nothing of it even though it had occurred just across the square from his family villa, because he was being strung up facing a pillar of

Suzanne's bed at the time, in her room with the thick walls and noise-dampening draperies and having his legs held up and stretched out at either side by Mueller and Kant, while Reins fucked him from behind.

He did recall afterward that Reins kept going to the window on the front of the villa and peeking through the curtain, so it was highly possible that the captain had prior knowledge of what would happen with Samuel that night.

The next day, Henri found there was no need to make excuses about not going to the bakery, as the bakery was closed up tight. So was the butchery. And so were the stables, the stable manager, Pierre, having melted away without calling in the two fuck sessions Henri had promised him. The baker, butcher, and stable manager, as well as more than half of Henri's rugby team had taken to the countryside to form a resistance group.

As tough a choice as it was, Henri's giving in so readily and easily to the wants of Hauptmann Reins had worked in the Ballard men's favor. If the soldiers had not billeted in the Ballard villa, the family's source of bread and meat would have evaporated. Instead, Reins had forced both businesses to remain open with new proprietors and more than sufficient food was being supplied to the Ballard villa kitchen.

The secret of the totality of Henri's collaboration with the enemy came out full blown in the village gossip stream not too long afterward when the captain decided he wanted to treat his unit of men to an evening of debauchery.

He commandeered the local maison close— brothel—on the edge of the village, complete with the two prostitutes who worked the two rooms above the barroom, and put on a lavish party. Henri didn't have a head for liquor and probably didn't know fully what he was doing when he was coaxed to stand on top of a table with the two women prostitutes, all naked, and danced a sensuous dance until each was pulled down by the eager hands of soldiers, laid out on separate tables, and gang fucked by a succession of randy and drunk German soldiers, all the time with their captain looking on, laughing and egging them on.

The brothel's staff—other than the two unfortunate prostitutes—fled the bedlam early in the evening. But they looked on from safe positions and all later attested to the willing wantonness and fraternization of Henri with the Germans when, long after the two prostitutes had curled up into bruised, whimpering balls of withdrawal, Henri was sitting on Hauptmann Reins' lap, riding his cock, and waving his arms like he was an American rodeo star.

After that all doors in the village were closed to Henri—with the exception of the village church. The next afternoon, when Father Christophe entered the main sanctuary, it was to find Henri lying, belly down, arms outstretched in front of the altar and murmuring prayers of confession. In the day's light he fully understood what his drunken behavior the previous night had revealed to the village. His ability to be a chameleon was abruptly being compromised.

At the soft voice of the priest, Henri looked up. He groaned. He had hoped it would be old Father Marc who would be there to hear his confession, but it wasn't. It was the younger Father Christophe.

"Come. Rise. Come through with me and we will discuss this," Father Christophe said. In the father's spare cell behind the church kitchens, Father Christophe gently pressed on Henri's shoulders to make the young man sit down on the side of his bed, raised his cassock to reveal he was naked underneath and in erection, and, cupping Henri's chin, guided Henri's mouth to his cock.

An hour later, when Father Christophe, one of Henri's regular hookups in the village, had fucked Henri in a side split from behind in a spoon position on the cot to ejaculations by both, Father Christophe said, "I can hear your confession now."

Henri dutifully confessed his sins in trying to be the chameleon and to the best he could for his family under the conditions of the German occupation. Christophe took the confession, named the penance, which was mild, but added the word of advice, "The resistance here will become violent, I'm afraid, son. It would be in your best interests to withdraw to somewhere else considering what the village is saying about you."

It hadn't been a full confession, as Henri had heard that he wasn't the only one cooperating with the French—that Christophe was falling into their line too and was fraternizing with the enemy as much as Henri was. Indeed, as the priest led Henri back to his sleeping cell, Henri caught a glimpse of a young German soldier withdrawing down a corridor.

Henri didn't think really that he needed to be told that he should leave the village—and he wondered who heard Father Christophe's confession and suspected that much of the melancholy in the priest's voice in giving him this advice came from the regret the advice would end this occasional trysts in the priest's bed. He was trapped, though. He knew the priest was right, but there was Grand-Père Ansel to think of. What would befall him if Henri just left? It was Henri's responsibility to put the well-being of his family first.

Oh what a pickle his attempt to play chameleon to solve problems that were insolvable had placed him in.

\* \* \* \*

By listening to the Hauptmann and his two attendants converse, Henri was able to discern that the occupation of the village was in trouble, both because the resistance here was threatening to swamp the resources the Hauptmann had been given and because the resistance in nearby Bordeaux was necessitating the retrenchment of forces there. Bordeaux was, by far, a higher priority for occupation than this small village was.

Increasingly Reins was showing his worry and concern—and his fear. The soldiers he had under his command were drawn closer to the Ballard villa, strengthening the defenses here, but acknowledging the weakness to the activities of the resistance elsewhere in the village and surrounding countryside. His worry was shown also in the frenzied way he and his attendants were using Henri's services throughout the day—like each fuck might be their last.

As active as Henri had been before, although he'd never been involved in threesomes before now nor been put in the positions of bondage and cruelty before as now, he had never been double penetrated. Now that was happening routinely, with the third usually using his mouth at the same time. Henri had no idea how much crueler Gerhard and Johan could get, with regularly now riding him on all fours on the floor while digging the heels of their boots into his calves and beating every exposed surface with a riding crop. Only the young soldier, Hans, held back from this—satisfied, no doubt by Henri's nightly visits to his bed for more intimate and loving fucking.

Having the Germans comfortable with his presence, though, helped Henri in the timing of what he knew needed be done. This was brought to a head by Hauptmann Reins himself one night over dinner.

"I'm afraid we pull out tomorrow," he informed Henri. "We have been called to pull back to Bordeaux to strengthen the defenses there."

"I . . . I will miss you," Henri answered, halfway believing it himself. He had not done much self-analysis of his response to the captain's form of lovemaking—halfway in fear of what he had to admit his response was—arousal, and to a high degree, pleasure at the cruel

195

use of his body, especially now by the gaunt and grizzly Obersoldat Mueller, who made no bones about testing Henri to the limit. Catholic that he was, despite the light penance Father Christophe had given him, Henri knew that he deserved what Mueller was doing to him. And, to his embarrassment, he longed to have more of what Mueller did to him.

"You don't have to miss me. You are coming with me," Reins said. "I am comfortable with your services. I don't see the need to find a new young man who will serve my needs as well as you do. I'm sure you realize—and appreciate—that I could have you thrown into a camp at any moment for deviant behavior and have not done so."

This was the way Henri realized it would go with Reins and it was the direction in which Henri had tried to develop the relationship. It wasn't a final answer, he knew. He no longer believed there was a final answer that would save him. But this could save his family and help his country.

He crept away to Grand-Père Ansel to tell him in as limited way as he could what he must do and why—although he was sure that the old man had known all along and hadn't seen any better choices for Henri and the family than the one Henri had made.

"You must go now, Grand-Père, by the secret door in the fence to the neighboring lot." The villa was guarded front and back by German soldiers and the two adjacent house had been commandeered and vacated. But there was access across the lots through hidden doors in fences that had long been devised and maintained by the residents.

"You must find the resisters. I know that the butcher, Giles, is leading them. You must call me out as a German collaborator and say that you and the aunties have managed to escape me. And then, after the Germans have pulled out—I am going with them—you must live as quietly as possible. You and aunties must learn to be chameleons. The Germans may return, and, when they do, it may be for all time."

Understanding, Ansel hugged his grandson, and, with tears in his eyes, shuffled away to the secret door into the neighboring lot.

Before returning to Reins and his attendants for a last frenzied night of demanding sex in the Ballard villa, Henri told the cook to put out a breakfast on the buffet in the dining room early in the morning and then, herself, to use the secret door to escape—and to assure Giles, in the function she had been serving of slipping messages to the resistance from Henri, that he would continue to do all he could to get whatever information on German plans and movements back to the resistance as he had done all the time he was with the captain.

"Ahh, you should not be taking all of this on yourself, Monsieur Henri," she objected. "You have been the best of patriots yourself, sacrificing yourself like this—letting the villagers, and now, even your own grandfather, believe you are a collaborator. When you are not."

"I am whatever I have to be, Lisle," Henri responded, knowing that the safest way to continue life as a chameleon was to maintain pretenses as much as possible. "Grandfather is too infirm to be expected to keep the secret. So he must not know yet. And you must denounce me in public after I'm gone as well. If justice prevails, Giles and the others will vindicate me someday when the Germans have been expunged from France. For now my collaboration must be believable."

The next day Henri rode out of the village of Blaye-et-Sainte-Luce in Hauptmann Gerhard Reins' open staff car, not knowing what the future held, but continually looking for the opportunity to use chameleon love to survive.

Reins sat close to him on his right and Mueller on his left, and they were barely on the road when both began to fondle his body and put upon him—with Mueller even managing to reach into the folds of his clothes, grasp his balls, and squeeze to the point of making Henri gasp and want to faint. It would have been so much better to be able to sit next to the young golden god, Hans Kant, now in the front seat of the vehicle, who was so besotted with Henri now that he would do anything—including passing on plans of German troop movements and intentions.

Still, the chameleon in Henri made him work up all options. The last thing he wanted to have happen to him was to be exposed as a male-on-male prostitute and sent to a camp. He'd rather die than that. When the car was stopped on the road for Reins to confer with a group of soldiers, Henri turned his face to Mueller and whispered, "It is my hope that someday you and I can be alone and I can enjoy the full attentions of your specialties."

Mueller glowered at him, his mouth twisting into a cruel leer. "Trust me, if I get you alone, I'll break you for all time."

It was an ultimate option for Henri. Something to keep in reserve in case his attempt at patriotism came to a dead end.

# Halfway

"I don't understand why I can't stay with you in Philadelphia," I said, trying to keep the whine out of my voice. Of course, I knew precisely why I couldn't, but I wanted him to say it. I wanted Larry to clear the air and admit to me that he had a family to go to in Philadelphia. I don't know what I'd do then—or what he'd do with the truth out in the open—but I was tired of his evasions. "You had no trouble with me staying with you in Harrisburg. If you don't have a family you don't want to know about me in Philadelphia, why would that be different from Harrisburg?"

That he had no trouble with me staying with him in Harrisburg wasn't exactly true either. We'd been in one of those small one-bedroom transient apartments at a Homestead Suite near the state capital complex, where he'd kept me pretty much locked down and he didn't bring anyone back to. I could understand that. He was an aide to some sort of important Pennsylvania state senator, and I was a rent boy he'd lured off a pole in a club. But it isn't like he'd just shown up at the club occasionally to take me out for a spin. We'd lived together for the two months of the spring legislative session.

"I told you, Angel," he said, the knuckles of his hands on the steering wheel white as we drove on I-81 from Harrisburg toward Philadelphia and his voice showing the tension as well, "I don't have a permanent home in Philadelphia. I stay with my parents. I hardly can take you there. I'll get a room for you somewhere."

A room somewhere. I almost snorted at that—and at the obvious lie that he was living with his parents when he was in Philadelphia. Still, it had been a small victory that he'd agreed to take me back to Philadelphia at all. He could have left me in Harrisburg—even have said he expected me to be there ready to be locked up in a hotel suite for him to play with when he came back for the fall legislative session. Fat chance of that. Although, who knows what I would have done. I think the club would have taken me back. I think I was a crowd pleaser when I was there—something different than the usual dancer rent boys. There were those who were turned on by half and half—halfway there, I thought of it. The boobs had been done, pretty much just buds but still a handful. I doubted I'd go further than that.

And nicely sensitive tits they were too. That's how, back in Harrisburg, Larry had cut off any discussions about his living arrangements in Philadelphia. Embracing me from behind, both of us on our knees on the bed. Larry running his hands up under the hem of the silky slip he liked me to wear, until he could cup and squeeze my breasts. Nuzzling my neck with his lips and then stifling my questions by possessing my mouth. French kissing me as he entered me with that big dick of his that always made me melt.

Chances were good that even if he admitted to me that he had a wife, two children, a dog, and a cat waiting for him in Philadelphia, I would be content with sitting in a small hotel room, waiting for the chance to have that dick of his working inside me and his hands squeezing my tits—just his; not a succession of drunken louts. But the evasions were driving me wild.

"Look, Larry, if you have a family in Philadelphia, just—"

"Oh, for the love of Christ, could you just get off that? Here, I'm pulling off the highway to get gas. This is the halfway point between Harrisburg and Philadelphia."

"Good," I said, as he nosed the Buick onto the off ramp. I barely caught the name of the turnoff, but laughed when I saw that it *was* a place called "Halfway." Not much of a place, though, just a few buildings on either side of the bridge over the highway. One of them, off to the south, was a gas station, though. "I have to take a piss and do something about this chipped nail anyway," I said. I looked down at my lilac-colored nails and the little chunk out of the index finger nail on the right hand.

"I'll just be a jiffy," I cheerfully chirped, as Larry stopped at a pump and I took up my purse and opened the passenger door.

"Take your time," he answered, his voice showing that he was still pissed at my wheedling at him on what we were driving into in Philadelphia. "Take all of the time in the world," he repeated, letting the words come out in little puffs of relief of tension.

I should have paid more attention to what he said—and the way he said it. When I returned from the ladies room, the Buick wasn't standing at the pump. It wasn't parked over at the side, either. And I looked across the road to a greasy diner with semitrailers parked next to it and to the small strip motel beside that, one with the sign Halfway Diner and the other with the sign Halfway Motel, and still there was no Buick.

Then I looked back at the pump. The small duffle bag with some of my stuff in it was sitting next to the pump. My gaze went to the gas station window then, where I saw two guys, one thin and young and the other burly and not so young, staring at me like I was the afternoon entertainment just about ready to give them a show.

I walked over, perched on the duffle bag, and lit up a cigarette, just like I knew where Larry had gone and that he'd be back in a few minutes. Inside, though, I doubted that Larry was coming back for me. This was typical Larry—running out in the middle of what was not even an argument.

\* \* \* \*

"Uh, miss," and then as I turned my head toward the gas station building, the voice adjusted to, "Um, sir."

The younger, thinner of the two men who had been watching me from the station window was approaching me. He had a cooking pot, with lid, in his hands, holding the pot's handle with one hand and the pot lid with the other. I had the sensation of him hunting for his dinner and stalking something to trap in the pot by scooping the prey up. He was much to the same age as I was—perhaps just shy of twenty—and seemed embarrassed in approaching me. He wasn't exactly ugly, but he was scrawny, with a bad case of acne, and looked beat down.

His problem with gender identifying me was natural. From the back I could be taken as a woman, especially if my painted nails were in view, as they were just now, as I was still worrying the split nail. I was holding my lit cigarette out, supporting that arm with my hand on the elbow—sort of a Bette Davis pose, which I cultivated. And my hair was curly, full of body, with lighter blond highlights, and descended to my shoulders. It was one of my best features with men when I was having sex; they loved to run their hands through my hair.

When I turned, though, the possibilities skewed toward the male. I wasn't wearing facial makeup. When I did, I could easily pass as female. And my loose flannel plaid shirt and worn jeans weren't a help in discerning sex. The shirt was loose enough to hide my breast projection.

And I wasn't built big enough to noticeably fill out a basket.

"Yes?" I responded, giving him a smile, which made him blush. He was approaching me in jerks and starts. Looking past him, I could see the older, hulkier man standing in the window. He was much more like the men I usually encountered and serviced, and the expression on his face, although quizzical, could, I think, quickly go to interest if I vamped him. I had no intention of doing that, of course, but I sensed my vulnerability—and probably abandonment—and needed to keep all of my options open.

It was then that I realized what was missing. I was sitting on my duffle bag, but I'd also brought a suitcase. Nearly all of my clothes were in there. Thank god that my makeup kit was in the duffle bag. "Shit," I exclaimed.

"Excuse me? I'm sorry. It's just that—" The young man had taken a step back and was withdrawing into himself. Visions of turtle and shell ran through my mind.

"Sorry," I quickly said. "It's not you. I just thought of something unfortunate." I had to adjust my voice to a lower register than I had started in midsentence, thinking that it might be best to be male for the moment. "I'm sorry, I'll move from the pump if a car comes up. I'm just waiting for my ride to come back."

"It's just that . . ."

"Just what?" I asked.

He pointed to my lit cigarette and then to the pump. "A spark could set off an explosion."

Ah, the stealthy approach explained. "Sorry, I'll put it out." I started to rub it out on the sole of my loafers, but this sent the young man into panic.

"No, please," he exclaimed. As he did so, he held the pot out.

Ah, that explained too. I gingerly put the cigarette in the pot and he slammed the lid down like he was the hero of the bomb squad. The town was saved. My hero. I gave him another smile. I guess I could suck him off, but he hardly looked the type who would be much fun in a fuck. My eyes went to his crotch, but I couldn't tell. The jeans were baggy. Now the hulk in the gas station window . . .

"Is there anything I can do for you?" he asked. "It doesn't look like—"

"No, it doesn't look like he'll be back soon, does it?" I said, with a resigned sigh. "Is the diner across the street any good?" I said that as I stood and lifted the duffle bag. But before he could answer, I exclaimed another "Shit!" as the seam in the bottom of the duffle gave way and out spilled most of the contents. Some of the contents were sex toys, which caused the young man to blanche, retreat a step, and look totally embarrassed.

They weren't his sex toys being revealed, though. I downgraded the possibility that he could be any use to me in exchange for servicing. The hulk in the gas station window, on the other hand, was sporting a big grin.

I turned the duffle over and scooped the escaped contents back in it.

"It's the best diner in town." The guy at the pump said in a meek voice. And then he laughed, releasing the tension in the air. "I guess you'd have to say that it's the only diner in town—and that this isn't much of a town."

"Thanks," I said, wedging the turned-over duffle under my arm. "I guess I'll give it a try. If the guy in the Buick comes back—"

"I'll tell him you are over at the diner," the young man said, hurriedly as he backed off. "And the motel over there isn't too expensive if you need . . . my name's Dan. I work part time over there too. The other guy, in the station, is Gus. If there's anything . . ." He sort of let that trail off, though. I think he was so overwhelmed by the situation that he didn't hardly know what to say. I felt from the way he was hopping around and backing off that he couldn't wait to get back into the building to tell Gus what he'd seen fall out of my duffle. I was pretty sure that Gus knew better than Dan what had been on display.

On second look, he looked sort of cute. The shyness became him, and when that acne was gone . . . well, he was at least worth a smile and having on my side.

"Thanks . . . Dan . . . you've been very helpful. My name's Angelo. When the Buick comes back."

"Yes . . . sir . . . I'll tell him you're over at the diner."

And then, as Dan skittered back into the gas station building, I clumped across the road, stopping every few steps to ensure that I still had control over the duffle. As I drew close to the diner, I could see through the picture windows that several sets of eyes were watching me.

I laughed. It was probably the most entertainment these people had in a month of Sundays. I guess it was something that I could still laugh at this predicament.

All were silent and facing the door as I entered the diner. All men, no women. I found this a bit disconcerting and, for no reason I could put my thumb on, foreboding. I found myself sorry I hadn't pulled my hair back in a pony tail or hadn't painted my nails that morning. Without my facial makeup I was halfway between here and there. I wasn't sure which to be. So, I stayed as neutral as possible.

Directly opposite the door, which jangled and almost made me jump when I opened it, standing behind a lunch counter, leaning into the counter with his arms spread wide and hands pressed into the back edge of the counter, was a tall, dark-headed, thin guy wearing a short-sleeved white shirt that showed sleeve tattoos on both arms and a spider web tattoo on either side of his neck running right up under a scraggly beard. His eyes were boring into me and he had a half grin on his face.

"Been sittin' over there for a while, ain't cha?" he said in a gravelly voice. "Been left to fend for yourself?"

"He's just run an errand," I answered. "I decided I was hungry and the young guy over there recommended this restaurant."

"Not likely," came a deep voice off to the side, which was met with laughs from more than one. Seven men of various ages and sizes—all definitely blue collar, though—were sitting in booths on the north side of the diner. It immediately registered with me that these must be the guys who matched up to the bunch of semis parked in tandem at the side of the diner. I looked over to the other side of the diner. Back in the corner, sitting in a booth, was a big-muscle dude, probably in his fifties, with wavy gray hair and the look of money about him. A blue denim shirt and pressed jeans and a peek at very expensive cowboy boots in the space under the booth. He also had some sort of flashy ring or two that were catching the light and reflecting off the diner walls and ceiling. He was smoking a cigarette, nursing a cup of coffee, and appeared to be reading a newspaper. Only appeared to be doing so, though, I could see. He was as interested in me as any of the others were.

While I was still looking at him, he lifted his coffee cup to indicate he wanted a refill, and the guy behind the counter was there so fast with a pot that I surmised that the older guy in the corner was the big daddy of this tiny burg.

While the tattooed waiter was gone, I gingerly put the duffle on the floor, being careful that nothing fell out—with the thought that if one of my toys saw the light of day in here, the truckers would have me on the floor and using it in nothing flat. I'd had considerable experience with long-distance truckers. Once again I missed the leavening effect of having a woman present.

The tattooed waiter returned. "What can I get you?"

"Serving breakfast or lunch?" I asked.

"Yes," he answered.

I took a quick look at the menu and ordered a big breakfast. I probably should have taken inventory of what was left to me first in monetary means, though, as I suddenly realized that most of my cash and all of my credit cards were in the suitcase that was inside a Buick somewhere down the road toward Philadelphia. I did have some cash on me. Just not enough to be throwing it around on "everything and the kitchen sink" breakfasts.

That didn't stop me from cleaning off my plate. Who knew where my next meal would be coming from?

Between trips to the big daddy table and the truckers' corner, the tattooed waiter hovered in front of me on the other side of the counter while I ate, giving me a half leer.

"Any buses to Harrisburg stop here?" I asked. He was just standing there, making me uncomfortable. I figured conversation would lessen the tension in the diner. The truckers, who probably were being boisterous before I came in, were huddled together, giving me looks, and whispering and sniggering among themselves.

"Nope," the tattooed waiter said.

"I'll be happy to give you a lift to Harrisburg," a voice boomed out from the trucker's corner.

"You ain't goin' in the direction of Harrisburg, Sam," another said. Laughs all around.

"I could lift you, easy," sniped another voice, followed by sniggers.

"Any place around where I can get a duffle bag," I asked the tattooed waiter, deciding that it was best just not to get into a conversation with the truckers, although I probably should have just taken the trucker up on the ride, even knowing what it would cost me. I had a strong feeling that time spent here was going to cost me that anyway.

"There's a consignment shop across the road, next to the gas station," a voice from the other side of the diner said. A more commanding, assured voice. The voice of "I get what I want." A little shiver went through my body. This was the kind of man . . . well, this was the kind of man I gravitated to. The information had come from big daddy in the corner.

"Now, ain't that convenient?" the tattooed waiter said. "Only five buildings here, and all of use to you."

"Five buildings?" I asked. I looked out the window and saw four, two on this side of the road and two on the other. The gas station and two-story consignment shop on the other side of the road and the diner and motel on this.

"Yep," he continued, with a leery smile. "The gas station got you here, the consignment shop will get you a new duffle, this here diner fed your stomach, and, if you'd like, I'll show you the motel next door."

"Or you can get a ride with me to Harrisburg," the trucker who had offered the service spoke up.

"Yeah, for a ride of another kind," another one chimed in. Laughter on that side of the diner. The tattooed waiter just smiled at me. No reaction from the big daddy corner.

"That's four buildings," I said.

"You missed the big, rambling one on the other side of the highway bridge?" the tattooed waiter asked. "I figure you can get a job there, if you've been just dumped here by that fancy Buick."

"Thanks for the breakfast," I said, rising and putting money for it down on the counter, including a generous enough tip not to get any backtalk on that, even if I could ill afford it. "And for the direction to the consignment shop." I said this to the waiter, not trusting myself to speak directly to big daddy in the corner. He was just the sort of man who only needed to beckon and I'd be there. And this wasn't the place or time for that.

When I got out of the diner and was looking both ways to cross the road—although there wasn't much danger of busy traffic out here in the middle of nowhere—I looked north across the bridge over the highway. Sure enough there was a rambling two-story building across the bridge with a high fence around a lot behind in and more semis parked beside it. I could read the sign, a gigantic lit-up neon on top of the roof. It said "Halfway Adult Bookstore."

The place looked entirely too large to be just a bookstore and video shop. I'd been around the block; I knew what else would be going on there. So, I hadn't fooled the guys in the diner one bit.

\* \* \* \*

"Yes, of course. We have a few right over there. Anything else you need? Anything else I can do for you? I saw you sitting over at Gus' station. You been abandoned or something?"

God, had everyone in this frickin' town been watching me? And no women?

"I may need some clothes too until my ride gets back," I said. "Do you . . . oh, yes, I see the rack over there." Who was I fooling? If Larry was coming back for me, I wouldn't need to be buying any more clothes. "But maybe not, depending on how expensive . . ."

"Short of money?" He asked. "Not a problem. There are always adjustments . . . trades." This made me look at him. Maybe his early forties. Not particularly muscular but not bad looking. Not fat either. No sign of a beer belly or anything. Not fully white, though. There was something else in him. Black? Hispanic? He was giving me a steady look—an assessing one. I don't think he missed much. The painted nails and the blonde highlights in my long hair. He'd been standing at the door as I crossed the road—like he knew I was coming to him. Had I betrayed something in my walk? So many things to think about in transitioning back and forth: the voice, the walk, the way I held my arms. The men in the diner had picked it out almost immediately. Who would expect them to be so savvy in a backwater like this? Maybe it said something about what went on in this backwater.

So, who was I fooling.

"Maybe you need some underwear?" he asked, giving me a steady look. He was holding up sheer panties, not briefs. "Or maybe something like this?" He held up a slinky red, satin sheath dress.

As they say, the jig was up.

"I'm not sure I can afford any of this," I said, transitioning to what I sensed he wanted me to be. My stance went into that of a female and I gave him a come-on look. I let my voice go into a higher register. "My suitcase is in the car that hasn't come back for me yet." My helpless lass pose.

"And, so, you don't just need a new duffle bag"— he was helping himself to rummaging around in my slit duffel, not being visibly surprised at some of the items he found—"you could use more clothes and maybe a place to sleep."

"Yes, probably," I said. "But I don't really have enough to pay for—"

"Yes, I think you do," he said, giving me a meaningful look. "I live in the apartment upstairs—with Gus, who runs the gas station. We've got beds up there. I think you can provide more than enough to cover the cost of anything here and a place to sleep if you come upstairs with Gus and me."

At Kirk's request—he had told me his name was Kirk, and exchange, having taken the stance he obviously wanted, I told him my name was Angel—I straddled his hips on his bed upstairs, wearing just the red satin shift he'd picked out. He was naked, and his body was fine enough, the cock adequate for the need. He'd given me time to do some makeup, so that I was mostly female for him. He appreciated the part that wasn't, though, putting his hands on my buttocks and pulling me forward over his chest until, brushing the hem of the shift up, my hard cock was exposed to the attentions of his mouth.

I had already given him a blow job and he was working himself hard again while giving me some attention.

Raising his torso up to me, an arm went around my waist, pushing the shift up to below my tits, his cheek went to my bare belly, and his free hand traveled up to squeeze my tits and pinch my nipples. I gave him the sounds I was sure he wanted to hear. Coaxing my buttocks forward and down, I helped his sheathed cock head center on my lubed and puckered entrance and then, as he gasped and groaned, I descended on his shaft.

His lips went to my nipples, and as we rocked back and forth and he panted, I murmured, "Yes, big boy, fuck me deep. Yes, just like that. Fuck me, fuck me."

As we rocked against each other I sensed we weren't alone in the bedroom. The hulk from the gas station—Gus—had entered the room at some point. He was pulling his clothes off and had his meat out. He was erect and, where Kirk was adequate, Gus was much more than adequate. He was big, tall, and heavy—but much of the heaviness was in muscle. Whereas Kirk was more bookish, Gus was just the sort of guy who came into the bar I'd worked at in Harrisburg and paid for hard use of my ass.

He came up on the bed behind me, straddling Kirk's thighs with his knees. His hands went to my breasts, and he leaned my shoulder blades back into his hairy chest. "I don't want to wait for a turn," he murmured in my ear. "Can you—?"

"Yes," I answered before he finished. He was my kind of guy. I wanted him inside me. Strangely, though, as he pulled the shift off of me in one movement and pushed my chest down onto Kirk's, causing my buttocks to rise to the need of his slow invasion of me on top of Kirk's buried shaft, my thoughts went to the commanding presence of the man in the diner—the obvious bid daddy of this tiny burg of Halfway—and fantasies of him being inside me.

Gus began to pump, squeezing my breasts hard, latching onto the side of my neck with his teeth, as Kirk encased my cock in one of his hands and started to stroke me.

"Yes, Daddy, yes. Fuck me, fuck me. Fuck me hard."

Where I slept that night wasn't a problem. I was wedged between Kirk and Gus on the bed they apparently shared. I'd been shown a bedroom I could use, but I didn't use it that night.

\* \* \* \*

I stopped out by the road in front of the consignment shop to catch my breath and steel myself for what came next. It hadn't rained here since the landing of Noah's ark on the mountain, I didn't think, and each passing semitruck, entering or exiting I-81 raised dust up to my ankles. That's all I could see moving hereabouts. Semis. Not that the small groupings of buildings were lifeless. Just that everything was on hold—and watching me. Kirk was standing into the doorway of the consignment shop, watching me as I paused at the road. Gus and the shy Dan were stationed at the gas station window, watching me. The tattooed waiter in the diner was just outside the diner door, back against a window column, one leg bent with the sole of his boot against the diner wall, smoking a cigarette—and watching me. Faces of men—truckers—inside the diner: all were turned to me, watching me.

I wasn't anyway in one direction today yet. I was half way, my hair pulled back in a pony tail, no facial makeup, but still the lilac nail polish, and I was wearing a tight T-shirt from the consignment shop. Today I had tits that showed. The satchel I'd taken from the consignment shop was stuffed with makeup. I had the red slinky shift and lacy panties folded into the purse as well. Kirk had told me to take anything I wanted from the shop—and to come back to bed.

With a sigh, I set my shoulders and turned and walked toward the bridge over I-81—headed for that flashing neon Halfway Adult Bookstore sign beckoning from across the bridge.

Over breakfast Kirk confirmed my assumption that there was more going on at the bookstore than books—that there was a gay bar behind the store front and rooms upstairs. He said this was the place that men who wanted men gathered from all over central Pennsylvania. This had come out when I remarked that I hadn't seen any women around here yet.

"You wouldn't," he'd answered. "Half way is strictly a man's world. But half men are welcome here too—especially welcome," he'd been quick to add.

I'd asked about work around here and places to stay.

"Mostly small farms around here," he said. "Pretty self-sufficient. You could work part time right here in the shop, but there's not much need for extra help. You can, of course, bunk out upstairs for as long as you want. But if I was you . . . and knowing now what you're prepared to do for a man . . . well, I'd go over to the other side of the bridge. They'd eat you up over there, I'm sure. That's where you could make money. Afternoons here in the store; evenings over there."

"You say they have a bar going?"

"Yep, they sure do."

"And entertainment? I worked the pole in some bars in Harrisburg."

"Then you'd find work over there. Just assert yourself and what you have to offer in the storefront and I'm sure they'd be eager to show you what's happening in back. But to work there, you have to pass muster with Mr. Kincaid."

"Mr. Kincaid? Who's he?"

"He owns the operation over there. Hell, he owns all of the operations here. The rest of us just work for him. You want to work here, you have to work for him too. And work hard for him. But whatever you do, don't let him take you back to his farm."

Ah, the big daddy I saw in the diner, I thought. Yeah I could work for him. "What's at his farm I wouldn't like?"

"The same that he'll give you a taste of in deciding to hire you. The same, but much more. Young men who go out to his farm with him never come back—at least not to here."

"Thanks, I'll keep that in mind."

And I did keep it in mind all the time I was walking toward the bookstore. I paused in the middle of the bridge spanning I-81, and stood there, looking down on the traffic roaring past. Semis. A whole bunch of semis. But cars too. I found myself picking out the Buicks and wondering about Larry. Wondering if he was having second thoughts and would come back for me. I found myself leaning over the parapet, thinking about how easy it would be just to pitch over the side into oncoming traffic. Change it all here. Not being half of anything anymore. Being a whole, mangled corpse. Visions of Larry coming back to me and coming upon my crumpled body in the middle of the roadway below. He'd be sorry. Yeah, right.

What scared me was that I found that attractive—a viable option.

I thought about this Mr. Kincaid. I had dreamed of the man in the diner fucking me while Kirk and Gus were doing that last night. Being given the hint that he was demanding, taxing, in sex by Kirk didn't change my attraction to him. Rather the opposite. That scared me too.

Nearly everything scared me in my life of half this, half that. But, hell, I found that attractive too.

I turned and marched on to the bookstore.

The store part itself didn't take up much room. It was obvious that there was more going on here behind the scenes. The parking lot was full of semis and yet I was the only one in the store, other than the clerk, when I entered. The guy, a gawky nondescript guy other than the big biceps and covering tattoos, was hunched over the counter, staring into a muscle-builder magazine when I entered. He looked up and suddenly was all attention.

"Yes, may I help you?" he asked, giving the impression that he would move mountains to help me.

"I'm looking for work," I answered. "I dance the pole in Harrisburg, was dropped here without ongoing prospects, and have been told there might be work for me in whatever is behind this store." I had decided not to start off with any lies. They quickly caught up with you in a dive like this.

"That's a distinct possibility," the guy answered, giving me a big grin and almost whistling for me. "Not my call, though. Come on to the back. You're in luck. Mr. Kincaid is here."

"You have a john I can use before I go back?" I asked.

"Over in the corner. You want company?" We both knew what he was proposing—and that he was just flirting. The way he was treating me like visiting royalty pretty much revealed that he knew I was above his pay grade in terms of servicing.

I had been prepared to work my way past the bookstore clerk if that was necessary, but it apparently wasn't necessary, so I just smiled and said, "No thanks." But I added, "Maybe later." No sense burning any bridges.

I spent several minutes in the john becoming fully Angel, and, when I came out with my hair down, my face made up, and wearing the panties and the red satin shift, the clerk's eyes bugged out and he actually did whistle.

"God damn," he said in a hoarse voice.

"Can you show me how to get into the bar?" I asked, using my breathy Angel voice, cultivated from watching numerous Marilyn Monroe movies.

"God Damn," was all he was able to say, but he did usher me to a door at the back of the store that was shielded by a beaded curtain. That opened to a smoky room, with a low hub bub of voices coming from a smattering of men hunched over tables. Sitting alone at a table, facing the room, at one end of a bar, was the same man I'd seen in the diner. Undoubtedly Mr. Kincaid.

All sound stopped for a few seconds when I appeared at the door and then it started again in earnest.

The clerk went over to Kincaid to tell him what I was interested in doing for this operation, and Kincaid waved me over to his table.

"Russ Kincaid," he said, as I sauntered over to the table, remembering to use my hips. He didn't ask me to sit down, so I stood there, letting his eyes undress and ravish me. "I understand you're an entertainer and looking for a job."

"I'm Angel," I answered. "Yes, I'd like to do a gig here. I've danced the pole at some bars in Harrisburg. As you no doubt figured out, I was stranded here. Need to make some transportation money."

"You dance the pole? And, tell me Angel, do you lay on your back and open our legs too for a cut of the profit?"

"Yes."

"Tell you what. I'll give you a trial. Go over there and pick your music out on the juke box and do fifteen minutes of dancing on the stage there. Any of these guys who wants to take you upstairs afterward, you'll get half.

What they pay will depend on demand and what I think they can afford. After that there will be a private audition with me, though, to determine whether you come back tonight for a full session."

"Sounds fair to me." I didn't bother to ask how much half of a fuck session would be. I was lucky to get half, this being an audition and all. And maybe there wouldn't be any takers.

As I moved over to the juke box, though, the chance of there being takers was increasing alarmingly. The clerk in the bookstore must have made some phone calls, because there suddenly were about twenty men—of all ages and sizes and shapes—gathering around the stage, with its solitary pole.

I danced the pole, briefly in the red sheath, but then in just the panties for a half hour or more. After the first song, the crowd was asking for more and someone was at the juke box bringing up another song. Kincaid didn't stop the show until after the sixth song and until after men stopped drifting back to his table to consult with him.

Afterward, the bartender ushered me upstairs to a room with a bed, a straight chair, and a dresser, and told me that I might as well lay on my back at the foot of the bed, strip off the panties, and open my legs.

Wham bang, right after that a quick succession of four guys were shown into the room, their hard dongs already exposed, and got right down to the business of fucking me—two in the missionary position and two doggy style. They must have been on a time clock, because there was little talking and they all worked to an ejaculation in less than fifteen minutes each.

Afterward the bartender reappeared, told me to put the panties and shift on again, handed me $200 in cash, and told me that Mr. Kincaid was waiting in his car out back.

"He's not doing it here?" I asked, afraid that he was going to take me out to his farm—where Kirk had warned me not to go.

"He has a room he likes to use at the motel across the highway," the bartender said.

Kincaid drove a fancy Mercedes. He said nothing in the short ride, but when we got to the motel, instead of going immediately inside, he pulled my face down into his lap and made me give him a blow job. His cock was long and thick. Somehow I'd known it would be.

Dan from over at the gas station was at the desk in the motel office when we entered. His eyes went big and his face revealed a look of concern when he saw me enter with Kincaid.

"I'll take the key to room 8, Dan," Kincaid said.

"Yes, Mr. Kincaid," Dan said. As he turned to take the key off the rack, he flashed me a warning look. I was touched that there was someone—anyone—who cared what happened to me.

In the room, which I realized Kincaid kept and prepared for just this sort of session, the big hunk beat the hell out of me before fucking me. As the door clicked shut, locked, he caught my cheek in an unexpected backswing that sent me reeling across the room and landing belly over the foot of the bed. He pulled me up by my hair, spun me around, and punched me in the stomach. I doubled over, and he pulled me up by my hair again and slapped me twice.

None of it was full force, but I was fully cowed and malleable now, just going into whatever position he wanted and giving him anything he wanted. What he first wanted was to rip off the shift and panties, force me down on all fours on the carpet, mount me, and fuck me hard. His hands went to my throat, and as he rhythmically pumped me deep, the pressure of his hands took me to the brink of unconsciousness and back until, as he gushed his cum, he didn't release the pressure and I blacked out.

218

I woke to the sound and the feel of the lashes on my back and buttocks. I was spread-eagled, belly down, on the bed, my wrists and ankles restrained at all four corners of the bed. He lashed me with the hand whip until I was fully awake and moaning and begging him to fuck me again. I much preferred that to this. When he came down on top of me, entered me, and began to pump, I whimpered the, "Yes, Yes, fuck me. Fuck me, Daddy, fuck me hard," that I knew he wanted to hear.

I must have passed the audition, because when he was done, had dressed, and released my restraints, he said, "You start at the bar tomorrow night at 8:00 p.m. The room you were in there is yours to sleep in. You may use this room until then. Get plenty of rest."

And then he was gone. I heard the powerful motor of his Mercedes start up and then silence. I lay there, assessing the damage, which wasn't all that much. Some welts and bruises. Once started, Kincaid gave me the impression that he was holding himself in check for now, but that he had so much more to give of what turned him on. I was still money in the bank to him now. I pulled myself up into a fetal position and moaned deeply.

"Are you OK?"

I turned my face toward the door to the room. Dan was standing there, looking very concerned.

"I will be," I answered in a weary voice. "Maybe in a hundred years."

"I have something that can help. Some salve. But it's over in my room behind the garage. If you give me a few minutes, I'll go over and get it and—"

"No, not here," I muttered. "I don't want to spend any more time in this room than I have to."

"I understand," Dan said. His voice was gentle and it was as if he really did understand—that this was a common occurrence here in Halfway. Suddenly, the little village wasn't benign anymore. I had now met the owner, the führer of the town.

"Can we go to the salve?" I asked, sitting up on the side of the bed, with effort. "In my satchel there. my shirt and trousers, please."

With trembling hands, Dan helped me to dress. He blushed as he touched tender skin. I knew what he'd like to have. I also knew that he probably was the only man in town who wouldn't simply take it given the opportunity and power to.

He was just as sensitive in applying the salve to my back and buttocks when we were sitting on the single bed in the small room he had off the back of the garage across the road from the motel. He clucked and groaned as he rubbed on the cream as if the wounds, the slight pain—I didn't want to overrepresent how much real damage Kincaid had done—were his as much as mine.

When he was done, I slid down onto my knees on the floor, pressing in between his knees.

He looked down at me, paralyzed with shock, a rumbling coming up from deep inside him, as I unzipped him and fished out his cock. He was hard, of course, and it was a very nice cock, maybe the nicest physical attribute of him. I rubbed the shaft against my cheeks and looked up and gave him a saucy look.

"God . . . no . . . you don't have to do this," he stammered, his face contorted and beet red.

"That's why I'm doing it," I said, "because I don't have to. I'm doing it because I want to."

He groaned and laced his fingers into my hair at the back of my head. There was a momentary pull of my head, as if he wanted to pull me away, but then I had his cock in my mouth and was sucking hard on his bulb. With a shudder, all of the tension went out of him, his hands cupping my head began to fall into the rhythm I was establishing of my lips gliding up and down his shaft, and he moaned in sheer ecstasy.

I didn't have to, and Dan certainly didn't expect me to, but I stretched out on his bed on my back then and let him explore my body with his hands at will—which he did at great length. He didn't suck me off, but he did stroke me to an ejaculation, and I gave him an award-winning performance with that, arching my back, writhing my hips against the slow pumping of his hand, grasping his elbow with my hand, whimpering for him, and, upon ejaculation, crying out for him to fuck me as I shot my load.

With coaxing, he took me in a side split from behind, and as long as he was behind me I could imagine it was the hunkiest of Hollywood actors mining my channel. There was nothing wrong with the size of his cock and what he could do with it. There was a brief awkwardness when I realized he had nothing in the room in the way of lube or condoms, but I was able to supply them from my satchel.

He fucked me slowly, shyly, continually asking me if it was good for me—if anything else he could do would be better. And it *was* good for me—especially when compared with the fast and furious fifteen-minute-max pokes by the truck drivers in the room over the bar on the other side of the bridge.

He apologized when he was finished and said he had to get back to the motel.

"No need to apologize. I wanted you," I said. "You took care of me with the salve. And then you really took care of me." He blushed at that. "Can I stay here tonight?" I asked, it suddenly occurring to me that the three places in this clutch of buildings that I now had rooms—the consignment store, the bar, and the motel—were all places I didn't want to be tonight.

"I don't know," he stammered. "I'm nothing like what you—"

"I want to spend the night here, with you, in this bed," I said.

This evoked a small smile, a deepening of the blush, and the hanging of his head. "Of course you can

221

stay here tonight," he said. He turned and headed for the door, but then stopped, and turned back to me. "And whenever you want to leave here, I'll drive you anywhere you want to go. I got a car right next to the room here."

I found that touching. After he'd gone and I'd showered in his small bathroom, I left to show up again at the consignment store next door. I'd promised to work a short shift there, and that's where the rest of my clothes and stuff were.

I had to laugh when I left his room and got a look at his ride. It was an old Buick LeSabre. I had arrived here in a new Buick and chances were good I'd leave in an old Buick. There was probably some irony in that, but I didn't want to think about that just then. At least it wasn't a semitrailer.

* * * *

I asked the bartender at the club what the usual lifespan of a pole dancer and rent boy at the club was, and he said "about two weeks." Thus, when at the two-week mark Julio, a cute little Hispanic trick, showed up to share the duty with me and another Hispanic, Juan, who had been here before and seemed a permanent fixture at the place, I wasn't surprised.

What surprised me more was how extensive Kincaid's holdings were. He had an "On the Road" special posted on the board behind the door into the bar, and I hadn't been working at the club for more than three days when I learned what that meant.

"This here is Mick," the bartender cum club manager told me one evening. "You'll be driving with him to near Philly to a truck plaza where Mr. Kincaid owns another club like this. He'll leave you there and you'll work the pole there until there's another 'On the Road' special from there back to here—or to near Harrisburg, where Mr. Kincaid has a club at another truck plaza. Got that?"

"But what's in it for Mick, here?" I asked. "What's so special about the special?" Mick was a big bruiser of a bearded mountain-man type who looked heavy but most of it was in muscle. He was maybe forty, tricked out in cowboy duds. He was leering at me like he would try to eat me in two bites.

"Mick here will have privileges with you between here and where he takes you and for three hours after delivery."

Mick proved to be quite virile and a quick reloader. He had his money's worth in the compartment behind the cab of his semi before he'd even driven out of the club's parking lot. He stopped four times between here and Philly and banged the hell out of me in the back of the cab.

In those two weeks I did an "On the Road" turnabout once to both the Philly and the Harrisburg ends. I usually, when in Halfway, slept in the room above the bar where I serviced men. Sometimes I just had to get out of the environment, and then I'd go to Dan in his room behind the gas station. He was always happy to see me. And I was happy to be with him too. He never got over the "lucky me" aspect. He'd been to massage school before becoming a "little bit of everything" at the Halfway gas station and motel, and whenever I came to him, full of tension from what I had to give men at the club, he relaxed me with a full-body massage before we had sex. He had magical hands, and I invariably had an ejaculation before we got to the main bout.

And when we did get to the main bout it was unlike having sex with any of the men at this club or the ones I'd had sex with before—even Larry. Dan improved in expertise with each successive fuck, and I quickly forgot he was no physical beauty because what he could do with his hands, tongue, and dick were a thing of beauty in themselves. Besides, he noticeably upgraded his wardrobe and was hitting the antiacne drugs hard since I arrived.

I had encounters with Kirk and Gus, too, the pair living above the consignment shop, but only on a couple of occasions. Being doubled took something out of me.

During the two weeks, Kincaid continued to show up at the club of evenings and oversee all that transpired. I could sense his eyes on me whenever I danced the pole and they followed me as I ascended the stairs with a john tagging behind me. I was waiting in fear and anticipation for the time he'd call me to go with him—and not just to the motel. When, as Kirk had warned me, that he'd tell me he wanted to drive me out to his farm.

That declaration came shortly after Julio was added to the roster of pole dancers, at the end of my first two weeks at the club.

As I'd come downstairs from servicing a john and was passing his table, Kincaid reached out and grabbed me by the wrist. "Tonight I want to take you home with me."

A shudder went up my spine. I knew it was a command, not a request. "Sure thing, Mr. Kincaid," I answered, and I turned from him so that he couldn't see the fear and concern in my face and moved toward the stage.

I didn't make it to the stage. Another hand shot out as I was moving between the tables, and I looked around, in shock, to see that the hand belonged to . . . Larry.

"Do you have to go back on stage just now, or can we talk for a few minutes?"

"I have a few minutes," I said, as I tried to control myself, still upset from the summons to Kincaid's farm after the show tonight and wondering how I was going to get out of that. I sat down at Larry's table. "Buy me a beer or I can't be sitting with you," I said. "And when the bartender comes over, slip him an extra twenty or I'll have to leave."

It felt good to make Larry pay to have to talk to me.

"I've missed you," he said when the bartender had been satisfied and we both had fresh beers. I didn't touch mine. I didn't want a beer. I needed some sort of escape plan. The irony didn't escape me that Larry was here. He wouldn't have come back, I didn't think, unless he wanted to pick up with me again.

"On your way back to Harrisburg?" I asked. "I wasn't aware that they'd called a special legislative session."

"They haven't," he responded. "I came from Philadelphia and am returning there—with you, I hope. I'm sorry; I shouldn't have left you here—to have to be doing this."

"No, you shouldn't have," I answered. I wasn't going to let him off the hook on that.

"I asked about you at the gas station and they told me you worked here. They remembered me letting you off there."

"Of course they would," I snapped at him. "It's not like people get abandoned on their doorstep every day of the week here."

"I said I was sorry. This isn't going well."

"Did you expect me to be all smiley face? You left me with nothing. Even took my suitcase. I had to rebuild here from nothing."

"I've missed you and know it was my fault—that I was in the wrong. I've come back to beg you to come to Philadelphia. To live with me in my apartment."

"Have you consulted with your wife and children on that—or the parents you say you live with?"

"There's none of that in Philadelphia. I just didn't know if I wanted to be living with a man openly—a half man, a transvestite. I'm not out; you know I'm not. Now, having tried to make it without you, I know that it doesn't matter. I need you. We can make it work."

"I don't know. I'll never know when the next time is coming that you'll abandon me somewhere."

"I won't. I promise."

He looked so hopeful. And it was a way out—a miracle of a convenience coming right at the right time, like this was some sort of Hollywood movie script. Everything coming together neatly in the end, and the happy couple riding off into the sunset in a new Buick to enjoy the happy ever after.

"You have your car here?"

"Yes, I'm parked out front."

"Let me get my things together then, and I'll meet you out there at your car in a few minutes."

I stood up from the table and prepared to walk away, but his hand shot out and he momentarily arrested my movement. He looked up at me with grateful, puppy dog eyes. "I'll treat you right this time, baby. It all will work out for the best. Trust me."

"I'm sure it will all work out for the best," I answered. As far as trusting him, though . . .

When I'd pulled what little I had together in the duffle I'd paid for in servicing two weeks previously, I left by the rear staircase and out the back of the building. Coming around the side of the building, I peeked around the corner and was able to pick out Larry's Buick. He was sitting in the driver's seat with his eyes glued to the front entrance of the place, assuming, I guess that I'd exit through that door.

Keeping semitrailer trucks between the Buick and me, I went out to the road, walked hurriedly across the bridge, and to the other side of Halfway.

Dan's eyes lit up when he saw me enter the door to his room behind the gas station.

"Get up and get dressed, Dan," I said. "It's time for you to give me that ride back to Harrisburg."

"Sure thing, Angel," he said, standing up immediately and reaching out to the chair beside the bed where he had his jeans and shirt folded. No argument and no hesitation. I could see that he was distressed, though, and disappointed.

"If you want, you could scrape together anything that you want to keep, and end up in Harrisburg with me," I said. "I'm sure you can get a job there that's better than you have here—maybe as a masseur. You have magic hands."

No hesitation there, either. His face lit up like a Christmas tree. I had no doubt what he wanted to do but he still asked, almost as if in disbelief, "Are you sure?"

"Yes, Dan, I'm very sure," I answered. And I was. It was time for me to settle down and to go more than half way in some direction too.

# Ever Rest at Evernew

"I don't right think he'll last the night, Massa. Land, I don't know what's taken' away the cream of our young men on this plantation."

"Leave me with him, Elvie. I'll see if I can give him some peace."

He watched until the woman had left the hut and then went over and silently shot home the bolt on the door. Returning to the pallet that took up much of the leaning, rough-wood cabin and was perched on a dirt floor, he looked down at the young darky who had once been so handsome, so robust, so giving and willing. He pulled the blanket away from the now withered, wasted body of the young man, naked save for the scrap of a loin cloth, the ebony slave still showing hints of the fine specimen he'd been just months before.

Some sort of wasting affliction.

He knelt down beside the young man and took the young slave's torso up into his arms, tenderly handling the now-thin body, stroking the chest and running his fingers around the navel on the flat belly.

"Can you hear me, Samuel?" he whispered in a low, soothing voice, his mouth close to the young man's ear.

"Yas, Massa," came the weak reply.

"I've come to give you rest, to smooth your journey home."

"Yas, Massa, thank you, Massa," the whimpered response.

He reached down with his free hand and loosened the knot of the loin cloth, pulling it away from the young man's privates. The cock lay long and limp against the slave's thigh, but it showed signs of life—greater signs than elsewhere in the young slave's body—as he encased it in a hand and coaxed it to stiffen. He nuzzled Samuel's neck with his lips and slid the points of his bicuspids down the side of the throat. Samuel rewarded him with a weak, but deep moan and the greater stiffening of his cock.

The master fumbled with the buttons on his own breeches, releasing his hardening cock. He coaxed Samuel's upper leg up and on top of his thigh, pulling Samuel's buttocks into position.

Samuel gave a low moan. "Yas, Massa. Please, Massa. Take Samuel to heaven, Massa."

"I am going to give you release now, Samuel," he whispered in the darky's ear.

"Yas, Massa," came the distant reply.

Samuel whimpered and gave a little jerk of his body, as the cock slowly pressed at his anus, invaded the channel, and began a slow, throbbing rhythm of penetration, short withdrawal, deeper penetration, short withdrawal, deeper penetration.

Samuel sighed and moaned, his own cock stiffening under the stroking hand of the master.

His face was turned toward that of his master, and his mouth was being pressed open by an insistent tongue for a deep kiss.

The stroking inside Samuel's passage picked up with intensity, and the young slave groaned from deep inside his collapsing body.

Then his mouth was free of the kiss and the lips were moving back to his throat. His head was being tilted away from the lover's searching lips, stretching Samuel's neck, exposing the barely throbbing vein there.

The slicing of the bicuspids into the vein in his throat was no more than a pin prick to Samuel now, and the sensation of the sucking of his blood through the embedded teeth came into sync with the now slow-pumping of the cock inside his channel as well as the stroking of his own cock encased in the master's hand.

"Massa, Massa, Massa. Take me, Lord," Samuel murmured. "Take Samuel on to paradise."

As Samuel gave his seed in a weak release, a stronger ejaculation creamed his channel deep, one last slurp at the throat was sounded, and Samuel's eyes rolled up into his head.

After gently laying Samuel back down on the pallet, rebuttoning his own fly, readjusting Samuel's loin cloth, and covering the young slave's fading body with the blanket, Philip DuCarde rose, looked around the cabin to see that all was in order, silently shot open the bolt of the door, and, a new spring in his step, emerged from the hut.

"He is resting now, Elvie," he said to the old slave woman sitting on a wooden bench across the path running in front of slave row. "He is at peace. But I am afraid that you are right—that Samuel will not last the night."

* * * *

Looking down on the orchestra level at Natchez' Institute Hall from the shadow of the box I was in, I was surprised at the turnout. The hall, construction having been completed the previous year, 1853, was the pride of Natchez, the only performance hall of its size and splendor on the Mississippi River between Memphis and New Orleans. The building, on South Pearl Street, almost on the banks of the Mississippi, had been designed for opera, and an opera was what had brought me, and so many others, out this evening.

I had come out of curiosity. Others apparently had come to observe who was and was not there. Institute Hall had quickly become the center of society in Natchez. I doubted that many had come because of the opera being performed, financed by an anonymous donor. I had made it my business to try to find out who had commissioned this, as my parishioners would expect me to. But I hadn't been able to find who had brought the controversial 1828 Heinrich Marschner opera *Der Vampyr* to the American south.

I tuned my ears into the gasps of discovery early in Act One as those in the orchestra section below learned of the content of the opera. I let my eyes wander around the hall and then drew back a bit into the shadows of my box as I saw, directly across from me in another box, the visage of the man who must be Philip DuCarde.

The DuCardes had been a prominent family in the area, owning various plantations on the eastern bank of the Mississippi both north and south of Natchez. Philippe DuCarde, a widower, though, had left suddenly and mysteriously some eighteen years earlier under conditions that were buried in the hazy gossip and legend of the areas. Something about questionable behavior and an uprising in society. I mainly was attentive to the stories behind this because my father had been a close associate of the DuCardes and had existed under something of a cloud in the city for some time after Philippe's departure. My father was too prominent in the town, though, to suffer for long—and suffer he did, from some sort of wasting disease after that, and he died some eight years later when I was barely eleven.

I hadn't withdrawn into the box soon enough, as I saw that the younger DuCarde was staring intently at me and turned to his companion—a friend of mine named

John Purnell, a young lawyer in the town—and gestured toward me. I was slightly disturbed to see John with him, but I was more disturbed by the aspect of John. I had not seen him in the last couple of months. In that time, he had been taken with some sort of sickness. He was pale and seemed listless. I marked the need to talk with him afterward. We were too close for me not to give him whatever help and solace I could in this condition. It occurred to me that he had not been to confession since the last time we were together—which was an occasion that begged for confession—by both of us.

As the curtain was being drawn for the first interval, an usher appeared at the back of my box and delivered to me, in a white-gloved hand, a note. "If you please, Father Hamilton," the usher whispered, "Mr. Philip DuCarde wishes to meet with you in reception room B during the interval." The note said essentially the same thing. I looked over to the other box as the lights came up in the hall and the hubbub of excited twittering crescendoed in the hall below. DuCarde's box was empty.

When I was ushered into reception room B, the attendant set the lock from the inside of the door, withdrew, and clicked the door shut. I was alone with Philip DuCarde, who was leaning his buttocks back on the top edge of a lounge chair, with his arms crossed over his chest and his eyes boring into me.

I thought of them immediately as boring, possessing eyes. They were in stark contrast to the rest of his visage. They were pale blue and compelling. Otherwise, he was a dark young man, not much older than I was, a product of the Cajun strain of families settled all up and down the lower Mississippi. His hair was dark and wavy, his face sharp-featured. He was of medium height, but his body was muscular, finely proportioned. His dress was elegant, more the style of European capitals than Natchez, a pioneer town still, despite its pretensions of culture and refinement, acquired via King Cotton wealth.

He was smiling knowingly at me, the line of his mouth slightly cruel, his teeth gleaming white and somewhat wolf-like, but not, in any way, subtracting from his attracting looks. I immediately was put on my guard. I had seen him with John Purnell, who knew me as no one else in Natchez did. I felt at a disadvantage—almost hunted, although I had no idea—at least not yet—why I should feel that way—other than the slightly canine aspect of the man's visage. I worried what John may have told him about me.

I also have to admit that I felt sexually aroused, and I worried about this too. I too easily fell under the spell of men like this. This younger DuCarde was a man of sensual beauty, with an aura of danger about him that I couldn't help but feel compelling.

"Is this Father Hamilton I see before me?" he asked. His voice was a smooth baritone, giving me the sensation of caressing my eardrums. All of the vibrations he was exuding were dangerous both to who I was supposed to be, rather than the paths I sometimes took, and to the weakness I had for certain strains of men. Everything about him was strongly male, overtly sexual. My mind raced with the image of me writhing under him, both of us naked, me fully possessed to my quick by his manhood, spiked to the ground by what now curled between his thighs.

"Yes, and I believe you are Philip DuCarde, master of Evernew on the Mississippi. I know your family was prominent here in years past and that several plantations along the river have remained in your hands. I, of course, along with many others, I'm sure, welcome you back into the parish. I hope to see you at mass."

"Our families were very close at one time, I understand," he said. And, yes, I did notice that he didn't respond to the invitation to appear at the mass.

"Yes, our fathers were close friends," I answered. "I barely knew your father before he departed." As I said that, though, my memory was stirred and I almost gasped at the realization that Philip DuCarde was the spitting image of my admittedly hazy image of his father. My mind probably was just rectifying the two, I reasoned.

"Extremely close friends, Yes," he said as he languidly pushed himself off the chair back he had been leaning on and came very close to me. "Intimate friends." His hand came up and touched my cheek. For some reason I didn't back away from him. Weaving through my mind was a voice—his voice—saying, "I will have you. I will possess you fully."

"I believe your father was ill when we moved away," he was saying out loud. "I do hope he recovered."

"Somewhat," I answered. "It was some sort of disease of lethargy. Somewhat like the mosquito-borne malaria so prevalent around here. But then not quite like that in symptoms. He recovered a bit but never completely."

"That's sad, I liked him immensely," DuCarde said, with a sigh that came across as not quite genuine. I didn't get the impression that he cared much how my father had died. "I am hoping that you and I can be very close friends too—intimate friends. You know, you look so much like your father did."

"Intimate friends?" I said, the echo in my voice of what he said showing a waiver.

"Yes, intimate. I think you know what I mean."

He wouldn't have been any older than I was when his family left Natchez. How could he know that I looked like my father? But then, I'd had the same thought about his father. Strange, though, that I couldn't surface a memory of Philip from that time.

The touch of his fingers was burning into my cheek. I have no idea why I permitted him that intimacy. But then, after what he next said, I had no choice.

"The intimacy between Philippe and your father was no different from what John has told me about your visits with him to the male brothels of New Orleans. I believe he said you are partial to muscular darkies. I believe you and I are going to be very intimate friends."

That was it, then. John Purnell had told him of our visits together to New Orleans—of our escapes from our roles in Natchez and giving in to our natural proclivities.

"You are a beautiful young man, Ham," he said, backing me up to the wall beside the door out to the corridor. "I wish for the same sort of intimacy with you that was shared with your father. The same that John says you share with the dominating prostitutes in the male brothels of New Orleans. Can you have such an intimacy with me, Hamilton? Can you open your thighs for me and let me in? I find the prospect arousing. I've never fucked a priest before."

He had me backed up against the wall, pressing my body with his, one of his hands cupping my basket, the other cupping my chin, stretching my neck up, and, after possessing my mouth fully with his, running his tongue down the side of my throat, over the vein I felt throbbing there.

I have no idea why I didn't resist him. But, of course, I knew why. I had wanted him inside me since I'd first seen him from across the theater.

"You are hardening nicely, Ham. You will spread your legs for me, won't you?"

"Yes," I answered, lost to him, both because of what he now held over me, thanks to John Purnell, but also because of the sheer magnetism of the man himself. His hand found my balls within the material of my tight breeches and he squeezed, causing my eyes to water. His teeth were sliding down the vein in my neck.

The bell rang for the audience to reform for the next act of *Der Vampyr*. DuCarde released me and gave a low laugh. "I want to drive you out to Evernew after the opera. To my home. To my bed. I want you to open your thighs for me there. I will fuck you as you've never been fucked before."

"Yes," was all the response I could give.

During the next interval, I descended to the lobby. I wanted to find John Purnell. I did so, but so shocking did he look—suffering from some form a malaria, I wagered, something that was draining him quickly—that he spoke before I had a chance to.

"I didn't tell DuCarde anything, Ham," he said. "He already knew—from sources in New Orleans. He demanded that I arrange an introduction with you. I'm his lawyer—and, as you can guess, a captive to his knowledge. He wants you to come out to Evernew. Something about witnessing papers or something. Perhaps a will. Nothing I am putting together for him, though. I'm sorry, Ham. I didn't tell him."

I would have spoken, to assure him it didn't matter because I was lost to Philip from the first moment I'd seen him, but DuCarde was there, nearby, now. The theatergoers were shrinking away from him, as if recognizing there was some strong force in their presence, as he moved toward us. I couldn't face standing here, in the lobby, chatting nonsense with him and John, the other theatergoers watching us, as I fantasized about him moving his hand up my thigh and to my privates, turning me, and covering me close from behind . . . penetrating me.

I couldn't fault John. And John obviously didn't know the full import of DuCarde's interest in me. I couldn't take standing here in a crowd with DuCarde, being both drawn to and repelled by him. Such was the magnetism of the man that I would have spread my legs for him right there in the reception room, if he had demanded it of me. I fled up the stairs to the side of the theater my box was in before DuCarde reached us.

I would be standing there, dutifully, on South Pearl Street, waiting for DuCarde's carriage to appear after the opera, even though my own lodgings at St. Mary Basilica rectory were but a short walk away on South Union Street. I would be standing there, knowing what I was moving toward—both fearful and melting in anticipation. Trapped by the threat of what the man knew but afraid—no, knowing—that I would have gone with him even without the threat.

* * * *

It was happening much sooner than I anticipated. We were still within the city, moving toward the river road and thus on toward Evernew, when DuCarde was covering me on the seat of the closed carriage. I was sideways on the bench seat, one knee on the seat and the foot of other leg on the floor of the carriage, leveraging on the sole of my boot to meet his thrusts with answering thrusts of my own. Both of our bodies were covered by his black cape, which rustled and undulated with the rise and fall of his buttocks as he trapped me under him and fucked me.

My breeches and undergarment were on the floor of the carriage, as was my clerical collar, which twinkled at me in the reflection of the passing light outside the carriage windows reflecting on the pure white of the collar—reminding me of how far I was going astray. I was hanging onto a side strap by the carriage window for dear life, as DuCarde covered me from above, both feet buried in the bench seat, leveraging for deepest penetration, and relentlessly plowing my nether channel deep with his cock.

No question or acquiescence was voiced between us as we settled in the carriage. He merely bored his eyes into mine as I started to disrobe and then presented myself, my private entrance, vulnerable and submissive, to his will.

My black shirt was pulled down to my shoulder on the side facing the front of the carriage, and my neck was stretched toward the back of the seat, pulled there by DuCarde's hand cupping my chin. His tongue was running across the bulging vein of my neck. I felt the scrape of his teeth there, and I moaned. His cock was deep inside me, thrusting, thrusting, thrusting.

The carriage gave a lurch and we suddenly were tumbling onto the floor and toward the right, as the carriage turned over on its side.

Quickly redressing, DuCarde and I both climbed up and out of the door that had once been at the side of the carriage and now was on top. We weren't yet out of the city, and people were gathering around. I recognized some of them. Some were from my parish.

"It's the wheel, Massa," the grizzled carriage driver said, as he stood beside the turned carriage. He'd managed to free the horses, pulling the carriage in time so that they didn't go down as well. "The wheel done give way. I has sent George to the nearest stable for another carriage." George was the slave boy footman for the carriage.

Once of my parishioners came up to me. "Do you need assistance, Father Hamilton?" he asked. "My carriage is just back there. I can take you to the rectory, if you wish."

"Yes, please, and thank you, Francis," I said, turning an eye of both apology and fright toward Philip DuCarde. He had moved too far too fast. I needed a breather, some space, a little time to think this out. Most of the shock was directly to myself, though. I had been fully submissive, surrendering to him without any demand having been voiced. He had fucked me as if by natural right, and I had bowed to him.

DuCarde just smiled and said, "Another time then."

"Yes," I murmured. "Another time."

"I have unlimited time—and patience," he said as I turned to follow Francis Martin to his carriage.

We both knew that he only had to level his eyes at me and I would lie on my back and open my legs to him.

\* \* \* \*

Philip crept in through the back door of John Purnell's townhouse on Orange Avenue. The rest of the family was at evening mass at St. Mary Basilica. But John was home, upstairs, in bed, too weak to attend mass.

DuCarde moved silently up the stairs and to John's bedroom. Purnell was lying on his back in the heavy four-poster bed, breathing shallowly, his eyes gazing up into the canopy of the bed, not really focusing on anything. He flinched at the sound of DuCarde entering the room, but he didn't look down. He was barely moving at all, as if it would take all of the strength he had to turn his head.

"It is I, Philip, come to give you rest."

"Philip?" Purnell whispered. "Ah, Philip."

"You wish me to put you to peace, don't you?" DuCarde asked in the low, smooth, soothing baritone of his seeking voice.

"Yes, oh yes," Purnell answered, his voice quiet, resigned.

Philip walked to the bed and looked down at Purnell. He reached over Purnell's legs, grasped the hem of his night breeches, and pulled them off, leaving Purnell naked. His body was once robust; now it was thin, close to emaciation. He was a handsome young man still, though.

DuCarde carefully stripped off his own clothes, folded them, and laid them on a chair within reach. He placed his hands on Purnell's legs as he whispered, "Look at me, John."

With effort, Purnell looked down the length of his body and took in the magnificent naked body standing at the foot of his bed. DuCarde was in full erection.

"Do you want me to give you my peace, John? Say it. This is the reckoning time."

"Yes, Philip, oh yes. Take me away. Fuck me to paradise." Purnell now too was hardening.

DuCarde came up onto the bed, slowly, deliberately raising, spreading, and bending Purnell's emaciated legs as he moved up between them.

Purnell gasped and gave a little jerk as DuCarde pressed the bulb of his cock at Purnell's entrance, moved inside, and then pressed in to the hilt. He held Purnell's legs, bent, against his sides while he established a slow rhythm of the fuck.

Purnell looked up into DuCarde's face through glassy eyes. "Yes, Philip, yes."

DuCarde leaned his torso down toward Purnell's chest and covered the young lawyer's lips with his, pressing his tongue inside. Purnell sighed for him. A hand came up to Purnell's head, the fingers lacing themselves into his hair, pulling his head to the side and stretching his neck out. DuCarde came out of the kiss, lifted his face from Purnell's and smiled benignly down at the other man. His mouth opened in a smile. His bicuspids gleamed and showed large and pointed.

Purnell sighed and gave a little moan, his arms lifting with great effort and embracing DuCarde's broad back, as DuCarde lowered his face to Purnell's extended neck, licked the slightly throbbing vein there for a brief moment before the teeth sliced into the vein and the sounds of sucking began.

Purnell moved his body against DuCarde's, his hands pressing and releasing on DuCarde's shoulder blades, in weak rhythm to the rising and falling of DuCarde's hips, the plowing of his cock, the sucking sounds of the draining of the blood. He sighed, and weakly whimpered. "Yes, take me to heaven, Philip. I see the light; I hear the music."

His head flopped over to the side and his cock released a small spurt of cum as DuCarde ejaculated deep in his channel and lifted his head and howled to the canopy of the bed above him.

Purnell was breathing in very shallow, off-rhythm pants as DuCarde pulled his sleeping breeches back up his legs, dressed, and stole out of the room and the house.

\* \* \* \*

God, he was big, and going deep. Showing me no mercy. Crueler than he'd been in the carriage, able to reach deeper. God, I was loving this. I was on his bed—at Evernew—on my belly, buttocks raised on trembling knees, as, covering me close, trapping my arms above my head by gripping my wrists, he took me in long, hard, thick thrusts.

I had reached Evernew after dusk, brought by the carriage he'd sent for me in Natchez, both of us knowing I would come to him. The carriage had come to me in mid-afternoon, not long after I was back from conducting the funeral for John Purnell, and while I was rereading John's obituary in the newspaper. Some sort of wasting disease, the report said. Nothing more specific than that. Just like my father, although taken by it quicker. I had seen the hand of death on him that night at the opera.

Then I heard the carriage stop outside the rectory, the doorbell chime, and Mrs. Roberts bringing me the note of summons. It had told me to pack a bag and come at once.

"The return of an important family to the parish," I told Mrs. Roberts. "They must be made welcome. A very wealthy family. I will be gone at least for the night."

She had readily understood and helped me quickly pack, sending me off at the doorstep with a smile and a wave. I hoped she hadn't seen how badly I was trembling as I entered the carriage.

I entered the house at Evernew in the dark. The house was only dimly lit by candlelight. Philip stood at the railing of the bridging hall linking the two wings about. He was naked, his body gloriously muscled and proportioned, his dark body hair covering his chest, belly, thighs, arms, and groin in artful curls. His long, thick cock curving up proudly and cruelly from the curls of his bush. An animal, a wolf, ready to do animal coupling. Animal coupling with me. Primeval. Nothing but lust and need. He met me at the top of the stairs, pulling me close to him, grabbing the hair on the back of my head and arching my head back, painfully. His mouth possessed mine, forcing mine open, his tongue going deep. Pulling the tongue out he growled and bit my lip, drawing blood. Despite the involuntary yelp, I was grasping his bare buttocks with my hands, holding him close to me, feeling the hardness of him. I was already panting hard when he told me to go to his bed, strip, and lay on my belly.

When he came down on top of me, his chest went down between my legs, his hands gripping my hips. Coaxing me to raise up a bit on my knees, his hands went to separating and squeezing my buttocks, and his mouth alternated between opening my entrance and pulling my cock through my thighs to suck it and my balls.

I was writhing under him, moaning, panting hard, and begging for him to be inside me when he went up on his knees between my spread thighs, worked his thick cock inside me, and began to pump. He brought the silkiness of his chest down on my bare back, and I turned my face to his for a deep kiss. He ran his fingers into my hair and pulled my head to one side. His tongue licked its way down my cheek and onto my throat where it ran lovingly down the vein popping out of my neck from my head being turned hard to the side.

I felt a prick at my throat, but most of my attention was concentrating on the mining of my passage by his impossibly thick and long cock, seemingly growing in

242

possessing length and girth as he pumped me. A warm, sensual feeling overtook me—a feeling of well-being, of being in perfect harmony with the elements. I could feel the pulsing at my neck and hear the suckling sound, but it didn't alarm me. I was floating, feeling oh so sexy and well taken care of. I was moving my pelvis in consort with the thrusts of his cock, opening and closing my fists buried in the bedspread to the rhythm of the fuck.

I had never been fucked as divinely as this before. I sighed deeply and murmured, "Yes, yes, fuck me just like this. Fuck me to heaven."

"Or to hell," he muttered under his breath. It gave me no pause. He was giving me what I had dreamed of receiving from him. Heaven or hell? At that moment, I didn't give a damn.

Philip moved a hand under my chest. I sensed he wanted to turn me on my back and fuck me in another position. But then I heard him yelp and pull his hand away, like it had been burned. And as I saw it flash by, it *did* look singed. I couldn't really tell, though, in the dim light. He had pulled away from me and was off the bed. I saw his naked buttocks disappearing out of the door to the corridor as I sat up in bed. Instinctively, I reached for the gold cross that hung on a chain around my neck. It felt hot to my touch.

It felt like it was damning me. Of course I shouldn't be here, in a man's bed, being covered and fucked by a man, a man hirsute enough to give a delicious animalistic tinge to the coupling. I was a priest. This was one of the worst sins I could be performing.

But he was so compelling, so arousing—so much the natural animal performing naturally. I couldn't help myself. I slipped the cross necklace off my neck, left the bed, and tucked it into the pocket of my breeches. That wouldn't damn me while I was here. My eyes found the clerical collar, though, gleaming white. Pure, chaste. A purposeful symbol. A promise I had not, could not fulfill. That too I tucked away in a pocket.

I lay back on the bed, my legs bent and spread, pillows under the small of my back, ready and willing in anticipation for Philip's return. He didn't return that night, though. I waited, awake for more than an hour, moving a hand from my shimmering cock to my neck, where it felt like I'd been stung and was warm to the touch. Then back to my cock, encasing it, stroking it, dreaming of the euphoric world I'd been in while Philip was fucking me, a sensation of contentment and satiation as I'd never felt before from a man between my thighs, a monster cock inside me, growing and thrusting, thrusting and growing. I gave up my seed in three long arcs and, with a sigh, drifted off to sleep.

\* \* \* \*

The next morning I descended the stairs, wearing a white shirt and brown breeches. Banished were my black priest's vestments, white collar, and the gold cross necklace. I could not be a priest today. All I could think of was lying under Philip, becoming one with Philip. But I found no evidence of Philip about. Only elderly slaves, mostly women, and one grizzled old man, the driver of the carriage, who also seemed to function as the house's butler.

"No, Massa, Great Massa never appears in the day. He moves at night and sleeps in the day. I wouldn't expect to see him about again until this evening. He said that you might like to ride the plantation today."

Indeed I did choose that pastime as I waited for Philip to be about again—to, I hoped, renew his working of my body—working me in ways I'd never experienced before. I didn't know what had pulled him away from me the previous night. But I was determined for us to overcome that, to move on from where we had left off.

We had just reached a level of totally synchronized movement, getting the most from a glorious fuck. The sense of him feverishly consuming me was sending shudders up my spine.

It took me the rest of the daylight to cover Evernew and the adjacent DuCarde-owned plantations. I was struck while riding the grounds of Evernew plantation to find only women, of all ages, and boys and old men working the fields. I would have expected to see young men too. I had wanted to see young, muscular, black bucks working the fields, stripped down to the waist. Watching them and imagining one of them between my thighs, working my channel with a thick cock—like I enjoyed in the brothels of New Orleans; the only disadvantage of coupling with Philip. He wasn't a black buck.

But there were none to be seen at Evernew proper. The wonder of this was that there were children around. There were women of child-bearing age, in abundance. Some even with seeded bellies. They must have been plowed by some younger man rather than the bent-over old men I saw in the fields. But none were in evidence. So the scarcity must have been something happening fairly recently. I didn't connect that with the reappearance on the scene of Philip DuCarde.

As my wanderings took me farther from Evernew, I did begin to see young, black bucks working in the fields. They were as muscular as I dreamed under the strain of the hard field work. Near the banks of the Mississippi, I left the saddle of my horse, tying the reins to a tree near a puddle of water and a lush stand of grass to give the horse a respite.

The stand of trees was bordered by a cotton field on the other side of the stand of trees from the riverbank. I stood there, watching the slaves at work, admiring the physiques of the young, black bucks. One, in particular, was noticing me, as well. I recognized the look he was giving me—of lust and want—and a touch of anger. Those were the black bucks I paid for in New Orleans— the ones who wanted to break me as much as fuck me. It was the penance I pretended was sufficient—that they leave me broken and gasping, beyond satisfied. The sin and the recompensing penance combined in one.

I knew how to return such a look. I stripped off my shirt and gave him a smile. I knew that I had a body to please a man who appreciated a well-worked torso. He unlaced the codpiece of his breeches and let a huge, half-hard cock flop out, probably trying to shock me. I didn't flinch. I just stood there, staring him down, a smile on my face. He looked around for an overseer or other observing field hand and, seeing none, looked back at me and inclined his head, his hand going to his cock and giving it a couple of shakes.

I inclined my head in answer, turned, and slowly walked into the trees.

The big black buck fucked me as I reclined between the roots of a giant oak tree close to the bank of the Mississippi. Both of us made guttural, animal rutting sounds as he pushed his knees between my spread thighs, held my legs, bent, spread, and raised in the crook of his arms, and thrust hard and deep.

It was just the fuck I needed. No talking—indeed, I had no idea if he could speak English or not; his body was so magnificently native, tattoos crudely burned into the puckered skin of his chest and back, that he could have come straight out of Africa to between my legs. Just grunting and groaning, thrusting and breeding. Fucking like animals. Seeding me, but just taking three big breaths, grunting threatening, prepared to cuff me and put me back under him if I dared try to escape, which I had no intention doing. And then thrusting inside again, the cum permitting more vigorous thrusting. Me thumping and clawing at his chest while he, positioning his face close to mine to watch my reaction to the wild thrusts of his cock, sneering and, no doubt, taking out on me all of his hate and frustration toward his white overlords.

He probably expected me to die under his assault and then to just roll my body into the river. But I took everything he had to give and collapsed over to the side after he'd pulled out of me, grasped my hair, and forced my mouth down onto his cock to clean it. With just a grunt then, probably angry anew had his anger hadn't killed me, he was gone, melting away into the cotton field, his eyes scanning in all directions for evidence of an armed overseer, and I remained, whimpering and sighing as the golden fingers of the sunset spread across the wide Mississippi at my feet. Broken, but freed, I told myself by the penance I had taken—until the next time I strayed.

Philip was sitting at a grand piano in the main parlor of Evernew when I returned to the house, nearly hobbling, as I mounted the portico steps. His playing was expert. Yet another surprise about Philip. I wondered how many surprises there were in him that I didn't know about.

I started to shrug my shoulders back into my shirt as I entered the room.

"No, leave it off," he said as he saw me. "I am, as you can see, bare-chested too."

I certainly could see that. I normally wasn't aroused by hairy men. But the pattern of the hair on his chest and down the centerline of his torso was sexy and made me want to take my eyes lower than that. Knowing already how magnificently he was equipped didn't take the wonder away of imagining the view below the beltline.

"You aren't wearing your clerical vestments tonight. Good. Come here; sit with me."

I went to him. No mention of why he'd left me so abruptly the previous night. I did notice that his hand was bandaged, though. I didn't feel that he wanted me to ask about what had gone wrong, so I didn't. He pulled me down into his lap, facing the piano, and placed my hands on the keys. Positioning my fingers, he caused me to play a simple tune. His chin was on my shoulder, his lips buried in the hollow of my neck, kissing, licking, and nipping with his teeth there. I didn't think he even was looking at the keyboard, and yet he was able to manipulate my fingers to play recognizable tunes.

"You play remarkably well," I murmured.

"I want to play your body as well as I play this piano."

"I want that too," I admitted in a low, hoarse voice.

"I want you to come upstairs with me now," he growled. I could feel from the strength of his cock against the small of my back that he wanted me. "Just you, nothing from the church."

"No, nothing from the church," I murmured, laying my head back on his shoulder and turning my face to his for a deep kiss.

"Take me to hell," I whispered.

"You know I will," was his answer.

\* \* \* \*

Just like the black slave on the banks of the Mississippi, but harder, more intense. I was on my back on Philip's bed, my legs bent, my heels dug into the mattress, leveraging my counterthrusts upward, as Philip knelt between my thighs, slamming deep and hard up inside me. One hand trapping one of my wrists above my head to the surface of the bed. The other hand gripping my throat and holding my head hard into the mattress. I was clawing at his bicep with my free hand, gagging at the grip of his hand on my throat, fighting for air, but moving my pelvis in hard counterthrust to him, taking him as hard and deep inside me as I could. The black buck hadn't been able to take me out of this world. Perhaps Philip could.

Like the black slave, he brought his face close to mine, capturing my eyes with his pale-blue orbs to watch my reactions to the thrusting of his cock and the clutching of his hand on my throat. I stared back, a stare of willingness, acceptance, challenge. Do your worst, my gaze tried to convey to him. It's what I need. It's my penance. The sin must have its penance.

A leery smile from him, just like that of the black slave. The mouth opened. I saw the prominence of the bicuspids. I hadn't noticed how canine his smile was before. His hand left my throat and went to the side of my head, his fingers lacing into my blond, curly hair, pulling my head sharply to the side.

A brief look of triumph in his face and then the face dipped to my exposed throat. I let out a cry and jerked hard as the sharp teeth tore into my throat. Slicing deep, cruelly, feeling my blood pump from me into him, an exchange for the cum he had pumped into me.

Writhing under him, I fought, but not for long. The feeling of warmth, of well-being, of being as one with him, overtook me and I relaxed under his control—his physical, mental, and emotional control. I was fully his now, and we both knew it. He was going to fully use me and put me to rest. The thrusting of his cock continued, but not as frenetic as before, and I now discovered that I could move my pelvis in perfect sync with the digging of his cock, which was thickening and lengthening in consort with his snuffling, all-consuming feeding at my throat. My channel walls were stretched to the limit, ready to split and shred as his throbbing cock thickened, became increasingly demanding.

My knees moved with the fuck, moving out as his cock pulled back, sometimes nearly bringing the bulb back to the entrance and then coming in, hugging his hips close, as he plunged deep inside me. My hands went to his shoulder blades, opening and closing their grip on his hard flesh in perfect rhythm to the fuck. His sucking at my neck was in perfect rhythm as well.

"Yes, fuck me, suck me, take me completely, release me," I murmured over and over again, as I became lightheaded. I was floating on the clouds. Not a worry in the world. I knew what he was, what he was doing. And I didn't care. I wanted him to have as much pleasure as he possibly could off my body.

I roused in a double explosion, my eyes opening wide, cries in harmony—from Philip as well as me—as we both exploded in a massive, shared ejaculation. A flash of fright went through my body, as he pointed his face toward the ceiling and let out a haunting howl.

I was fully his.

I drifted off afterward, all quiet except for the sound of the suckling at my throat, Philip's cock flaccid, but deep inside me. Snuffling at my throat, a lick along the vein line, and then the prick once again of the teeth, and the sound of the ocean in my inner ears as my vein pulsed and Philip fed. The draining sensation, lightheadedness, the glow of a bright light from afar and the sound of eerie music.

It wouldn't be long now, I knew. Release was at hand.

When I woke, I was on my stomach. My arms and legs were extended to and tied off at the four corner posts of the bed. Pillows were stuffed under my midsection. The drapes were pulled, but I could see around the edges of them that it was daylight. I didn't feel as drained as I had the previous night when I blacked out. I was regaining strength. But I was restrained, so I wasn't going anywhere. My master wanted more pleasure from my body. I would hang on, not succumb now. I must give him the full measure of pleasure.

Nighttime again, lifting my buttocks in the air. Philip came down on top of me, stretching out on me, close. Entering my ass and beginning to pump. He grasped my hair and pulled my head to the side. His teeth slit into the vein at my neck, and he noisily began to feed.

I didn't care. I never felt as close to a person before as this—as well taken care of as this—as aroused and sensual as this. I set my pelvis in motion against his stroking, surprised a bit at how much effort it took. I drifted off into a haze, listening to the sucking sounds at my neck. Taken fully by my lover. Wanting him inside me, needing him inside me. Giving everything I had to my lover, because I couldn't get enough of what he gave to me. Jolted once more by the howl at the moment of ejaculation.

Suspended over the side of the bed, in Philip's arms, holding me close from behind, his cock up inside me, moving in and out, deep, shallow, then deep again. Not exactly standing on my own. I doubted I had the strength to stand. One arm around my midsection, palming my belly with his hand, holding me up, bent over toward the bed. The other hand buried in my hair, pulling my head back into the hollow of his neck and twisting it to the side. Teeth slicing into the vein of my exposed, shredded neck, sucking, suckling.

"Yes, yes, take me to paradise; take every ounce of pleasure you can from my body. I surrender all." Not knowing if I had had the strength to say that out loud. But it was what I wanted to convey. I wanted him to take me now, all the way, all the way to paradise. The paradise of that bright light, the ethereal music, the sense of sitting on a fence, not caring which side I fell on but feeling the sensation of the beginning of a slow fall—in some direction.

Barely awake again, head buzzing, having difficulty forming a thought. On my back. No restraints this time. None needed. I wasn't going anywhere. I could barely lift my hands, let alone move off the bed. Philip kneeling between my thighs, pulling my legs up to a bent position. My not being able to hold them there myself. Just letting

251

them flop to the side. With a little laugh, he pulled them up into his hips with his hands. Positioning his cock at my now-gaping hole, reamed to his requirements at his thickest, he easily slid inside, deep. Whispering in my ear, a voice of awe, "You have lasted longer than any of the rest."

Fucking me there, like that, to his ejaculation, his howl, my weak-flow response.

Too tired. Too tired to care. Craving for the sensation of the pulsation at my neck, the feeding of my lover, giving over everything I had, my very essence of life, to my lover.

Holding there, waiting to harden again, he lowered his face to mine.

"I'm going to give you peace now," he murmured, his smooth baritone voice honey to my soul. "It has been glorious, but it's time."

"Yes, take me to heaven," I whispered back.

He laughed, a low, guttural laugh. "Just so, or maybe to hell," he said. "You know, you were the best. Over the centuries you still were the best. I couldn't resist; I couldn't space you out. I had to have all of you at once. Your father was good, but you are the best, and you know why?"

"No, why?" I murmur, not really caring why, but he seemed to want to tell me. And whatever Philip wanted, I wanted as well. Anything, as long as he took me to heaven again, let me dance and float on the clouds to the sensation of his suckling at my throat. As long as he brought me to the bright light, the heavenly choir, the fence.

"Because you are a priest, of course. Taking the godly and bringing it low. Making it knuckle, bow, and scrape to me. Begging me for my attentions. I couldn't prolong that. I had to use you in one orgy of victory over heaven. The dark forces winning. Truly, I tell you, that I take you to hell."

"I was never a very good priest, you know. I'm not sure I count for much in either heaven or hell."

It wasn't the right thing to say to him—at least he obviously didn't think so. But I was beyond rationalizing or gauging what I was saying. Still, it was the simple truth. I now fully realized it. I would be no loss to the church. I wanted him to stop talking and to go back to fucking and sucking me. And I could feel him going hard again inside me. Raising his anger had helped make him hard. He began to fuck me hard. Thrusting deep, cruelly.

It was what I wanted, though. The only penance I knew to offer. He was leaning in, his face close to mine again, a hard leer on his face.

I turned my head to the side, exposing my neck to him. Offering him the ultimate sacrifice. It was the first time I had offered my vein to him. His eyes opened wide, and I gave him the beatific smile I had learned to bestow on parishioners at the seminary.

"Your sins are forgiven, my son," I murmured.

His head dove down, his teeth cruelly digging into my neck. The sucking, hard and cruel, commenced immediately. This was it. We both knew that. Painfully, slowly, I moved my hands down to his buttocks and held them there as he thrust hard up inside me, again and again, angrily, insistently. I grasped his buttocks to me and weakly moved my pelvis with him, wanting him to know I accepted him to the end.

I was floating again, off toward heaven again. At peace, entirely satiated and at one with Philip's body, every part of his body synchronized with mine in the working, the draining of mine. I felt my ejaculate spread up his belly. My hands fell away from his buttocks, my body fully his now to do what he wished. I stretched my arms out straight from my body, my body completely open to him.

"Take me, I am fully thine."

I heard the music, coming in gently over the sound and feel of suckling at my neck. My ears were buzzing underneath the sound of the music, which was fading away. I felt myself totally relaxing, beginning to fall away from the fence, hearing the sucking sounds of his mouth, the slap, slap of his thrusting cock.

The howl as he released his seed. But a different sort of howl—more forlorn, ending in pain and frustration, rather than one of victory.

I felt so at peace, so "I don't care," so loving of the release he was providing me, so . . .

\* \* \* \*

I was surprised—disappointed—when I woke up and realized I wasn't in heaven—or the other distinct possibility, hell. That wouldn't have surprised me in the least. I was lying on Philip's bed, and daylight was filtering around the edges of the drapes on the window again. Somehow, I had survived the night—unless, of course, this was what heaven—or hell—were like. Wouldn't that be ironic? Heaven—or hell—was Philip's bedroom at Evernew?

I lay there for some time, taking inventory. I was semiparalyzed, but the slow increase in aches and pains—and the sound of my own groans—informed me that I was beginning to regain strength. But I knew I would not survive another night of this. I had no idea why I hadn't passed in the previous night—or maybe the night before that. I'd lost all concept of time. All I knew was pain, and the heightened awareness of how much higher my sexual satisfaction could soar than I ever realized before.

Not that that was doing me much good. It was something to contemplate if I survived another sunrise.

My attention was arrested by the clinking sound approaching up the staircase. I looked down the length of my naked and bruised body and saw the grizzled old driver cum butler walk into the room carrying a tray laden with food on porcelain plates. He lowered the tray to the foot of the bed and went over to the windows, one by one, and pulled the drapes. Blinding light flooded the room.

"I thinks you need to try to eat your fill of this food and rest a while before trying to rise, Massa," he said as he turned and walked over to the side of the bed. There was no sign of judgment in the old man, and, indeed, I presumed that he had seen all, knew all.

"Philip? Master DuCarde?" I managed to croak out. My throat was dry, and I realized that I was ravenously hungry as well as thirsty. How many days had I been on this bed?

"Massa Philip, he done packed up and left before daybreak," the old man said. "I think it be a while before he visits Evernew again." Did I catch a glint of a smile float across the old man's face?

"Left?"

"Yas, sir. And I think you be needin' this back," he said, as he drew my gold cross on the chain out of his pocket and handed it to me. "Sorry. I had to borrow it for a bit last night." The satisfied smile on his face spoke volumes to me. "If I was you, young Massa, I'd be keepin' that closer to me in the future. And I'd be lookin' at it and thinkin' about it more, too."

I had to admit that he had a good point.

# Summer's End at Spirit Lake

The next-to-the-last weekend had now descended for the gang at Spirit Lake before summer ended and we scattered again to our respective colleges and "whatever" activities. Giddiness was high, which is saying something for the group of friends from the affluent Atlanta uptown district of Buckhead, but we'd been on the other edge of giddy every weekend we'd come down to the lake. Somehow I think we all knew this would be the last summer we'd gather at my parents' big old Victorian "cottage" on the Woodland side of the lake. It just wasn't the same without David Alexander, our erstwhile leader. The titular role had devolved on me—it was my family's vacation house we came to for our partying and debauching—but I just couldn't live up to David's role in the group—nor did I want to.

It was Saturday afternoon and, having mostly recovered from the party the night before, the six of us had piled into Danny Alexander's '55 fire-engine-red Cadillac Series 62 convertible for a "who knows where?" boredom-fighting road cruise, which Danny decided would be a slum run around the lake. The white-black class line, still strong in the Georgia of the mid fifties, ran down the middle of the lake from north to south. On the western side of the lake, on the outskirts of the town of

Woodland, the manicured shoreline was lined with piles of Victorian-style wood monstrosities on verdant lawns owned by rich families like mine, the Maddoxes. The other side of the lake, with the small town for coloreds—the folks who served us on our side of the lake—that we called Coon Town, was where the "others" lived. The shore on their side of the lake was swampy and mostly undeveloped, just waiting for the vacation resort developers of the sixties to "gentrify" that side of the lake and push the coloreds out.

Although this was the second summer for the Alexander family's Cadillac convertible to be strutting around the lake—last year with Georgia University tennis star David Alexander in the driver's seat—it hadn't had quite the same impact this year on the Woodland side. A year-old bright red Cadillac convertible was still a head turner, but not so much with tall, gangling, trying-to-get-on-the-Georgia-basketball-team little brother Danny behind the wheel. This Saturday afternoon Danny's attempt to live up to his brother's aura had apparently caused him to decide to try to wow them with the car on the Coon Town side of the water.

As the current supposed leader of the "Wild Ones," I should probably have been doing the driving, but the Alexander senior's dictum had been "No one but Alexanders at the helm of the Cadillac," and the six of us wouldn't have fit in my jet-black '54 Ford Thunderbird convertible anyway.

The six of us—once seven, with a leader, and now a loosely and mournfully bonded six—the tight little group from Buckhead, known as the Wild Ones. There certainly were more than those at the summer weekend parties at my family's lakeside cottage whatever night the Wild Ones were in residence—some added partiers coming by land and others by boats on the lake—but by day we reverted to the core group. Everything revolved around the six of us in this Cadillac rounding the northern head of the lake and nosing our way toward Coon Town.

The three young men in the car all were jocks—or, in Danny's case, a jock wannabe—at the University of Georgia in Athens, having been a "group" under the tutelage of athletic standout David Alexander since our high school days in Buckhead. The young women in the car also were from the Buckhead neighborhood, but, as they'd been jock groupies since high school, try as they might, the group just didn't revolve around them—certainly not in Georgia in 1956.

The group had always revolved around David Alexander, state tennis champion in his senior year at Georgia the previous year. As I've noted, a loose version of leadership had devolved this summer to me, now a college sophomore—my sports at Georgia were rowing and swimming—mainly because I, Lee Maddox, had the summer house at the lake and David was irrevocably gone. The "honor" had been dumped in my lap when David, out of college and newly in the Air Force, had nosed his P-80 Shooting Star training jet fighter into the ground at Moody Air Base near Valdosta the previous fall. Danny was trying to fill in his big brother's shoes in the group, but until he actually made the Georgia basketball team, he wouldn't be fully believable. He also hadn't achieved the maturity even of the college freshman that he was.

The third young man, Thad Price, an upcoming junior at Georgia, had age seniority in the group now, but, despite being a star All-State fullback on the Georgia football team, he'd had his head rattled on the field a few too many times to be making decisions about nearly anything.

Of the women in the car, Chas—who, for obvious reasons we had named thusly to avoid her given name of Chastity—was the floater, also known as the group punch. Anybody and everybody who had tooled around with the

Wild Ones from Buckhead's North Atlanta High School on had had her, with no one claiming her as a steady. Everyone had had her but me, that is, with that missing dangler on her charm bracelet driving her nearly crazy. I'd already had to remove her hand from my crotch twice on our Saturday afternoon ride around the lake. I was wedged in the middle of the backseat of the Caddie with her to my right.

She should have known why I hadn't had her, but she was ever the optimistic dreamer.

To my left was Maggie Campbell, who was still half drunk from the previous night—her usual condition in her grief. Maggie had hung on David Alexander from early days in North Atlanta High and had followed him to Georgia U. He'd been everything to her, and she hadn't been fully sober since his death. She was trying to substitute Danny for him, apparently thinking that clinging to him and keeping him between her thighs was the answer to her grief. Danny was taking advantage of that. While Chastity was trying to paw me in the backseat, Maggie was leaning forward in her seat, pressed against the back of the driver's seat, running her fingers through Danny's hair and nibbling on his ear. There was a frenetic, surrealistic aspect of Maggie's hanging on Danny, as if it disgusted even her that she clung so tightly to him—and that he wasn't David, and could never be David.

The other two in the front seat were plastered against each other, giving Danny plenty of lateral room in the land boat to try to see the road through Maggie's waving fingers. Thad Price and June Milton had also been a couple from North Atlanta High days, when he was a standout on the football team and June was a cheerleader. June, like Chas, wasn't going to college. Chas was majoring in adding men to her charm bracelet and June was majoring in leading Thad down the aisle as soon as he graduated from college. None of us were hurting for money—all were attached to lucrative family businesses—

so jobs didn't need to be a large part of our future planning or present concern.

We were strutting through Coon Town—I couldn't put the low speed Danny was taking on this stretch of the road any better than that—when he swung the Caddie into a rundown Texaco service station that I wasn't even sure was open.

"What are you doing, Danny?" I asked from the backseat. "We don't need gas. You filled it when we hit Woodland on Thursday."

"I want to help the local economy," he said, with a sneery laugh that told me this was the least of his motivations.

Then, as we pulled up to a rusting gas pump, I saw that the place was open. A massively built, the emphasis on built, black guy came sauntering out of the ramshackled service bay and headed toward us.

"Say, isn't that the guy who sometimes plays the banjo to LeRoy Brown's piano back in Woodland?" Chas asked, suddenly all attention to the guy with big chest and bicep muscles, trim waist, and bulging crotch.

Maggie confirmed that we had, indeed, seen him on the banjo at the honky-tonk called just that, the Honky-Tonk, on the edge of Woodland, where we went when we wanted to slum on the white side of the lake. I knew that his name was Sam Jackson. He was about our age and could have flattened Thad in a football game or any other sport I could name. A big, strapping, handsome black. Wearing just coveralls and barefooted, showing bulging biceps and the promise of the same from his pectorals along the edges of the coverall bib.

"Can I do for you?" he said, as he walked up to the car.

"Yes, indeedy, you can do for me," Chas muttered under her breath, although possibly—and purposely—not low enough for Jackson not to hear her.

"You sell gas here, don't you?" Danny asked. His voice was condescending. He'd stopped here for everyone within sight along the dreary street lined with leaning shacks to admire the shiny red Cadillac.

Sam nodded, not showing any belligerence, but not showing any subservience either.

"Well, then, fill 'er up, check the oil, clean the windshield, and you might shine up the white walls while you're at it."

I was feeling embarrassed at Danny's behavior, but I dared not get involved or show even that I knew Jackson from anywhere. Maggie still was hanging around Danny's neck from the backseat, and Thad and June didn't seem to know there was anyone around but each other.

Chas made no bones about being impressed by the big black, though. She was humming and flashing him her glamour eyes and had unbuttoned the top two buttons of her blouse.

Sam did the full requested servicing that had been asked, with Danny badgering him about how he was doing it—and how fast he was getting it done. Just egging Sam along to see how far he could get. I was doing what I could to pretend I wasn't here. I'd probably say something to Danny later about demeaning a person of color needlessly, especially on their own turf and regardless of their relative size, but anything I did now would be like lighting a match to a bonfire. Chas, shaking out her long, blonde, curly hair and sticking out her chest, was following everything Sam did with her eyes. She was virtually begging for eye contact, which the big black wasn't giving her.

When he was done, Sam said, "That'll be $2.50 for the gas." He said nothing about the other services.

"Pay the boy," Danny said gruffly to Maggie, barely containing his irritation that he hadn't gotten a rise out of the black giant. As Maggie dug the money out of her purse, Danny reached into his own pocket, extracted a

261

quarter, and flipped it toward the attendant, who caught it deftly in his hand. "Here's something for you, boy," Danny said.

Still no rise, but there might have been if the black guy hadn't just turned around and sauntered back to the station office.

Danny moved to start up the engine, but, standing up from her seat in the back, Chas declared, "Wait for me, I gotta visit the ladies."

Danny fumed a, "Christ Almighty, why didn't you do it while the black boy was pumping the gas?" but, ignoring him, Chas just maneuvered around the spooning couple in the front seat, got the door open, and was sashaying her butt in an exaggerated dueling-cats-in-a-burlap bag roll toward the service station office in the wake of the big black guy.

A few minutes later she returned, a scowl on her face. "Let's get outta this dump," she said as she climbed over Thad and June and landed in the backseat.

"What's with you?" Danny said over his shoulder as he started the Caddie up. "You're all unenthused all of a sudden."

"The ladies back there wasn't worth peeing in," she answered, taking a long look at the condition of her manicured and purple-glossed nails and turning her face toward the side of the car.

Somehow I didn't think that the condition of the ladies room was her problem—she certainly didn't ask us to stop for a pee on our continued journey around the southern end of the lake and back to my house. She didn't even try to paw me anymore—just sat there and stewed, looking at the scenery with no indication of actually seeing it. Maggie continued trying to be a scarf around Danny's neck. Most of the way home, however, Danny was taking looks to his right in the front seat. I figured I knew why. June's panties had been tossed into my lap and she was on Thad's lap, facing him. Her blouse was open and Thad's

262

face was buried in June's very nice rack. She was bobbing up and down on his lap, and I decided there was no reason for me to sail her panties back to the front seat for a while.

\* \* \* \*

I was wandering around the living areas of the cottage on the shore of Spirit Lake that night, hearing discussions on all sides of me, above LeRoy Brown pounding out Scott Joplin's "Maple Leaf Rag" on the piano, of how much everyone missed David Alexander and wasn't it a shame that David wasn't here and how much livelier the parties were when Alexander was sitting on the piano and thumping on its side as LeRoy punished the keys. And these weren't even members of the Wild Ones. These were summer-only friends who had the huge houses we all called cottages at the lake too who had descended by car or boat and half of whose names I didn't even know—or had bothered to remember. Most of the owners from the lake came from the Macon area, not Atlanta, and most of them were going to out-of-state colleges.

Thad and June and Maggie and Danny were off humping each other somewhere. Chas was making the rounds and pulling guys out of the melee for quickies in her room upstairs. She had tried me twice, to no avail, but she wasn't having much trouble with the local guys. Everyone was frenetic, panicking that this was the next-to-last weekend of the summer and they hadn't been laid enough, hadn't gathered enough memories of the good life at Spirit Lake in the summer.

Well, I missed David too. In ways these shallow, socially safe young people would never realize.

I walked through the open French doors at the water side of the living room and down to the dock. I stumbled onto the pier and to the water end of it, plopping down in one of the scruffy-white wooden Adirondack chairs pointed at the lake. I looked over to the other one, half expecting to see David sitting there. But of course he wasn't. He had been, though, last summer, on the next-to-last Saturday night of the summer season on the lake, coming out to where I was sitting in one of the chairs, smoking a cigarette, and seeking a muffling of LeRoy Brown back in the house, pounding away on Scott Joplin's "The Entertainer."

"You need to give up those smokes if you're going to take the state swimming crown," he said, as he reached me at the end of the dock and settled in the other chair. He was a magnificent specimen of a man just out of college. Dark complexioned, in a half-surly, bad boy look that was transformed the moment he gave you a smile. His hair was dark too, and he never seemed to be able to shave close, but on him it looked good. The women at college opened their legs instantly for a man who looked this good. He was shirtless, having stripped his off while walking to the dock. It was a hot night. I'd taken my shirt off too. I felt young and immature, not yet fully developed, in contrast to him. His was a mature man's body; my body was still working at it. I was a swimmer, blond and smooth chested, the chest muscled well enough, but not deeply—just enough development to serve the needs of a sleek line knifing through the water. He was hirsute, deeply tanned, broad- and deep-chested, already a muscular man, nipples puffed out on bulging pecs. A god to those of us in the Buckland Wild Ones—to the whole community of youths on the western shore of the lake.

Any woman cavorting back there in the house would go with him in a flash. I think that's why he usually kept Maggie Campbell close—to ward off women throwing themselves at him. She had been safe, malleable, and uncomplaining since high school. Maggie wasn't with him now. He hadn't brought Maggie down to the dock with him. My body tensed up. It was always dangerous when he dropped Maggie before searching me out.

I was well aware that he wanted something from me—without Maggie being around—and that he almost desperately wanted to be the first one to take it from me. We both knew I would give it to some man someday. We both knew that he wanted that someday to be tonight—and from him.

I pointed to the large crystal tennis trophy he'd brought out—his prize for winning the state title early in the summer. He wasn't carrying it around so much to brag as because of how much beer it would hold. It was at least half full now.

"You're ragging on me about fags . . . and training for sports," I said, "and yet you're walking around with a gallon of beer sloshing in that trophy?"

I had stopped after speaking the word "fags" and looked away, as he had done. I regretted the use of the word. There had been moments throughout the previous year at college, where we had reached a point where I knew what he wanted—what he wanted to ask of me, demand of me, take from me—but when I couldn't bring myself to give him the answer he wanted. It wasn't that I didn't want to give him that answer. It was because I was scared. It would change everything, completely reorder my life. Still, I knew that someday I would cross through that one-way beaded curtain. In the summer of 1955 that wasn't something you decided to take on lightly—if at all—though. You were expected to hide it—to not have such thoughts and desires at all.

"Well, I didn't bring the beer out here to share with you," he said with a laugh, even as he handed me the trophy and I took a deep draw off it. "My sports training days are over anyway."

"But you have to be able to fit in the cockpit of that fighter jet you've volunteered to learn to drive," I said. I couldn't help making my voice sound a bit bitter.

"I've told you not to worry about that."

"Anything that takes you way from Atlanta . . . from Athens . . . from here, at the lake, makes me sad," I answered.

"And away from you?"

I didn't answer that. I just looked away from him, toward the dark shoreline across the lake, not wanting him to see how close to home it hit with that question.

"Maybe if you'd—"

"Please, David, don't put this on me. I couldn't start something with you and lose you so soon afterward."

"This is it, bub," He whispered, pulling his chair close to mine and reaching over the arm of my chair to place his hand on my crotch. "Who knows if there will ever be another summer like this?" he murmured. "You know what I feel, what I want."

He was unzipping my shorts. I didn't stop him. I was trembling.

"I know you want it too. You've said as much. Your body is telling me as much. One kiss. That's all I ask for and I'll zoom up in the air—in my jet and beyond."

I looked down at my shorts, the fly open. "That isn't all you are asking for, is it?"

"No it's not. If not now and I have to go away and come back, we both know I won't have been first. And you know how important that is to me. What it will mean for us in the future. We both know what you want and that it will only be a matter of time. Surrender to me. You want to."

My face was turned toward his. I'm sure he could see the tears on my cheek. He came in with his lips for a kiss and I didn't deny him. He was fishing my cock out of my fly and fisting it. I couldn't hide from him that I was hard for him. And I didn't deny him this either.

"Oh, Lee," he muttered and was out of his chair, kneeling in front of me, taking my cock in his mouth. "This is it, isn't it? This is the time for this," he murmured as he came off the cock with his mouth and encased it with a hand.

"David, no. No . . . not here," I managed in a strangled voice. "Anyone can come out here and see us. There's a houseful of people in there." The Joplin rags had ended, and LeRoy had moved into Cole Porter and Hoagie Carmichael mood songs. They would be slow dancing in there now, dancing close together, building up for "laters." But some couples' "laters" could come sooner, and they might drift out here to fuck on the sloping lawn between house and water.

"But you'll go with me? You'll let me fuck you? You will surrender your virginity to me?" he raised his face to mine, pleading. It wasn't in David's nature to plead. He was giving me a great honor. But then, of course, I was sure that I wouldn't be the first to have been debauched by him, to have fallen to his puppy-dog charm.

"I'm scared—"

"I'll be gentle. I'm off to Valdosta in two weeks, Lee. Don't deny me this. Listen to what LeRoy is playing inside: Cole Porter's 'Anything Goes.' He's playing that for us. Here, come with me."

He fucked me in the voluminous backseat of the Alexander '55 fire-engine-red Cadillac Series 62 convertible that his family had just bought and he'd driven so proudly to the lake, bringing his younger, rising college freshman brother, Danny to the lake with him. Danny, who even now, while David was popping my male cherry in the back of the family car, was upstairs in Chas' bedroom losing his virginity to her.

David was gentle—at first—lying on top of me across the backseat of the car, between my spread legs, my left ankle hooked on the top of the backseat and my right on the top of the front bench seat, and with him, cooing to me and holding his hand over my mouth to stifle my deep groans, moving inch by inch up inside me with his thick cock. My luck to be deflowered by a horse-hung man. In the end, though, when he was three-quarters of a foot inside me, he lost control and started pumping in earnest. I struggled against him then, but only briefly, and it was no use. He had me folded in his arms and immobilized, his pelvis moving hard against my buttocks.

The struggle was perfunctory. By then, despite the pain-pleasure, I wanted no less from him. His cock was all possessing, his kisses like wine. I never wanted him to stop sucking on my nipples; sending his cock revolving deep inside me; causing my channel walls to ripple from the pleasure of him; finding and rubbing, rubbing, rubbing my prostate with his bulb until I exploded in arcs of cum to his intake of breath and steely strokes. Again, and again, and again. It didn't end with me giving up my cum for a man the first time, even though that first time exhausted me. He drove on to a significantly later finish, as I just clung to him, putty in his hands, and moaned.

When he was done—and I had been undone—he said he didn't want me to leave him that night. He was a puppy dog about it, begging me not to leave him, as, he said, the brief period in the car left him wanting me more. He said it would be OK if we didn't fuck; we could just cuddle.

I couldn't say that I wanted him to leave me either. He drove to a seedy motel at the north end of the lake that couldn't decide whether it sided with the Woodland whites or the Coon Town blacks and fucked me all night in various taxing positions, leaving his girlfriend, Maggie, roaming through the lake house, nudging couples apart to ID them, and wondering where David was. She eventually found Danny, pounding furiously on Chas' locked bedroom door—where Chas was adding another, different charm to her bracelet—and led him away for each to console the other—laying a foundation for more intimate consolation when David's jet took a nosedive a few months later.

The morning after David's all-night debauchery of me in the seedy hotel, I stumbled out of cracked-tile shower, sore as hell, with little sleep and with only a towel around my midsection. I caught David sitting on the bed, just in his Skivvies. He had a penknife and his belt in his hand and he was carving a notch in it. It was just one of many notches carved in that belt.

"What are you doing, David?" I asked.

Giving me a mischievous grin, he said, "What do you think? You know what I'm doing. Ah, come on, don't pout. You knew it would happen. You were one of the easiest ones. You wanted it so bad it was hardly any challenge at all."

The bastard. I think what hurt the most was that it was just a notch, indistinguishable from the others. Nothing special to him.

But, such was the charm, self-confidence, magnetism, and child-like audacity of the man that, rather than getting mad, when he held out his hand and said, "Come here, come to me," I let him pull the towel away, bend me over the bed, and fuck me again. Even then I knew that what I had given to him and a relationship between us didn't mean to him what it meant to me and that the notch he added to his belt was more an ending for him than a beginning. Still, such was my attachment to him that I would take what I could get for as long as I could get it.

Late August to early November didn't leave much time for David and me. In fact, beyond the last weekend of that summer at Spirit Lake, there was only one brief, glorious weekend in October in my studio apartment at college in Athens. And even during that weekend he didn't seem totally mine, seemingly thinking of his military duties much of the time and taking an inordinate interest in another student on my stair hall. I wouldn't be surprised to learn he'd added another notch to his belt before leaving for his military duties that Sunday evening.

As I never felt he was mine anyway nor did I feel that he had taken anything from me that I wasn't ready to give, I just appreciated what little time I could have of his. I think I had a premonition he wouldn't be coming back to me from the military.

I snapped out of the reminiscence to rejoin the summer of 1956, sitting on the dock, outside my family's lake cottage, where the next-to-last weekend of the summer was being celebrated and mourned in appropriate debauchery mode. LeRoy was on the slower Cole Porter songs now. It was his lot to play almost to the bitter end. He wasn't really a guest at the party; he was black; he was hired to be here. I sat through "Night and Day" and "Begin the Beguine." Couples were beginning to drift out onto the lawn to start their evening fucking. One couple already was at the other end of the dock, rocking against each other, playing "hide the hands." How much they missed David, they were saying, between moans and giggles.

I looked at my watch. Good thing it was time to be gone. I couldn't have stayed around for much more of this on this next-to-last summer party night. The rowboat was right there at the end of the dock, gently tapping against the pier. I moved down to inside the boat, untied the rope anchoring it to the dock, and pushed off with an oar.

I wasn't going to be state champion in anything this year if I didn't practice, practice, practice. I pushed away from the lights and laughter of the party into the wet darkness of Spirit Lake.

\* \* \* \*

I rowed all the way across to the eastern side of the lake, in quick time. Rowing that distance normally was a piece of cake. Tonight, though, I wanted to punish my lungs and empty my brain of thoughts of David—pull in more pleasurable thoughts—and so I rowed double time.

270

Reaching the other side, which was swampy at the shoreline rather than dressed with concrete rip-rap like on the wealthy, white side of the lake was, I struggled out of the boat and pulled it onto the shore. Struggling up the grassy verge, I plopped down on my butt, facing the water, and looked toward my lit-up house on the other shore.

I could still hear LeRoy playing the piano, the sound coming in on the breeze across the lake in more gentle, melded tones than as heard from my dock—and, most certainly from inside the cottage. Hoagie Carmichael this time. "Stardust," "Georgia on My Mind." LeRoy had his favorites that he played forever, from one summer through the next. Those who came to the parties at the cottage expected it and, in truth, had grown used to it as a nonintrusive background partner and shield to their fevered and lecherous business.

They'd be swaying against each other in the living room now. She'd have lost her panties somewhere and would have a knee hooked on his hip. He'd be inside her, undulating to the beat, moving his dick languidly inside her. Sighing in the living room, moaning on the grassy slope between house and water, cries of passion in the bedrooms, pans swept off the counters and hitting the floors in the pantry. Probably even the springs of the fire-engine-red '55 Cadillac Series 62 Convertible bouncing up and down as Danny fucked Maggie in the backseat, Maggie dreaming of being fucked by David, and Danny frantically trying to fuck David out of Maggie.

I wondered if they knew that David had grabbed my virginity from me in the backseat of that car. It was what I mostly was thinking of as we drove around the north end of the lake earlier in the day as I, smiling regretfully for the camouflaging effect it provided, removed Chas' hand from my crotch again, and again, and again.

In the dark now, sitting on the grassy slope of the eastern shore, I was hard. But it wasn't for anyone across the lake, at my family's vacation house. I already was shirtless. I pushed my shorts and briefs down, off my legs, and took my cock in my hand. Slowly beating myself off—putting my mind to discerning and matching the meter of the strains of "In the Cool, Cool, Cool of the Evening" wafting across the lake from LeRoy's long, sensuous fingers on the piano keys. I had more than once thought of LeRoy playing me with those sensuous fingers.

I hadn't exactly been celibate since David had plucked my cherry.

I didn't flinch from within my reverie when my thighs were encased in beefy, brown, rugby-player-muscled thighs, thighs that then moved over mine, hooking my legs and teasing them apart, trapping me there. Muscular chocolate-brown arms encircling my shoulders; wet lips pressed into the hollow of my neck; a huge, hard cock pressed against my back, running up the small of my back; warm balls pressed to the base of my spine; a beefy brown hand covering mine on my cock and taking over the beat of my meat.

The cock was the thing. The muscles were very nice in their way. The handsome face didn't hurt. But though I tried to recapture over the last year at college what I had briefly had with horse-hung David, not before there was Sam had there been a man who could—who would—fill me almost to splitting me and make me come in great arcs of cum as David then could—as Sam Jackson now could. That Sam Jackson was now preparing to do.

By freak accident I had met Sam in the lake—in the lake's water itself. I was swimming laps across the lake and back to my house, stealing a march on the hard training that was to come when I returned to the University of Georgia in September. And there, right before me, completely unexpectedly, in the middle of the lake, had popped up the wooly black head of a man.

272

The shock of it had made me swallow water and sputter. Sam had put me in a lifeguard's hold and paddled me to the Coon Town side of the lake, to this very shore. I probably would have been all right on my own, but the shock of his sudden emergence from the water had knocked the wind out of my sails. As I had been swimming I had been dreaming of that last time, in my college room shower last October—of David fucking me up against the shower tiles with the water cascading over our steaming bodies. His massive cock invading and possessing me fully, stroking hard and deep.

We had both been swimming naked, the black man and I. His nakedness was magnificent. The mouth-to-mouth resuscitation had moved from the clinical to the passionate.

"Do you? Will you?" he had murmured.

"Fuck me," I had replied.

Still half in the dream state of David covering me from behind in the shower and possessing my lips as his staff invaded my channel, I grabbed the initiative, embracing the black man's broad back in my arms, digging my nail in the bulge of his shoulder muscles, weaving my calves around his thighs, possessing his cock in a death grip of a hand and guiding him inside me. He was hard and strong. I was yielding and moaning. If I hadn't had a big cock before, I would have been beside myself in pain, but I had, so I was in heaven.

And I was fucked. Hard, deep, horse-hung thick and long, and at great length. Black buck fucked.

That's what white women who walked in Atlanta alone were threatened with in those days: "Some black buck is going to take you and do the unspeakable to you." I didn't take it as a threat, though. I contemplated it in my wet dreams.

Thus had Sam been included thereafter in my nightly rowing exercises during the weekend days of August of the year 1956. And in that next-to-last Saturday evening of summer at Spirit Lake for the year—I made a point of checking the statistics some time later—in which there were 492 reported lynchings of black men in Georgia, many for sexually messing with someone of white color, Sam Jackson fucked me hard, with no inhibitions on either side. He totally merged his black body with my white one as LeRoy Brown's fingers on the keys across the lake reverted to Cole Porter's "I've Got You Under My Skin."

He had slowly pitched me forward until my cheek was pressed into the grass. Working his way in licks and kisses down to my buttocks, his broad hands pulled my butt cheeks apart, and I groaned as his tongue went for the gold. He covered, mounted, and thrust inside me and fucked me hard and long in a no-prisoners-taken doggy fuck. He was more brutal and consuming than he'd ever been before, and I was afraid the taking was some sort of retribution for my not having spoken up that afternoon at the gas pump.

I was equally scared that I had responded to this cruel taking with as much want and passion as I did. My dreams of a black buck taking me were being fulfilled.

"No," he whispered to me later, as we sat cross-legged, yoga style, my legs on top of his thighs, my ankles crossed behind his trim waist, and the bulb of his cock pressing, but not yet entering my entrance. "I would not have wanted you to say anything. I get that a lot when white folks drive through town and need gas but aren't happy they're paying a black man for it. That guy, despite his height and his Cadillac—probably his daddy's Cadillac—is just a pipsqueak in his brain. He isn't worth a fight."

He had Danny pegged to a T. "But why? You took me almost in anger just now. Don't get me wrong, I loved it. I'd take it every which way from you. But you haven't been that demanding before . . . well, the first time, I guess, but I almost took it from you that time, I wanted it so bad."

"Yes, you did want it bad, didn't you?" he asked, with a grin, pressing his forehead to mine. He looked down at his long, long, thick cock, poised there at my hole, the bulb resting at my throbbing entrance, his staff too throbbing in anticipation. His glance downward caused me to look down too.

"I badly wanted to give it to you too. You, know, I watched that arrogant white guy fuck you in the backseat of that Cadillac last summer. Ever since then, I'd wanted to fuck you too. You know I'm going to give it all to you again," he said, calmly, matter-of-factly. "I don't usually go into the hilt, but today you get it all. And you want to know why, don't you?"

"I want it all. But, yes, I want to know why."

"I'm just sulking and looking for someone to hurt. You're leaving. You're going back to that fancy university town in Athens. You're probably now going to go back to that party of yours across the lake and fuck one of those hottie white women who was in the car today. Another week and you'll be gone. I won't be here when you come another summer, you know. I can't stay here any longer."

"But don't you have family here?"

"I got no one. And nothin' in this hell hole of a town. Or anywhere else, for that matter."

"I understand," I said. He made me stop and think. Who did I have here myself? My mom dead, my dad in New York most of the time, my step-mother clubbing her life away inside a martini glass in Buckhead. This was why I could use the Spirit Lake house every summer and trash it. No questions were asked when the bills came in to put it back together again. No questions were asked whenever I cashed a check. No one even asked where I was when I cashed the check. They were just glad that their relationship with me could be covered with a check.

What was I doing in Georgia anyway? Look at us, Sam and me. Him a black buck, me a white twink. Who cared what we did—other than the good people of Georgia? Who the fuck were we hurting by making our kind of love? We were committing a felony here in Georgia law, the two of us sitting close together, Sam just having fucked me; Sam about to fuck me again. A double felony. Not only were we both men, but he was black and I was white.

Can't do that here in Georgia in 1956. Not that it even mattered that it was illegal. Who would wait for the law in Georgia when there were so many strong, low-lying tree limbs conveniently nearby? It wouldn't be me they were hanging, but they'd make me watch—and then a couple of them would take me off in the bushes and fuck the shit out of me to make the point that you couldn't be queer in Georgia. So, what the fuck were we even doing here in Georgia? Who would give a fuck if we just disappeared?

"I doubt I'll be coming back next summer either," I then said. "It won't be the same. It wasn't the same this summer. But, don't worry, I won't be fucking any women when I go home tonight. I'll go straight to my room and dream of you fucking me—even with you doing it with a bit of anger behind it."

"That's the other reason I'm going to fuck you hard again," he said, with a grin. "You want it hard from me."

I couldn't tell him he was wrong.

"You don't fuck women?" he asked, doubling back on our earlier conversation.

"No, I don't. I can't help it; I only want it from men." I didn't ask him the obvious question, but he answered it anyway.

"I fuck women. I fuck both men and women. I like it both ways, so I do it both ways. White men don't seem to put any brakes on about fucking black women."

"I don't care," I said. "as long as you fuck me. As long as you fuck me again . . . now . . . and give me all of it. Make me remember this."

I was trembling when he placed a strong hand at the base of my spine and, our foreheads pressed together, my eyes locked by his, began to pull me into him, onto his cock. He released my eyes than, and lowered his, causing me to look down. His hands grasped, squeezed, and separated my butt cheeks.

"Here it comes," he muttered and continued pulling me into him. I watched, panting, groaning giving little cries, as inch by relentless inch he made it all disappear inside me. I dug my fingernails into the meat of his biceps on both sides and arched my head back in a cry to the sky as wild, wiry black pubic curls pressed into and mingled with trimmed blond silk.

Giving a grunt, he rose up on his feet, maintaining his hold on my buttocks. I, in turn, maintained the lock of my ankles at the small of his back, but I pulled my claws out of his biceps and let my arms fall behind me, reaching for the grass. My weight, such as he gave over, was resting on my shoulders. I looked up the line of my body to his magnificent, black, sweat-slicked torso, every muscle bulging, struggling to burst out of his skin, as he pulled my channel on and off his cock. Harder, deeper, deeper, harder. Stretching up for my tonsils. Faster, harder. Forever. The glorious shared gush of release.

Another chorus of "I've Got You Under My Skin" floating across the water.

The cottage looked like a battle zone when I returned. Everything that could be pulled down onto the floor or set askew was. There wasn't too much breakage, though, as was understandable. We'd already had another entire summer to tear the place apart and trash anything that wasn't nailed down. My father hadn't bothered to check the house out for years. Among the wreckage were bodies, strewn about in twos and threes and even fours. Legs and arms entwined. Clothes in tatters and pushed away from flesh. Still a twitch here, a movement of crotch against crotch or buttocks there.

No one was at the piano. I found LeRoy Brown on the leather sofa in the library. Naked, he was stretched out on top of Chas, whose face was turned toward mine, eyes slitted, and locked in an expression of total satisfaction. They were the only couple I could see on the battleground who were still fucking. She had two sofa pillows under her hips to give him a good angle, and he was languidly moving his long, gaunt, black body in pushups above her. He was taking long strokes— extraordinarily long strokes—in her maw of a cunt, much too cavernous to feel tightness from the invasion of his cock. Not being able to help myself, I took in a long breath as nearly a foot of shaft came out of her cunt and then let the breath out as it slid back deep inside her.

He wasn't wearing a condom—which was a detail that I was to remember of the night.

I just shrugged and trudged upstairs to unlock and enter my bedroom. I had locked the door against invasion by anyone else, knowing that the next-to-last party at my family's Spirit Lake house would end in precisely the shambles that it did. If I didn't have the fortitude to prevent the party, at least I could preserve a retreat for myself—and for my dreams of Sam—and, still, of David.

\* \* \* \*

The very last weekend of the summer of 1956 at Spirit Lake arrived. I had driven from Buckhead to the lake in my '54 two-seater Thunderbird. Danny, Maggie, and Thad had come from Athens, where Thad already was into week-day football practice, in the Alexander family Cadillac. I'd made one stop on the way down from Atlanta, and what I'd gotten was burning a hole in the floor under the driver's seat of my Thunderbird. By agreement we were hooking up at the Main Street Café in Woodland before going out to the house. Chas and June, their time totally free of any obligations, had stayed on at the lake house during the week to bring some semblance of order back into the house before one last shove over the edge of debauchery this weekend. Chas had her MG Sprite, so they were good to go for transportation.

"One more weekend," Danny said as we were sitting in the booth at the café. "Then it's back to school." All four of us nodded; it was the four us, the remnants of the Buckhead Wild Ones who were starting back at the University of Georgia in Athens next week.

"You got a letter from the basketball coach yet?" Thad asked, turning to Danny.

278

Danny looked away, gave a sigh, and then said, "God, I miss David."

"So do I," Maggie said in a small voice. I looked at her. It was obvious she did miss David, at least in comparison to Danny. In other circumstances, when we got back to school, I'd take her aside and tell her she needed to get on with her life—that Danny never was going to be David—that David wasn't exactly a saint. That, in fact, she should stop trying to live in the shadow of any jock. That being a groupie for horny jocks was so high school. She had a good head for figures. She could make something of herself in her own right. Maybe I'd write that to her instead.

Thad looked at me then. "I'm team captain again, so I'm in solid on the football team. How about you, Lee? You heard from Coach Tomlin yet?"

Coach Tomlin. I sure had heard from Coach Tomlin, the swim team coach. He'd written about how anxious he was to have me back at school. How much his balls ached from not having me there. How hard he was going to fuck me when he could get me under him again. As if Coach Tomlin of the "not so much cock and even less stamina" knew what hard fucking was. Yeah he wanted me back. Pretty stupid of him to put it in writing like that, though. Not that I'd do anything about it, other than ensure he wrote me good letters. "Yeah," I answered. "Coach Tomlin's written me. I'm good to go for the year."

"Just one more weekend here this summer," Maggie said in a small voice. "It just hasn't been the same this year."

Each of the other three of us chimed in agreement in our own way and then each sank into his or her own thoughts, thoughts that were interrupted by commotion at the door and the sobbing, half hysterical exclamations of the woman standing inside the door, clothes in disarray, face puffy and bleeding.

All of the men in the café rose from where they sat, suddenly warriors, avenging knights in white armor. All the women shrank away from the sight, taking faint. It so easily could have been them. Every face in the café was white, of course, and steeped in avenging anger. Everyone was thinking "black buck."

279

The waitress behind the lunch counter was the first one to react, moving quickly to Chas and putting an arm around her. "What is it, sweetie? What's happened? Who's done this to you?"

"That big black man over in Coon Town. The one that pumps gas at the Texaco station over there," Chas burst out. "He beat me when I said I wouldn't. And then he . . . he . . . he was too strong. See the bruises on my arms . . . my legs? Then he . . ."

All four of us came shooting out of our booth—Maggie, Danny, and Thad moving toward Chas, who took a couple of steps in their direction as well—me going around them, to the door, into my Thunderbird, and roaring toward the north end of Spirit Lake.

Sam was calmly standing at the gas pumps at the Coon Town Texaco station, clipboard in hand, and checking the meters when I drove up.

"Nice ride," he said, as I pulled the Thunderbird to a stop next to him. "Very nice ride. Don't see Thunderbirds on this side of the lake often. Maybe you'll give me a ride in it someday. I'll ride you and then you can ride me in that car maybe." He laughed at his own joke but then could clearly see that I wasn't laughing.

"Get into the car, Sam." I said.

"Want to give me a ride now?" he asked. "Want to go somewhere on our last weekend together and fuck like bunnies and ride around in your fancy Thunderbird between fuckings?"

"Stop that, Sam. Just get into the car. They'll be here any minute, I'm sure. We got to get out of here."

"Why? Who's going to be here? Out of here to where?"

"Does it matter, Sam? Just get in the fucking car."

He got in the car.

I took a road straight east, not a main route north toward Atlanta or south toward Macon and Athens. I'd turn north when we got closer to the coast.

"What's this all about, Lee?" Sam asked.

I told him.

He was quiet for a moment. I had expected to hear a denial from him. But I didn't.

"Sure I fucked that woman," he finally said. "She wanted it bad. Came pestering me. Pestered me every day since you came riding in with the pipsqueak at the wheel of his daddy's Caddie that day. I finally gave her what she wanted. Every day this week. You weren't here. But I didn't beat that woman. I didn't have anything to do with that. She wanted it and I wore rubbers. You weren't here and I wasn't in the best frame of mind. All you rich whites got to me. She wanted it again this weekend and I told her I was finished, that she clung too much, demanded and expected too much. But I didn't beat on the woman. I don't beat women. I don't have to beat white women to get it from them."

I keyed in on him saying he wore rubbers—at about the same level as hearing his disclaimers that he'd beaten Chas. I believed him. But Chas *had* been beaten. She was crazy, but not crazy enough to do that to herself. Then I remembered that LeRoy hadn't worn a condom when he fucked Chas last weekend. If there were repercussions and Chas pushed her case of vindictiveness by producing a black baby, Sam would be in even more trouble—if he hadn't already been hung from a tree by then. This was Georgia in 1956. LeRoy certainly wasn't going to step up to admit that he'd barebacked Chas, that was for sure. And I couldn't blame LeRoy for that—not even for spiking Chas. She went with any and every man, of whatever color. That was on her.

I also didn't see LeRoy as a woman beater. No, Chas had picked up one too many casual fucks and had gotten more than she'd bargained for—and then decided that Sam was her most-likely scapegoat.

Not that the Georgia boys in white sheets, passing for armor, would choose to believe that.

"It's OK, Sam," I said. "We'll be OK. I'm heading north. We can blend in in the North. I got enough under my seat to get us started and there's more where that came from."

"You got to be at college next week," Sam said.

"They have swim teams and classes in business at good colleges in the North too," I said. "I'll have no trouble getting letters of referral from Georgia U. As long as you are willing to be with me, we can make this work. And even if you don't want to be with me for long, I can give you a new start. If you want to be with—"

"What do you think?" he murmured, turning toward me, reaching a hand over and unzipping me, finding me hard. "You had planned this anyway, hadn't you? The white woman had nothing to do with this."

"Only the urgency of getting you out of town, out of Georgia," I answered. "Yes, I hoped you'd let me take you away—or take money from me to get a better start in life if you wouldn't go with me. Does that make you angry?"

There was silence for a few minutes and then, "Not at you. No, that's all good where you—we—are concerned. It's better than thinkin' you just don't want to see me lynched for fuckin' a white woman. But how far do you think we'll get in the South, a white boy with a black man in his car?"

"We'll find a lay-by somewhere to hole up until dark—when we're well away from the lake. A couple of days, driving at night, and we'll be across the Mason Dixon line. Then nobody will care. I'm not running from anybody. I have nobody to run from. I can get us through this. I only have you to run to, to run with, if I'm not being too presumptuous, too pushy."

"No, course you're not. Maybe for this daytime lay-by—I like the sound of the word 'lay'—you can find someplace quiet and real private, maybe next to a river. I like fuckin' you next to water."

"If you don't stop beating me off, I'll run this car off the road," I said, but then, quickly, I added, "not that I want you to stop."

"I think I can do one better," he said, with a laugh. "I put my head down, maybe no one will notice that you have a black man riding with you in a fancy Thunderbird in the South." With that, he leaned over, pulled my shorts and briefs down to my knees, took my cock in his mouth, and ran a finger down between my thighs and up to—and into—my puckering asshole.

We went for miles and miles without anyone seeing a black man in my passenger seat.

One thing was for sure, though, I was going to have to find a private turnoff real fast. And the other thing that hit me was that, though I'd been thinking this was the worst end to summer at Spirit Lake, I, in fact, was going to remember it as the best summer's ending I could ever wish for.

~

# About the Author

**Habu** is one of the pen names of a former supersonic spy jet pilot, intelligence agent, male model, movie actor, and diplomat. A wild youth in Southeast Asia was spent enjoying whatever sexual opportunities came his way, and much of his gay male writing is about recalling incidents from those days and inventing ones he'd perhaps have liked to experience. He now leads a very quiet and ordinary happily married family life.

An American, he is a published mainstream novelist and short story writer under another name and in another dimension of his life. He has written or cowritten (with Sabb) approaching 1,000 published short stories and over 100 published erotica e-books, primarily of gay fiction but also memoir, straight fiction and ménage fiction. His hand and creative writing can be seen in stories and books by habu, sr71plt, Dirk Hessian, Shabbu, and Stephen Kessel—among unrevealed others that might surprise readers. The fictionalized GM memoir *Flying High, Diving Deep* is loosely based on his life experiences. He can be found at the adults only gay male site www.BarbarianSpy.com, which he shares with Sabb and Dirk Hessian.

You can send feedback about this e-book directly to habu, or send general feedback on this e-book to www.BarbarianSpy.com.

Our authors always like to receive feedback, and appreciate it when readers post reviews at distributors and other sites.

# BarbarianSpy

## FOR LITERARY HEAT

**Not all books listed below may currently be on release.**
\* indicates the book is available in paperback and e-book.

### BOOKS BY CHRIS CROSS

**Multisexual Adult Romance**
Pulaski Square
Chocolate in Vanilla (MF)
Christmas with Chris (MMF) (MM) (MF)

### BOOKS BY ALEX LOCKHEED

**Transgender Romance**
Meeting Jenna
**Transgender Other**
Being Sarah

### BOOKS BY DIRK HESSIAN

**Xtreme Historical Erotica**
The King's Men
Shores of Tripoli
Prophecy of Noto
Pretender's Fate

**General Historical Erotic Romance**
To the Hessian Hills
Fire Down the Valley*
Constantinople*
The Beautiful Way*
Blue and Gray
Colonel's Treasure
Beginning of Time
Labyrinth

### BOOKS BY HABU

**Gay Erotica**
**Memoir Faction**
Flying High, Diving Deep*
**Xtreme Erotica**
Chain Gang Banged (Short Story)
Tramp Steaming*

Escape to Girne
Silas' Choice*
Last Call
Choke Hold
Apyko: The Greek Pimp
Visits of the Schlange
Second Coming: Emile La Cour Unleashed*
Vortex: Sacrificed by Curiosity*
Dark Angel Sounding *(in e-book & included in Sounding:Ultimate Control paperback)*\*
Sounding: Ultimate Control (*Print Only*)*
Sounding Five *(in e-book & included in Sounding:Ultimate Control paperback)*\*

**Romance**
Bangkok Summer Seduction
The Photograph
Inevitable Case
Turn to Love
Rain Check
Built for Pleasure (Sci Fi)
Danny's Choice*
Pull of the Groove
Sugar n Spice Christmas
Friday Nights with Lenny (Christmas Romance)
Snowy, Snowy Nights (Christmas Romance)
Tank n Bull
Sail to the Sun
War Letters
Ravens Roost
Caribbean Cruise Top to Bottom
Arena Stage
Trading Partners (Valentine's Day)
Four Coins
Lower Than the Heart (Valentine's Day)
Brambleton
Gotta Keep Trying
Finding Amnad
Platres Conclave

**Other Novels/Novellas**
Temptation's Clutches*
Descent into Chaos
Escape to Girne

Journey Through Abilene
Harmony and Dissonance
Stallion Station
Racing With the Devil (espionage suspense)
Prepared in Cape Verdi
Gilded Cage
House on Park*
Anything for Ambition
Dance of the Ravishers
Hard Knocks U*
My Neighbor's Spa*
Man's Man: Tales of a High Priced Gay Hooker*
Trip Money
The Indian Doctor
Sailorboy
Home to Fire Island
**Murder Mysteries**
Inevitable Case
Vanishing Laura
Death on a Ping Pong Table
Clint Folsom Mysteries Compendium Volume 1*
Death to Blonds - Stolen Judgment (Clint Folsom Mystery)*
Clint Folsom Mysteries Compendium Volume 2*
**Gay Erotica Anthologies**
Earth Cry*
Shunga
Habu's Christmas Balls
Eight in D*
DevilMENt
Silas' Choices*
Stallion Station (A Novella in Parts)
Eleven to the Dogs*
Fifty Seventy*
Spy Tails 001*
Spy Tails 002*
Doubled*
Doubled Again*
Tails in the Tropics*
Tails in the Med*
Tails in the West*
Rough Riders*
Grab Bag 1*

Grab Bag 2*
Grab Bag 3*
Grab Bag 4*
Grab Bag 5*
Grab Bag 6*
Grab Bag 7*
Grab Bag 8*
Grab Bag 9*
Beyond the Beaded Curtain*
Habu's Christmas Balls
The Sporting Life*
Fetish Galore!*
**Literary Gay Erotica**
Cairo Surrender*
The Handyman*
Homeward Bound
Journey to Mirage*
**Bisexual/Menage/Multisexual Erotica**
And Eat it Too
Two Men, One Woman*
Every Which Way
Summer of Denial
Death on a Ping Pong Table
Cruising Gigolo
13 Ways for Halloween
Luther*
The Indian Prince*
**BOOKS BY SABB**
Driver Reliever
Hiring in Hollywood
The Legend of Holleystone Grange
Surprise Encounters*
She is He
Wrong Man
Loyal to his King
Barbarian Tales - Book One - Traveler's Tales*
Barbarian Tales - Book Two - Journeys Begin*
Barbarian Tales - Book Three - The Inheritance*
Barbarian Tales - Book Four - Road to Persepolis*
**BOOKS BY SHABBU**
Velvet Interrogation
Finding Jason

Dirty Pool
Operation Black Jade
Cigars!*
Angel in the Barn
Gayly Complicated*
Despoiling David
The Tree of Idleness*
I Met a Man
Rough Road to Happiness
**BOOKS BY STEPHEN KESSEL**
**Gay Romance**
The Forever Man
Two Chances
**BOOKS BY KIM BLACK**
**Lesbian Romance**
Transfixed on Tammie (F/T lesbian)

www.ingramcontent.com/pod-product-compliance
Lightning Source LLC
Chambersburg PA
CBHW021335250626
47155CB00002B/704